Praise for *In the Language of Miracles*

A New York Times Editors' Choice

"Assured and beautifully crafted . . . Hassib is a natural, graceful writer with a keen eye for cultural difference. . . . [She] handles the anatomy of grief with great delicacy. . . . *In the Language of Miracles* should find a large and eager readership. For the beauty of the writing alone, Hassib deserves it."   —Monica Ali, *The New York Times Book Review*

"A riveting and important book. It drives home the fact that no matter what religion we practice or country we are from, we are more alike than we think. [*In the Language of Miracles*] narrows the gap between us and may make us a bit more tolerant, understanding, and accepting."
          —*The Missourian*

"Impressive . . . From [Hassib's] first page to her denouement we can be gripped and moved by a study of the fault lines within an immigrant family."   —*The National*

"Hassib writes with an authority uncommon in debut writers; in this important book, she weaves the beauty of Arabic culture with the harsh realities of modern American life with exceptional insight and poetic ease."   —Bustle.com

"[A] sensitive, finely wrought debut . . . Sharply observant of immigrants' intricate relationships to their adopted homelands, this exciting novel announces the arrival of a psychologically and socially astute new writer."   —*Kirkus Reviews* (starred review)

"[A] stellar debut . . . Thoughtfully examining the role of religion and prayer, parents and grandparents, this rich novel offers complex characters, beautiful writing, and astute observations about the similarities and differences between the Egyptian and American outlooks on life. It would be difficult to find a better book for any discussion group; highly recommended."   —*Library Journal* (starred review)

"Topical both in its take on race relations and in its depiction of a troubled young man with ready access to firearms . . . Hassib is a capable writer, especially when dealing with the interpersonal. Her natural use of language resembles that of Khaled Hosseini." —*BookPage*

"A family reckons with tragedy amid a storm of suspicion in Egyptian author Hassib's debut novel. . . . [*In the Language of Miracles*] offers fascinating insight into the lives of American Muslims, and the prejudice with which they contended in the years after 9/11." —*Publishers Weekly*

"[An] admirable debut . . . Hassib does fine work portraying a family divided by culturally and generationally divergent reactions to a harrowing situation, and the novel builds to a gratifying crescendo as the memorial nears and tensions rise." —*Booklist*

"Spoken words are all powerful in Rajia Hassib's masterful book about thought versus action. Whether the characters are explaining, questioning, or stating their deepest beliefs, though, conversation never creates anything; it's the human response to the life that subsumes us, whether we're active or passive. In the face of tragedy, and even great happiness, abstractions fall away; the personal and particular endure. It's a very moving book." —Ann Beattie

"Smart, nuanced, and culturally dazzling, *In the Language of Miracles* is a heartrending story of Egyptians and Americans, of two families whose lives are intertwined and then unraveled by fate. Hassib's writing has an intoxicating quality that made this a page-turner, but by the end, her beautiful story surpasses its characters in its unflinching investigation of tragedy, mental illness, and healing across two cultures in conflict." —Zoë Ferraris, author of *Finding Nouf* and *City of Veils*

"Rajia Hassib's *In the Language of Miracles* is a tautly told story of one family's grief and the quiet but daunting burden of survivorship. She has deftly captured their individual struggles as they swim through the deep waters of loss and blame. We turn page after page and hope, as all bereaved do, that there's a chance for healing."

—Nadia Hashimi, author of *When the Moon Is Low* and *The Pearl That Broke Its Shell*

"Rajia Hassib's timely novel is a gripping, hold-your-breath exposé about being Muslim in post-9/11 America, where the heinous act of one can demonize all. But it's also a universal, multigenerational, immigrant tale. The old-world, Egyptian grandmother's bungled English, her prayers and incense, rub against her American-born, tech-savvy grandchildren's bungled Arabic and Western music. It's an intelligent, beautifully rendered reminder that no matter our ethnicity or creed, we all long for acceptance and a place to call home."

—Marie Manilla, author of *The Patron Saint of Ugly*

"Rajia Hassib has a finger on the pulse of two languages and two cultures. She deftly spins an honest tale of a family reeling in the wake of tragedy, all the while exploring the subtle complexities embedded in communication, culture, and human relationships."

—Laila Halaby, author of *Once in a Promised Land*

Rajia Hassib was born and raised in Egypt and moved to the United States when she was twenty-three. She holds an MA in creative writing from Marshall University, and her writing has appeared in *The New Yorker* online, *Upstreet*, *Steam Ticket*, and *Border Crossing* magazines. She lives in West Virginia.

In the
LANGUAGE
of
MIRACLES

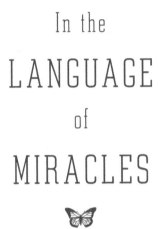

RAJIA HASSIB

PENGUIN BOOKS

PENGUIN BOOKS

An imprint of Penguin Random House LLC
375 Hudson Street
New York, New York 10014
penguin.com

First published in the United States of America by Viking Penguin,
an imprint of Penguin Random House LLC, 2015
Published in Penguin Books 2016

ISBN 9780525428138 (hc.)
ISBN 9780143109150 (pbk.)

Printed in the United States of America
1   3   5   7   9   10   8   6   4   2

For Kamel, Sarah, and Yousef

In the
LANGUAGE
of
MIRACLES

PROLOGUE

When Khaled fell sick at age nine, his grandmother descended on his parents' house and promised him healing. Armed with incense, a thermos filled with holy water from the Zamzam Well in Mecca, and a frayed pocket-sized book of prayers, Ehsan arrived at Khaled's bedside ready to fight any and all misfortunes that might have befallen her favorite grandchild. His illness, she insisted, had to be the result of an evil eye, its malice aggravated by her daughter's negligence of the simplest methods of protection from such wickedness. "Not a single blue ornament on display in the entire house! And when was the last time you played a recording of the Qur'an in the kids' rooms? How do you expect to protect them?" she chastised her daughter again and again. Khaled, with his jet-black hair, green eyes, and that coy smile that always caused Ehsan to burst into a recitation of the sura of Al-Falaq to pray for his protection, was particularly vulnerable to the evil eye. His mother's insistence on throwing him an elaborate birthday party a few weeks earlier must have been the last straw. "Why parade the boy around? Why invite people's envy?" Ehsan would repeatedly mumble as she tended to the sick child. They might as well have injected him with bacteria and saved the money spent on the inflatables.

Khaled, aware of his favored status, had not thought it strange that Ehsan would travel from Egypt two months before she had originally intended, risking a flight into JFK on the heels of the blizzard that ushered in 1996, probably spending the ten-hour journey imagining her plane

1

tumbling down in the middle of the unfamiliar snow she still feared beyond reason. On the day of her arrival she walked into Khaled's room, flanked by his parents and followed by his siblings, Hosaam and Fatima, and sat on the edge of his bed, the thermos held tightly in both hands. In a whisper that implied her words were meant only for his ears, Ehsan told Khaled the story of the holy water she had requested specifically for him, water her sister had carried all the way from Saudi Arabia to Egypt and that she in turn had carried from Egypt to the United States.

"This is blessed water," she said as she unscrewed the thermos lid and poured just enough to moisten a washcloth. "It is water that has run since the time of the prophet Ibrahim, peace be upon his soul. It is so pure it can heal the sick. If you were in the middle of the desert, one sip only would quench your thirst for days. This water," she continued as she put the thermos on his nightstand and held the white washcloth up for him to see, "runs out of the deep belly of the Arabian Desert, yet in this scorching heat it still comes out ice cold. This water will make you all better."

Khaled listened to her, struggling to make out the words, which she pronounced in an Arabic he found different from the one his parents used and yet familiar, since he had spent months out of each year in the company of his grandmother either at his home in Summerset, New Jersey, or at hers in Alexandria. Keeping his eyes on her lips helped him understand her better and also filled him with comfort; years later, he would still remember how unfamiliar his own room had felt, crowded as it was with his entire family. Hosaam's bed, the upper of the bunk beds, loomed heavily over Khaled's head the whole time, and throughout his feverish nights he would wake up imagining the bed was slowly lowering and eventually flattening him, and he wondered what his mother would do when she walked into his bedroom in the morning and found her son sandwiched between the two mattresses. Hosaam had not slept in his bed for days, having been banished to the living room both to protect him from potential infection and to give his brother some rest. Sitting on the edge of Khaled's bed, slowly dipping the washcloth in the small bowl now filled with Zamzam water, Ehsan's large body managed to make his bed seem more solid and less overcast in the shadow of his brother's. Looking at her, he could also ignore his other fears: that Fatima, standing in the corner, would accidently topple over the Lego that he had stacked on his desk, or that Hosaam would look under his bed and find the ladybug he had discovered crawling on their windowsill that morning, so rare in January, and that he had placed in the little jar with holes in its lid to keep safe until he could figure out what to do with it.

Ehsan put her hands under his armpits and lifted him into a seated position as she instructed her daughter to grab one of Hosaam's pillows and place it behind Khaled's back. Gently, Ehsan pushed his shoulders until his back settled in a Khaled-shaped groove in the pillows. He did not feel like sitting up, but he did not object. Ehsan, clad in permanent black since her husband passed away thirty years earlier, was not a figure he was willing to defy. Besides, as she leaned over him, adjusting the pillows, Khaled enjoyed breathing in the smell of incense, rosebud soap, and spices that always clung to her dress and her white veil, and the verses from the Qur'an that she hummed under her breath reminded him of her home and filled him with an unrealistic expectation of freshly baked cake and cold, frothy lemonade.

"How does the water work?" Fatima asked. She had inched closer to his bed, keeping to his left-hand side where their mother, Nagla, sat. The youngest of the three siblings and barely seven, Fatima's Arabic was the most riddled with an American accent that Khaled knew she was trying hard to mask. He looked at her and smiled. The sun, shining through the window behind the illuminated strands of her black hair, framed her face in a messy halo. He was grateful she had asked the question he had in mind but would not ask in the presence of Hosaam, who was leaning against the door frame, watching him.

"It works any way you want it to," Ehsan answered as she started folding Khaled's sleeves up. "If the sickness is in your stomach, you drink it and it takes the sickness away. If it's on your skin, you wipe yourself with it and it heals you."

"But . . . Khaled's lungs are sick. How will you get it there?" Fatima's eyes widened and teared up, her lower lip trembling as she looked at Khaled.

"Oh, we don't have to get it there," Ehsan said, laughing. Khaled laughed, too, relieved. "We'll just wipe his chest and face with it, and maybe give him some of it to drink."

Slowly, Ehsan started unbuttoning the front of Khaled's pajamas. Her hands, rough with years of cooking and cleaning for five children and twelve grandchildren, rubbed against his feverish skin and he winced. When she was done, Ehsan pulled the pajama top open. Khaled immediately started shivering, looked around him at his mother, his sister, and his father and brother, both standing by the doorway, and instinctively pulled the shirtfront closed. Ehsan, who had just had time to reach out and grab the washcloth from the bowl, looked at him and laughed.

"What's wrong, boy? Are you shy?"

"I'm cold," Khaled said, blushing. Fatima retreated into her corner and sat on the floor, pulling both legs up to her chest.

"Don't be silly, Khaled; it's just us," Nagla said, pulling his shirt back open. Khaled's lower lip quivered and he looked at his older brother, who was grinning down on him.

"Do you know the story of the Zamzam Well, Khaled?" Ehsan asked as she slowly touched the wet washcloth to his chest. Khaled, the fabric cold and prickly against his skin, felt his eyes well up and shook his head so that he would not have to speak.

"Well, it goes like this: The prophet Ibrahim, peace be upon his soul, took his wife, Hagar, and their young son, Ismail, out to the desert as he went in search of God. This is the Arabian Peninsula, you know, and the desert there is hotter and drier than the inside of a brick oven on an August day. So he set up camp for them between two large hills called Al-Safa and Al-Marwah, and then went up one of the nearby mountains, where the angels had told him he should go," she said as she gently stroked his entire chest with the cloth. She paused for a moment, murmuring prayers and verses from the Qur'an as she moved the washcloth in circles. When she was done, she pulled out a dry towel and started patting his chest.

"Hagar and her child waited for so long, they ran out of water, and Ismail started crying of thirst. His mother, desperate and aggrieved, ran up one hill, hoping to see someone who could help her, but there was no one there. So she ran back down and up the second hill, again looking for help, but saw no one. Seven times she ran from one hill to the next, the cries of her son piercing the empty desert, and still she found no help. Finally, she fell to her knees by her son's side and asked Allah for the help no humans had given her. And what do you think happened next?" She leaned close to Khaled as she buttoned his shirt.

"What?" Khaled asked, his eyes fixated on her face.

"Young Ismail struck the ground with his heel and water spouted out of it! Water so pure they each drank their fill and all sickness disappeared from them. Water so abundant it still runs to this very day out of the hot desert, just as it did thousands of years ago at the time of Ibrahim. This," she said as she picked up the thermos and held it high like a trophy, "this is water out of that same well that will not dry out until Judgment Day. This is water that God ordered to flow as He answered the prayer of one who needed Him, one who knew He was the only one to turn to in the hour of need. This is blessed water, and it is healing water, and it will make you all better."

Khaled looked at the thermos, his eyes wide. He could barely feel her stroke both his arms with the cloth as he looked at Fatima and saw her staring at the thermos, too. His parents exchanged looks, his father rolling his eyes, his mother looking away from Ehsan so that she would not see her smirk. Then he saw Hosaam, three years his senior, still leaning against the door frame close to his father, grinning.

"Oh yeah?" Hosaam said. "So this is holy water?"

"Yes, it is," Ehsan said without turning to look at him.

"So this water is going to make him better, huh? How's that? Is it antibacterial water or something?" Hosaam laughed at his own joke. Khaled saw his father give Hosaam a stern look that Hosaam either did not see or chose to ignore.

"Don't make fun of that which you don't understand," Ehsan said. Slowly, she turned and looked at Hosaam, holding his gaze until his grin collapsed into an uncomfortable smirk. "And mind your manners when you talk to me, boy. I'm not your mother."

"He didn't mean it, Mama," Nagla said, smiling at her mother and mouthing something at Hosaam behind her back, to which he waved a dismissive hand that his father quickly slapped down.

"This is no laughing matter, Nagla. You should know better."

"I know, Mama, I know. I'm sorry. The kids are just not used to this stuff."

"This *stuff* is not something you get used to. This *stuff* is something they need to learn to respect. You know what happens when you disregard stuff like that, Nagla."

Khaled's father snickered, and Khaled looked quickly at Ehsan, thankful she was still too busy pulling his sleeves down to notice his parents grimacing behind her back.

Ehsan stood and picked up the bowl and the thermos. "Still, they're your kids, and you can raise them any way you like. Here," she said as she turned around and shoved the bowl into Hosaam's arms, "make yourself useful and take this to the kitchen. And you," she spoke to Nagla, carefully handing her the thermos, "take this to my room. Let me have some time alone with the boy."

"Come on, Fatima," Samir said, holding out his hand. His daughter jumped up, ran to him, and took it. As the family walked out, Ehsan reclaimed her seat on the edge of Khaled's bed. Smiling, she reached out and pushed a stray strand of moist hair away from his eyes.

"You want to lie down again?" she asked. Khaled nodded.

Gently, Ehsan pulled the covers back and let him slide down before she pulled them back up, tucking them around him as he laid his head on his pillow. Then she sat back next to him, and softly and monotonously started reciting verses from the Qur'an, her right hand now stroking his arms through the covers, now his legs, and occasionally straightening his hair. Khaled closed his eyes. He did not care what Hosaam thought. He did not care what his parents thought. He believed everything Ehsan said. He believed because he could feel her coarse hand against his forehead but his skin did not ache anymore, and because he could already feel the tightening in his chest lessen and his breathing grow steady and deep, like he was finally able to pull enough air into his lungs to fill them all up.

"*Setto?*"

"What, *habibi?*"

"What did you mean when you said it was not good when people didn't respect stuff like that? You know, about the holy water?"

"Why do you ask?"

"I don't know. I was just wondering."

"Well, do you believe it?" she asked as she stroked his head one more time.

"Yes, of course I do."

"Then you have nothing to worry about, do you?"

Khaled did not answer. He thought he should ask her more questions, just to make sure nothing bad was going to happen, but his eyelids grew heavy, and her hand, suddenly lighter, seemed to push the questions out of his mind with every new stroke until he finally fell asleep.

WEDNESDAY

1

ENGLISH: The Lord gave, and the Lord hath taken away.

Bible

ARABIC: God gave; God took; God will provide compensation.

Saying

For almost a year, the Bradstreets and the Al-Menshawys practiced elaborate avoidance tactics, living next door to each other yet hardly crossing paths. Khaled noticed his parents' change of habits right away: Samir, after years of leaving for work at 8:00 a.m., started heading out a full half-hour earlier just so he would not run into Jim Bradstreet. Coming home, Samir no longer parked his car in the driveway and walked through the front door but squeezed his Avalon into the cluttered garage then slid through the barely open door and walked into the kitchen. Nagla abandoned her wicker armchair on the deck, moving her ashtray to a bench where she sat with her back to the living room wall, looking away from the Bradstreets' backyard and hidden from their view. Even Cynthia Bradstreet forsook her gardening and the backyard she had practically lived in for years. From his bedroom window, Khaled watched as her irises wilted and drooped and her herb garden succumbed to negligence, the tan spikes of dry dill and cilantro eventually covered by

11

snow, which, once it melted, revealed a rectangular bed of lifeless mud where the blooming garden once stood.

Then, just short of a year after the deaths, Khaled answered the door one evening and saw Cynthia Bradstreet standing on his parents' doorstep. One hand still holding the doorknob, Khaled stared at her, forgetting to step aside to let her in.

"Hey, Khaled," Cynthia said, moving closer to grab his hand. Khaled had grown four inches since he turned sixteen a year earlier, and she had to look up to meet his eyes. Despite the warm weather, her hand was freezing cold.

"Hey, Aunt Cynthia," Khaled said. Behind him, he heard his father's heavy step, followed by his mother's hurried one, and then Ehsan's shuffling feet and her voice, mumbling prayers.

Nagla served tea in gold-rimmed miniature glasses that wobbled on the silver tray in her unsteady hands. Khaled, terrified that his mother would drop the tray in Cynthia's lap, stared at Fatima until their eyes met and then nodded toward their mother.

"Here, Mama. Let me," Fatima said, taking the tray and passing the tea around before walking into the kitchen to serve Ehsan, who had settled in at the breakfast table the moment everyone else was seated and had started softly reciting the Qur'an, her oversized copy of the book resting under her palms, the print large enough for her to see without glasses. In the background her voice rang in a constant hum that Khaled missed only whenever it was interrupted, just as he noticed the combined noises of air conditioner, refrigerator, and running dishwasher only when the power went out in the winter and the house was suddenly drenched in silence.

Khaled, sitting at the bottom of the stairway, watched as his father sipped his tea, legs crossed in his armchair. Neither Nagla nor Cynthia tasted hers, though both women held on to the gold-rimmed tumblers, wrapping their fingers around them.

"I wanted to be the one to tell you," Cynthia said, raising her eyes to look at Nagla. "We're planning something for next weekend—for the anniversary."

Nagla nodded. "Yes. We saw the flyers."

"I thought you might have." Cynthia looked down. "Jim and Pat went a bit overboard with them, I'm afraid. They're everywhere."

Khaled had seen the flyer that very morning. Standing on the platform of the Summerset train station, waiting for the Amtrak to take him to New York, Khaled had turned around and found himself facing Natalie, her image centered in the flyer thumbtacked to the green felt, safely tucked behind the glass of the display case. She was wearing her hair in the asymmetrical bob that she had debuted only a few weeks before her death and a blue sweater that Khaled remembered seeing her wear to school. Looking at the flyer behind the protective glass, all Khaled could think of was the blue morpho butterfly, and how he had once told Natalie he would one day travel to South America and photograph his own, not catch it to put it on display, but watch it, follow it around, guess at the span of its wings, maybe even attempt to measure it, but then let it fly away unharmed.

Khaled waited for Cynthia to resume talking, his heart sinking. He imagined her asking his parents to leave town for the weekend of the memorial with no need to explain why the Al-Menshawys would not be welcome. He hoped that she would not be so blunt, that she would spare his mother the humiliation.

"We'll be planting a tree," Cynthia said. "At the park. A rosewood. They live very long, you know." Khaled reached out for his teacup, which he had placed on the wooden steps, sipped some of the minted black tea, burned his tongue, and put the cup back down.

"That's an excellent idea," Samir said, nodding. Fatima moved closer to her mother and perched on the arm of Nagla's chair, one arm wrapped around her shoulder. Khaled, watching her, smiled.

"I wanted to come to tell you in person." Cynthia addressed Nagla, but Nagla still kept her eyes down, intently examining the surface of her tea. Only one year ago, they would have both been sitting at the kitchen table, alone, the hot tea growing cold as they whispered and laughed.

"I knew for a long time now that I'd be holding some kind of service," Cynthia went on. Khaled strained to make her words out. Her voice, so soft, made it seem as if she were whispering the words for Nagla's ears only. "I need this, Nagla. Some closure. I've also realized, a couple of days ago, that I would never get closure unless I spoke to you, too." Nagla looked up, for the first time meeting Cynthia's eyes. "I want you to know that I don't blame you. I . . . not anymore."

Nagla nodded, quick, repeated nods, letting her head fall down again and her gaze rest on the tumbler in her lap.

Cynthia sighed. "Also—that whole memorial thing; I never intended it to be that public. When I first thought of it, I was hoping for something private, just for the family. But then Pat thought we should let people come, too, if they wanted to." Samir's eyes narrowed at the mention of Cynthia's sister. Cynthia went on, "Jim agreed, and now . . . Well, you've seen the flyers."

"I saw a couple of flyers today," Samir said, crossing his arms at his chest. "I'm sure everyone saw them. You'll have a good turnout."

Cynthia nodded, placing her tumbler on the side table. She had not once looked Samir in the eyes. She turned to face Nagla again, reached one hand out and touched Nagla's. "I know this might make you uncomfortable, but that was not my intention. I'm not apologizing for the memorial," she added quickly, "but I do want you to know that this is not meant for you. I also want you to know—I need you to know that I don't blame you for what happened," she repeated. Nagla nodded again.

14

"Okay, then," Cynthia said, getting up. Nagla and Samir followed her as she headed toward the door. Halfway there, Nagla's eyes froze on the door-side console with its assortment of framed photos. She hastened, overtaking Cynthia and Samir, and stood by the console, her back resting against its marble edge. Khaled's eyes met hers, and he understood. Of course. She was blocking Hosaam's picture, the one of him when he was twelve or thirteen, grinning in his blue-striped shirt, his expression infused with the discomfort typical of school pictures. Khaled held his mother's gaze, remained seated until Cynthia passed both of them on her way out. Only then did Nagla relinquish her spot, following her husband and standing by the door as Cynthia walked down the front path. Khaled followed, too, standing behind his parents and towering over both of them, watching as Cynthia turned to her own house, disappearing behind its front door.

Khaled let his parents walk back in and then slipped out. He looked around him at the quiet street where he grew up, familiar even in the darkness. Taking a deep breath in, he savored a comfort that daylight seemed to eradicate, a safe sense of belonging that had lately become people-shy, obliterated by the slightest glance of recognition from a stranger. Khaled walked up to the swing hanging from the white porch rafters, sat down quietly. The chains holding the swing up rattled. They would not creak if he did not push the swing. He stretched his legs in front of him, leaned his head back. Across from him and on top of the opposing row of houses, the cloudy sky hid all stars.

"Hey." Fatima's head was sticking out of the doorway. "Come back in. They're fighting."

"Why?"

Fatima did not answer but waved at him to hurry in before disappearing through the doorway.

"No, Samir. She was *not* inviting us." Nagla was sitting back in her chair.

"It was as good as an invitation," Samir said, hovering over her. "Why else do you think she came?"

"She was just being nice." Nagla paused, raised one trembling hand to her forehead. "Because that's how she is."

Samir sat on the sofa, crossed his legs. "Twenty years in the U.S. and you still don't understand Americans."

"What's there to understand?"

"That she took the trouble to come to our house. That she mentioned closure. Sure, it's nice of her. But there is more to it than that. She wants to make peace, Nagla. How can she do so if we don't participate?"

"How are we supposed to participate? There is no way they want us at this service, Samir. Think of how awkward it would be," Nagla pleaded.

"I'm not saying it won't be awkward; I'm saying it's necessary. If we don't go—especially after she came to our house to tell us about it—they will think we don't want to put this thing behind us."

"Who will think so?"

"Everyone!" Samir's voice rose. Echoing him, Ehsan's voice rose, too, reciting verses from the Qur'an. She had moved from the kitchen to the living room, sat in a corner chair across the room from her daughter and son-in-law, but had kept the holy book open in her lap, her lips moving rapidly as she continued her reading, barely audible.

Samir sighed. "Think about it, Nagla. This is our chance to be part of this community again. This service is an opportunity for us to show that we are on the same side they are on. That we regret what happened as much as they do. That we are not—" He paused, searching for words. "That we are not what they think we are."

"I don't know, Samir. We tried going public before, and that didn't go so well, did it?"

Samir stiffened up, blushing. "I was trying to help. To make things better for you and the kids. That's all I've ever done. What else would you have me do, huh? Just hide and wait it out? For how long?"

"We could always move, you know," Khaled said. His father turned and glared at him.

"We're not starting this again. And who asked for your opinion, anyway?"

Fatima, moving closer to Khaled, grabbed his arm and squeezed it. He said nothing.

"Just think about it," Samir resumed, leaning toward his wife again. "We could go together, as a family, showing our respect. Perhaps they would let me say a word or two, address them—"

"You want to speak, too?" Nagla interrupted him.

"The flyer said they'd welcome speakers!" Samir said.

"Yes, but not you! Not you!" Nagla got up, paced the living room. "I know you mean well, Samir, but I really think you're off, this time. I mean—can you imagine?" She paused, raised both hands to her face. "Ya Allah." She sighed.

"Why not me? See, this is the mentality that's setting us back. You're acting like they are right; like we are not part of this community."

"It's not about the community!" Nagla's voice rose. "It's about . . . about . . ." She choked up.

"It's about your refusal to support my decisions. Again." Samir's voice grew hard. Fatima nudged Khaled, took a step toward her parents, but her brother held her back. She glanced at him and he shook his head.

"I'm always supportive. When have I not been supportive?" Nagla stepped closer to her husband. "Why do you have to turn everything into a criticism of me? Can't I even help you see the . . . the . . ." she stammered, and then, in a gush, added, "the stupidity of your plans?"

"Eh ellet eladab di?" Samir protested. What kind of ill breeding is this?

Ehsan raised her voice again. "Hal jazao alihsani illa alihsan."

"Baba," Fatima said, stepping closer to her father.

"Watch your language, Samir," Nagla said.

"Look who's talking!"

"Fine," Nagla said, walking away from him. *"Mashi."*

She headed toward the stairs, started climbing up.

"Where are you going?" her husband yelled. "We're not through yet!"

"I am." Nagla did not pause, nor did she turn around. "You know what you want to do, go do it. That's how it always is anyway."

"I'll do what I want, yes. And I don't need your permission!"

Nagla slammed her bedroom door shut.

Samir, as if noticing his two children for the first time, looked at Khaled and then at Fatima. "And what about you two, huh? Do you have anything to say?"

Khaled shook his head.

"Good!" Samir walked to the kitchen, paced once around the breakfast table like a man on a pilgrimage, then walked out the kitchen door and onto the back deck. Khaled could see him through the bay window as he sat down on one of the armchairs, leaned forward, and ran his fingers through what remained of his hair.

"As stubborn as ever," Khaled murmured.

"He's only trying to help, Khaled." Fatima looked up the stairs. "You think she'll be okay?"

"She'll be fine. She's used to this."

"Psstt," Khaled heard. He and Fatima turned around to see their grandmother summoning them. She had closed the Qur'an and placed it on the table beside her, where Cynthia's untouched tea still stood. Khaled and Fatima walked up to her, Fatima sitting by her side while Khaled crouched down in front.

"What's going on? What memorial are they talking about?" Ehsan whispered.

"El-sanaweyya ya Setto," he said, trying to pronounce the words in his best Arabic. "They will be holding a memorial service for Natalie's one-year anniversary. The anniversary of her death, that is," he clarified unnecessarily.

"They're going to the cemetery?"

"No, not the cemetery. It's different, here. You don't have to hold a service at the cemetery. They're doing it at the park."

"At the park?" Ehsan said, raising her eyebrows. Khaled nodded. "I'll never understand the Americans," she sighed. Upstairs, a door slammed, and they all looked up, as if expecting to see Nagla's movements traced on the ceiling.

"What about your brother's *sanaweyya*?" Ehsan whispered to Khaled. "Aren't you going to do something for him?"

Khaled looked at Fatima, who was biting her lower lip, just the way their mother always did.

"I don't think so, *Setto*. We can hardly invite people over for him, you know," Khaled said.

"I know that, boy. I'm not an idiot," Ehsan said, slapping Khaled on the shoulder with the back of her hand. Her slap, surprisingly hard, almost made him topple over. He reached one hand behind him and steadied himself. "I just meant you, the four of you, and me, of course. Maybe just go over to the cemetery and read some Qur'an. Or ask people at the mosque to pray for him after the Friday prayer," she said, looking at Fatima. Upstairs, they heard another thud, perhaps another door slam, or a drawer pushed closed too violently.

"Why don't you go upstairs to her, *Setto*?" Fatima asked.

"I don't know," Ehsan said, glancing toward the back porch though she could not see it from where she was sitting. "What if your father wants to go up and talk to her again? I don't want him to find me there and think I'm snooping."

"He won't go talk to her now," Khaled said. "He probably thinks she should come and talk to him first. He always does that; yells at people and then expects them to apologize."

"Khaled! Don't talk of your father in such a disrespectful way!" Ehsan said.

"But he's always like that!"

"She's his wife, so what if he yells at her? Your grandfather, Allah rest his soul, used to chase me around with the broomstick. At least he doesn't do that, does he?" Fatima, glancing at Khaled, sucked at both her lips, and Khaled smiled, knowing she was struggling to stop herself from laughing at the image of her heavy grandmother dodging a broomstick. "Besides," Ehsan added, "he's the man of the house; he has the right to do whatever he thinks is for the best of his family."

"*Thinks* is the key word, here," Khaled mumbled.

"What?"

"Nothing, *Setto.*"

Ehsan sighed. "Such bad luck," she said. "Such bad luck has befallen this family. It's all because of the evil eye, of course. *Hasad.* People back home, they think of you here, living in this big house, driving expensive cars, and all they imagine is money growing on trees. They covet all that Allah has given you, and then look what happens. This!" She held both arms up in a gesture that encompassed their entire lives. Khaled looked at the console, at the picture of his brother's smiling face, slightly angled, so that he could not see his expression, only the sharp silver edge of the frame.

Sighing, Ehsan got up, headed into the kitchen, and opened the cabinet where she kept her incense kit. She pulled out the brass globe with its decorative perforations, the small box holding the dry incense leaves, and the bag with the pliers and the pieces of coal. In a moment, she would be resting the coal on the burning flame, letting it glow red and hot before she placed it on the layer of sand sitting in the bottom half of the incense burner. On top of it, she would sprinkle leaves of incense, let the fragrant smoke rise through the holes of the globe as she held it up by its three chains, swinging it in circles as she wandered the rooms of the house, chanting prayers.

Fatima picked up the abandoned tumblers still filled with tea and placed them back on the tray that she carried into the kitchen. Washing the glasses by hand, one by one, she occasionally looked out the window at Samir, still sitting on the deck. When she was finished, she walked out of the kitchen and up the stairs, where Khaled could hear her knocking on Nagla's door. He headed toward the stairs, too. He would go to his room, to his laptop, away from all this. He climbed only a step or two before he stopped to look once more at his brother's framed picture. In the kitchen, he could hear Ehsan's incantations. The smell of the incense, sweet and tangy like a mixture of cloves and rosebuds, slowly filled the air, and Khaled, turning around, started up the stairs again. Of course it was all bogus, he thought. No amount of burning leaves could have possibly made a difference. No incantations, regardless of how sincerely and incessantly uttered, could ever prevent disaster.

2

ENGLISH: Home is where the hearth is.

ARABIC: Whoever leaves his house loses prominence.

Samir and Nagla arrived in New York on a sunny morning in April 1985. Sitting in the station wagon, Samir thought how perfect it was that this car now zoomed through the Big Apple while Egyptian music drifted from the dashboard. His cousin, Loula, was driving, and he, sitting next to her, exhausted after the ten-hour flight, slid down in the seat, looked out the window, and listened to Om Kalthoum's voice mingle with car horns and jackhammers. The singer's voice, low, chagrined, and so deep he felt it came from the bottom of the earth, was rumored to have been so powerful that she had to stand six feet from the microphones to insure they would not break. The recording dated back to the fifties, and Om Kalthoum tenderly reprimanded a lover for his long-endured cruelty. Samir listened and knew the answer to his own destiny was as simple as an American car playing Egyptian music in New York: he could, he was certain, build a life for himself and his family here, while preserving their Egyptian roots. Om Kalthoum sounded better contrasted with the New York skyline and its pure blue backdrop of a sky than she did in Cairo with its dusty roads and overcrowded streets. The contrast between her familiar voice and his new surroundings highlighted the beauty of each in a way Samir had never experienced before.

Glancing behind him, he smiled at Nagla, who sat in the backseat next to a squirmy Hosaam, too busy to see Samir watching her. He looked as she tried to comfort their ten-month-old son and knew, right then and there, he would do anything to give them the life they would never have had a chance at, back in Egypt.

"So when do you get to start?" Loula asked. Over the phone a few weeks earlier, Samir had told her about the medical training he was to start in Brooklyn, only two hours from her home.

"Not until July. But I wanted to get Nagla settled in first."

"Do you know where you'll be staying?"

"The hospital has a couple of buildings they rent out of. I'll get in touch with them tomorrow and see what they can do for me."

"You should talk to Ahmed first," Loula said. "He might know someone who could get you a cheaper place. Sometimes these places they recommend cost an arm and a leg."

"I don't need a cheap place."

"Just to save up, you know."

"Thanks, but I think we'll be fine."

Loula did not answer. Born in Brooklyn to an American mother, she was Samir's first cousin whom he had seen only intermittently when she vacationed with her parents in Egypt. He suspected she was taking them in only because his uncle had insisted. Months earlier, Uncle Omar had assured Samir that he would have welcomed him in his own home had he not lived in Detroit. Loula was the only person Uncle Omar knew who might offer Samir temporary shelter.

Ahmed, her husband, Samir had met only once, and he had detested him. Tall and lanky, Ahmed had sat down in Samir's father's living room, legs crossed, the heel of his shoe facing Samir's father in unabashed neglect of Egyptian manners, and had spoken in an Arabic scattered with unnecessary English expressions that his then six-year tenure in the United States did not warrant. In contrast, Loula had talked almost exclusively in Arabic, stuttering as she searched for words, pronouncing the letters in a heavy accent that belied her features, so Egyptian she seemed fit to play the role of Cleopatra. Considering that she was born and raised in New York, Samir had found it fascinating that she could even converse in the language. He did not understand how she had ever ended up with Ahmed.

In the station wagon, Samir tried to let Om Kalthoum's voice soothe him again, but he failed. He did not know what had offended him more: Loula's implying that he would not be able to afford the hospital housing (which, to be honest, he was not entirely sure he could), or her suggestion that he ask her husband for help, a man who, Samir suspected, knew nothing more about Brooklyn than he himself did. Whatever knowledge Ahmed had amassed in his years spent in the United States, Samir was sure he would be able to catch up on shortly. He did not need help from anyone, and certainly not from other Egyptians whose only claim to expertise on all things American lay in the limited experience a few years had to offer. Closing his eyes, Samir reminded himself he would have to veer away from any unpleasant confrontations with Ahmed during the days or weeks he'd have to spend at his home, and, most important, he'd have to make sure he got out of there as soon as possible.

To his chagrin, however, he and Nagla ended up staying with Loula and Ahmed for three months. Only a day after their arrival, the human resources lady at the hospital, portly and with too-blond hair, had looked at Samir over her reading glasses and told him, one more time, in a slow English that implied he might have had trouble understanding the language, that housing for the residents was currently full. He'd have to wait until June 30, when the senior residents would move out and make room for incoming interns. Samir, explaining again that he had been told accommodations might be available a month or two before his starting date, had to sit and listen to her explain to him that the key word here was *might*. Nothing was available. Short of paying for a hotel room for eighty-some days, Samir had no other choice but to impose on his cousin's hospitality.

Loula was not as indisposed to having them as he first imagined. She and Nagla managed to use a mixture of broken Arabic and English to communicate, and in a matter of days Samir could see, to his relief, that the two got along well. Loula introduced Nagla to a plethora of baby products she had never heard of, from changing tables ("Really? A piece of furniture *just* to change a baby's diaper?" Nagla had later whispered to him) to baby gyms, swings, and all sorts of bottle-cleaning accessories. Nagla slowly started cooking Egyptian food for Loula and Ahmed, taking over the kitchen and preparing dishes of stuffed eggplants and green peppers, *musakka*, and baked fish in a casserole of potatoes, garnished with celery and marinated in lemon, cumin, and minced garlic. Within weeks, Nagla was spending as much time in the kitchen as she had at home, sometimes by herself and often with Loula by her side, trying to learn the exact way to wrap grape leaves around their stuffing. Nagla, Samir realized, was much, much more comfortable than he was.

Even Ahmed did not seem to mind having them, but Samir suspected that was mainly due to how much Ahmed enjoyed telling him exactly what to do.

"So you're really going to take that hospital housing place, huh?" Ahmed asked him one day. They were sitting on the back deck, where Samir found out anyone wishing to smoke had to go. Samir had not expressed his annoyance when Loula, seeing him light a cigarette inside the house only minutes after his arrival, had politely said, "Feel free to use Ahmed's ashtray." She ushered him to the deck, opened the sliding doors, shoved him outside, and closed the doors behind him, coughing. He had found the adjustment a bit cumbersome, especially considering how cold the weather still was in April. Especially considering that he frequently had to endure Ahmed's company.

"I am taking the housing offer, yes," Samir said, bending out of his

25

chair to flick his ashes into the ashtray on the table between them. Ahmed was smoking a cigar, and the wind, changing direction, blew the odorous smoke Samir's way. He got up and walked to the railing, stood leaning against it and looking at the hill in the distance.

"In *Flatbush*? You're going to live in *Flatbush*?" Ahmed asked. He was sitting in an oversized wicker armchair, both his feet resting on the coffee table, the cigar dripping ashes on the deck. Samir, hiding a vague feeling of alarm that started to creep up on him (what was wrong with Flatbush?), looked calmly at Ahmed and nodded.

"It's close to the hospital."

"You don't have to live close to the hospital. It's Brooklyn! You can take the subway, you know."

"I'll be on call a lot, and I don't want to be too far from Nagla in case she needs me."

"You can get a place in Bay Ridge. That's where all the Arabs live."

"I don't want to live where all the Arabs live," Samir said, his teeth clenched. "I want to live close to the hospital."

"Well, I don't blame you," Ahmed said, crossing his feet. "I wouldn't want to live too close to Arabs, either."

"That's not what I meant," Samir said, irritated. That man could not sit without showing the soles of his shoes.

"I'm telling you, they're not the best company, when you live abroad. Still, Nagla would make friends. And you'd be close to all the shops selling Egyptian food."

"What do you mean, they're not the best company? I'd love to live close to other Egyptians."

"Oh, so you'd love to live with fellow Egyptians, would you?" Ahmed asked.

"Yes!" Samir lied. He knew exactly what Ahmed meant, how people always warned to veer away from Egyptians and Arabs when you lived abroad, how they always said Egyptians would help you at home but stab you in the back the moment you set foot off Egyptian soil. One of his fellow medical students had sworn to him, only weeks earlier, that an Egyptian resident at a Florida hospital had assured him he need not apply there because they never took foreign graduates unless they achieved the highest scores in their medical equivalency tests. This same resident, he later found out, had scored in the seventy-sixth percentile and had still secured a spot. "He just didn't want me there, competing with him," his disgruntled friend had told him.

Everyone said Egyptians abroad acted as if preserving their own little piece of success required they make sure no one else shared it. Samir secretly believed this to be true. ("They will snoop into your business all the time, too," this same expert on expatriate Egyptians had whispered to him. "Come into your home unannounced and open your fridge just so they can see if you're living at the same standards you had in Egypt or if you had to tighten the belt.") Still, he hated to admit all this in front of Ahmed, and, even worse, hated to hear Ahmed criticize Egyptians and Arabs, as if he were not one of them. It was one thing to know the faults of your own people, he thought, but something completely different to speak so irreverently of them, as if you had somehow become better by virtue of a few years spent in the United States, in a large Connecticut house, with imported Cuban cigars that dripped ashes on the deck's gray wood.

"Yes," Samir repeated. "I would like to live close to other Arabs. But I've already signed the lease on the new apartment."

"Oh well," Ahmed said, his lips twisting in a sly grin. "I guess Flatbush it will be, then."

"Yes. Flatbush it will be," Samir said, gratified to have the last word.

A few months later, Samir had realized that Ahmed might have had a point regarding Bay Ridge. Nagla, having to stay home with Hosaam as Samir worked eighty-hour weeks, had grown irritated with isolation. She knew no one, and even as he encouraged her to take Hosaam to the park to meet other parents and make new friends, he knew she was too self-conscious about her limited English.

Plus, the apartment itself proved to be small and dark, with only one bedroom and a windowless living room stuck between the kitchen and bedroom. Even though they had both been relieved finally to take possession of their own apartment, walking in for the first time, Nagla's smile was not what Samir had hoped for. Her muffled comments and occasional "Oh, that's nice," as she walked from room to room felt more like polite replies directed at strangers. He knew she was comparing this space with the one they had left in Egypt, which his father had purchased for him years earlier, with three bedrooms and a large, airy living room, the full front of it made out of sliding glass doors that opened to an eighth-floor balcony with a view of the Mediterranean. The apartment in Egypt, he had felt like telling her, was better, yes, but what else was better? What else?

Time, he had hoped, might help Nagla get used to the apartment that was to be her home for the next three years. He was wrong. Only three weeks after they had moved, he walked home from work late one afternoon and found a fire truck parked in front of the four-story brick building. At the foot of the front steps stood Mrs. Russell, the landlady, talking to one of the firefighters. When she saw him approach, she pointed at him and said something to the firefighter, who laughed softly and shook his head. Samir, curious but not necessarily alarmed because he could see no fire, had tried to walk past them and up the stairs when Mrs. Russell held him by the arm and spoke in slow, deliberate English.

"You must tell your wife to be careful, or she will burn the building down!"

When he looked at her, puzzled, she repeated her admonishment, word for word, only slower and louder. "You . . . must . . . tell . . . your . . . wife. Be . . . careful. Building . . . will . . . burn . . . down!" For added emphasis, she pointed at the building, lifted both arms high above her head, and then let them both drop.

Upstairs, Hosaam was sitting in the crib Loula had given them, holding on to the rails and crying.

"Nagla?" Samir called. There was no answer, but he could hear whimpering. Before turning to head into the bedroom, Samir glanced toward the kitchen and saw a patch of dark soot on the ceiling. The entire apartment smelled like burned oil.

She was sitting on the floor, in the corner between the bed and the wall, her legs drawn to her chest, her face buried in her knees, sobbing. Samir, speaking softly, sat down next to her.

"Nagla, what happened?"

Looking up, Nagla covered her face with both hands and said, "I . . . was cooking. The . . . alarm," she said, sobbing, "the fire . . . alarm . . . went off. I didn't know it would. I was frying eggplants. I wanted to cook *musakka*."

Samir brushed her hair away from her face.

"I tried to get up . . . on a chair, to see how to turn it off. It was very loud and . . . Hosaam . . . was sleeping. I could not, and I went to ask for help . . . I went to Mrs. Russell. When we came back . . . I forgot, you see, I had the oil on the stove," she said, sobbing again. "It was on fire. I grabbed the pot and threw it in the sink, threw flour on it, and put it out. When I turned around, Mrs. Russell was not there. She called 911. She said . . . she said . . ."

"Shushhh," Samir said, pulling her closer to him.

"She said this is not Africa, you don't do that, you don't set fires in the house," Nagla said.

"Shushhh, it's okay, *habibti*, it's no big deal. It's okay."

"I was so embarrassed, Samir! I was so scared and so embarrassed. I mean, Hosaam was here alone, when I went to get her," she said, pulling away from him and looking him in the eyes. "I felt so, so stupid! What if something had happened to him?"

"It's okay, *habibti*, nothing happened. It was only an accident." He pulled her arms away from his neck and reached for her hands.

"Ouch!" she said, snatching her hands away from him.

Only then did he see her hands wrapped in kitchen rags, the palms burned where she had held the hot skillet, both hands peppered with already-swollen blisters.

Hours later, as he sat in the emergency room waiting for other doctors to treat his wife, Samir had thought about that apartment, that small apartment belonging to strangers who could tell him and his wife what they could and could not do, and he had thought of how miserable Nagla had been. He would, he promised himself, holding Hosaam tight, make it up to her. She would have her own home.

That thought was the one comfort he held during his three-year residency. Every trouble Nagla faced, he blamed on that apartment. Every time it snowed while he was at work, he would look out the window and think of her, trapped in a claustrophobic apartment with Hosaam, alone and undoubtedly weary of the boy's understandable whining as he, too, suffered from loneliness and boredom. If they had been in a large house, things would have been easier for everyone. Hosaam would have had more room to play, maybe even a backyard with a swing set, and Nagla would not have had to feel, as he suspected, that the move from Egypt had been a downgrade. The house would also be something concrete she could report back to her family; she could send pictures, show her mother and brothers that she was living well, that *he* had provided for her well, just as he should.

They started house-hunting a year into his residency. Samir would have started earlier, if he could, but it took him months to convince his father to sell his share of the family's automobile dealership to his brothers and wire him the money.

"Selling out now will cost you in the long run," his father had cautioned.

"I need this money now, *Baba*," Samir said, vexed that his father interfered in his plans.

"But how will you know where to buy? Why New Jersey? You'll have to commute for the next two years. And what if you decide to move to another state after you're done with your residency?"

"I won't commute for that long. I'm sure it will take us some time to find a good house, and by then I'll be closer to the end of my residency. I just need to start looking. And I like New Jersey. I've been researching the job market there. There is one small town I'm particularly interested in, a place that could definitely use another internist. I'm sure I'd be able to set up my own practice there in no time."

"*Insh'Allah* you will be able to," his father corrected him.

"Yes, *insh'Allah* I will," Samir said, irritated. His father, who had met Ehsan only a handful of times, sometimes acted so similar to her that Samir wondered if he should encourage the widower and the widow to spend their final years together, walking around their apartment, burning incense and reminding their offspring to say "God willing" whenever they spoke of their futures, lest they jinx the whole thing.

Samir, pacing the kitchen of his apartment, had heard all of this before, all his father's arguments against buying a house, all the precautions and what-ifs. But his father was talking to him from the balcony of his apartment with the Mediterranean view, sipping Turkish coffee his maid had prepared while he read the morning newspapers. Meanwhile, Samir was pacing a nine-foot-square kitchen, whispering so that he would not wake Nagla and Hosaam, wondering why he had to talk his father into sending him his inheritance, which he'd signed off to him already.

"I was actually considering waiting a bit, *Baba*, only things have changed now. I have some good news," he said, waiting for effect.

"What?"

"Nagla is pregnant." He tried to sound as cheerful as he could, pressing one hand hard against his forehead.

His father's exclamations of joy he had anticipated, of course. One more grandchild, one more heir, one more grandson (hopefully), one more human being to carry on his father's genes. Soon, Samir explained, Nagla would be too tired to house-hunt. If they could find a house now, he would have enough time to renovate or paint or change the carpets, so that Nagla and the kids (plural) would be able to move in as soon as he was done with his training, if not before that. Summerset, only an hour away from New York, was a small town where good houses were not abundant; if they found one, they would need to snatch it up before it was gone. "All I'm trying to do," he told his father, "is make sure my kids have a good home to live in. I only have your grandchildren's best interest in mind."

They found the house a couple of months before Khaled was born, just when they were both ready to give up house hunting in anticipation of the arrival of their second child. They had both gotten out of the car, stood in front of the white house with green shutters, and looked at it for a while before going in. Samir saw Nagla's face brighten up in a way he had not seen since Egypt, and he knew that this was their home. The wraparound porch. The red door. He did not care that it was four decades old, that three of the upstairs bedrooms shared one small bathroom, nor did he care that the carpets needed to be changed or that the porch awaited repainting. That the kitchen needed to be remodeled. Nagla stood in the breakfast-area bay window and looked at the backyard, a sunny patch of flat grass that faded into a forest of trees.

"This looks like something I've only seen in movies but never imagined I'd own!" she said.

"You like it?" Samir asked.

"Like it? I love it! It's a bit expensive, though, don't you think?"

Samir wrapped his arms around her protruding belly, rested his chin on her shoulder. "Don't worry about it," he assured her. "I told you I'd let you pick the house, and if this is the one you want, this is the one it'll be."

They closed on the house thirty days later, partly because he had told Nagla he would, partly because he had loved the house, too, but mainly because Ahmed had told him not to.

"Are you crazy?" Ahmed had asked. He and Loula had stopped by the apartment, as they often did when they were in town. Loula was in the bedroom, where her two kids played with Hosaam as she and Nagla talked. Samir and Ahmed sat at the kitchen table. Samir, usually embarrassed by their visits, which only reminded him how poorly he was providing for his family, had welcomed this one. He had printed out pictures of the house to show to Ahmed.

"What do you mean?" Samir said, irritated.

"For one thing, this house is *huge!* What do you need such a huge house for?"

Oh, so you don't like it because it's bigger than yours?

"It's not too big," Samir said, smiling. "I didn't want anything too small or too confining. Nagla will be staying home with the kids for a long while, and I want her to have a house she can enjoy."

"She could have enjoyed a house half this size, if you ask me," Ahmed said, pushing the photos back across the table to Samir, who picked them up, arranged them neatly in a pile, and said nothing.

"Besides," Ahmed added, "why don't you just rent? Give yourself time to see if you'll be able to set up your practice there. Also, give yourself time to save up, you know, before you spend every last penny you have on that house."

"I've already found a good place to set up my practice. And I'm *not* spending every last penny," Samir said through his teeth.

"It's your funeral," Ahmed said, shrugging.

Samir, blushing to his ears, glared at him. *Wait and see,* he thought. *Just wait and see.*

For months before they moved in, Samir and Nagla spent every weekend renovating and painting, tearing out old kitchen cabinets and counter-tops and replacing them with new ones. As they worked, Hosaam would trot from room to room, running in the freedom the large house af-forded, while a newborn Khaled napped in his car seat or, later, sat in his stroller, watching as his parents worked. Whenever Samir would finish one room, Nagla would take it over, painting with all the windows open. He loved to see the smile on her face as she pulled her roller down each wall as if her stroke imprinted every section that she touched with magical protection and promises of prosperity. Once done, she would hang curtains, move in their belongings a little bit at a time, clean and organize and then reorganize as she learned the house's every little nook and cranny.

In Egypt, they had never done manual work, mainly because labor was so cheap it was easier to hire professionals. But here, in New Jersey, Samir had learned that homeowners did all the renovating themselves. He had listened to his colleagues' conversations about remodeling with a newfound fascination. There was pride in their talk, a sort of boastful-ness inherent in ownership, in the fact that no landlady would walk up and tell them what they could and could not do.

Samir had assumed he would learn renovating just as he learned anything else: from books. When he found himself standing in the mid-dle of a half-demolished kitchen, however, he realized the amount of information he did not know was overwhelming. What was he supposed to do first, put in the new cabinets or the new tile? Did he have to replace entire cabinets, or just the cabinet doors? If he wanted to tear the cabi-nets down, how was he supposed to do it without damaging the walls? He felt overwhelmed. Suspicious by nature, he was afraid to hire con-tractors to finish a job he had started. He needed help, he knew. But he knew no one who could help him. More accurately, he knew no one he was willing to ask.

Ehsan would have said it was providence, because help did come his way, in the form of a six-foot blond young man with broad shoulders and an even broader smile. He literally stepped across their adjoining backyards and into Samir's kitchen one day, introduced himself, and within an hour was giving Samir much-appreciated advice. The young man was their new neighbor, Jim Bradstreet, and he was going to help him remodel the entire kitchen.

"Are you sure, Samir?" Nagla had asked when he later told her the news. "That's a lot of work! You really think he would want to help?"

"Of course he would! He's the one who offered. He literally was on his knees peering under the countertops before I even got his name!"

"But are you sure he was not just offering out of politeness?"

"This is not Egypt, Nagla," Samir said, waving an impatient hand. He was sitting on a stool in the apartment's kitchen as Nagla prepared dinner. "It's not like home; people here don't make offers like that unless they really mean it. And besides, it's still up to him. If he wants to, he'll show up. If not, he won't."

The following weekend, Samir took Nagla and the kids to Summerset. Only half an hour after their arrival, Jim stepped from his backyard into theirs. Samir, smiling broadly, looked at Nagla. *I told you so.* Jim was followed by a woman and a little girl close to Hosaam's age with white-blond curls that glittered in the sun. She ran right up to Hosaam and handed him a stuffed bunny with a blue bow tied around its neck. Hosaam took it, and both kids darted across the yard, following a white butterfly that the girl had spotted and pointed out to Hosaam.

Cynthia, a chubby brunette, had brought a plate of pastries. She handed them to Nagla.

"Welcome to the neighborhood!"

Nagla looked at the gift and smiled, murmuring thanks. She turned around to walk into the kitchen, realized the countertops had been removed, and stopped in place, pastries in hand.

"What was I thinking!" Cynthia said, laughing. "You don't even have a kitchen to eat them in. Come over to our place; I'll put on some coffee."

"I can't," Nagla said, looking at Samir.

"Of course you can!" Samir said, giving her an encouraging look.

"But, I mean, I don't want to be heavy," Nagla said.

Cynthia's brows scrunched together.

"She means she doesn't want to intrude," Samir said. Nagla blushed, and Samir strapped his arm around her shoulder. "It's difficult to translate from Arabic, sometimes."

"At least you can speak two languages!" Cynthia said. "The most I can say is *no hablo español!*"

"Seriously," Jim said. "Just go spend some time with her. It'll keep her out of our hair. She's such a chatterbox."

"I am," Cynthia admitted. She nodded at Hosaam and Natalie racing around the yard. "Besides, it'll be good for the kids."

Samir watched Nagla push Khaled's stroller across the lawn, nodding as Cynthia spoke to her.

It was at that exact moment that he felt the pieces of his life falling into place at last. As he and Jim walked inside to construct his new kitchen, Samir knew he was building not just a house, but his home, surrounded by good American neighbors, where his children would flourish and he and Nagla would grow old together.

3

ENGLISH: If you don't have something nice to say, don't say anything at all.

Saying

ARABIC: Whoever believes in Allah and the Last Day, let him speak benevolently or remain silent.

Saying of the prophet Muhammad, peace be upon his soul

Khaled could not sleep. For close to two hours he fiddled on Facebook, trying to block out the whispers seeping through the wall at the head of his bed, Ehsan's voice distinguishable from Fatima's, the words muffled and incomprehensible yet audible still. His sister and grandmother were the only two capable of discussing today's events—what were they saying? He doubted his parents would talk tonight. He didn't check to see if his father had eventually joined his mother in their bedroom.

On his nightstand, his phone beeped, signaling a text message—doubtless from Garrett, the only one who would text him that late. Garrett's message showed a picture of the flyer.

Did you see this?

Yes, Khaled texted back.

This Sunday.

Yes.

What will you do?

Khaled thought of possible answers to this question: Get out of town, stay in hiding, watch a *Star Wars* marathon. Instead, he typed, Dad wants to go.

WTF? Why?

Wants to give a speech.

Bad idea.

I know.

Man. Your dad. Should be banned from contact with public.

Khaled sighed, put the phone down. Of course Garrett was right. Ever since Cynthia had left, Khaled had been wondering which was worse: walking into that service knowing that nobody wanted them there, or watching his father actually get up and address the crowd.

Samir had a track record of unfortunate public announcements. A year earlier, he had spoken to the reporters who showed up on their doorstep on the heels of the police officers who came to talk to his parents. Khaled had let the officers in and had watched as one of them walked into the kitchen, where Nagla, towel in hand, raced toward him, her face blanching even before he spoke. She listened, intent, her eyes searching his face, and then she quietly lowered herself to her knees by the foot of the kitchen table, the towel in her lap, as if expecting a toddler to rush into her embrace. As the officer stooped down to talk to her, tears streamed down her cheeks, but her face remained expressionless, showing signs of only a mild surprise, a puzzled look that reminded Khaled of the way his mother sometimes stared at people who spoke too fast for her to catch up. He wondered whether she needed him to translate for her, whether the officer's English, like so many others', was beyond her grasp. But she did not. She had understood.

Standing in a corner, a terrified Fatima grasping his arm and sobbing, Khaled saw his father thunder down the stairs, almost tackling the officers, speaking so fast they barely had time to answer his questions. The other officer, the one who had stood in silence and looked around, grabbed Samir by the elbow and led him out of the kitchen and into the living room. Samir's questions spilled out in a mad rush. Where did it happen? Were there any witnesses? Did they check the surveillance tapes yet? Maybe someone put that thing in Hosaam's hand afterward. And how did Hosaam get to the park? He didn't have his car. Samir pulled at the officer's arm, wanting to lead him to the garage to show him, to prove to him that Hosaam did not have his car. Yes, he understood that Hosaam was dead, and Natalie, too, but how could they have found them in the park if Hosaam didn't have his car?

Khaled didn't pay attention to the reporters until later in the day, when his father left with a couple of officers, his departure accompanied by a plethora of shouted questions and clicking cameras. Khaled stayed in the living room, watching the reporters through the parted blinds as they set up camp across the street, cameras dangling from their necks and poised on their shoulders, lenses glimmering in the scorching sun. He did not know what else to do. His house had suddenly become alien. The police had evicted him from his room—Hosaam's room—as they rummaged through it. His mother, still sobbing in her bedroom, was in the care of Fatima, Aunt Ameena, and a couple of other ladies from the mosque, who had rushed to the house as soon as they had heard the news. He felt he should be with someone—but with whom? There was no one to be with.

He knew his father had returned when he saw the reporters look up the street in unison. Stepping out of the police car, Samir ignored their shouted questions as he walked up to his front door. Khaled waited on the other side of the door for his father to get in. He did not. Khaled walked up to the door, slowly opening it, and saw his father's back as he walked away from him and into the throng of the reporters, saw him lift one hand up, silencing all questions, and then heard him speak.

What he said made the eleven o'clock news as well as the front page of the local newspaper. Bud Murphy, one of Khaled's high school classmates, uploaded a file of Samir's speech to Khaled's Facebook wall. Khaled watched only once as Samir urged the reporters not to come to any rash conclusions, not to publish any accusations until the police uncovered the truth. The whole thing was a terrible misunderstanding. He knew what they were thinking, what they were preparing to report, especially with victims so young, but he begged them not to condemn his son. Especially since he had heard someone had driven by the two kids as they sat in the park, had tried to pull Natalie into his car, and, when Hosaam came to her rescue, he had—well, everyone knew what happened next. No, he could not tell them who his source was. But he was sure Hosaam was as much a victim as Natalie. One day, he had begged them. Just wait one day before printing unsupported allegations so the truth could come out.

What came out the following morning was the police statement the sheriff issued after watching the tapes recovered from surveillance cameras that monitored the Summerset Park Visitors' Center. Ultimately Samir could not argue with that evidence. Instead, he sank down on one end of the sofa, covered his face with his hands, and wept.

That day the reporters returned. Khaled watched from his bedroom as they again hovered at the edge of the yard, quietly waiting. Soon their cameras were clicking as they barked questions. Below his window Khaled saw Samir make his way to the reporters. His statement, again posted to Khaled's Facebook wall by Bud Murphy, was even longer than the previous day's. Samir was shocked, dumbfounded. He had no idea how something like that could have happened. Hosaam and Natalie had been friends since they were both toddlers. The Bradstreets were their closest friends. No, he was not aware of any mental problems his son might have been suffering. No, Hosaam was not a college student. He was going to go to college, of course, but he had decided to take a year off first. Yes, he had been speaking to his son, regularly, of course. Yes, Hosaam had still been living with his parents. They were very sorry. They were very, very sorry. He wanted people to know that he and his wife had not known, had not imagined . . . if there was anything they could have done to change things. If only they could . . . they were truly sorry. Khaled watched the footage of this statement on Facebook, read the forty-three comments left by his numerous Facebook friends and acquaintances, and then closed his Facebook account for good.

On the following day, the reporters showed up again. Samir spent the morning pacing the living room, occasionally parting the blinds to scowl at them. Fatima convinced her mother to get out of bed and walk down to the living room. There Khaled's sister sat next to their mother, coaxing her to eat a cheese sandwich and to sip tea with milk and honey. Nagla did not seem to hear Fatima speak. Khaled, sitting in an armchair a few feet away, watched as Nagla sat, back straight, hands folded in her lap, her eyes relentlessly watching Samir's every move. She had not slept since it happened, he knew, and her eyes were puffy, the hollows underneath them ashen. When Samir finally stopped pacing, he walked up to his family and explained, in short, hesitant sentences, that he felt he had to issue another statement to clarify things.

"Clarify what?" Nagla asked.

"Tell them we had nothing to do with this. Tell them he's really not . . . was not a bad kid." He stood straight, looking down at Nagla, and, were it not for his lower lip trembling, Khaled would have thought he was issuing a simple statement: *We should eat at Olive Garden tonight.*

Nagla got up slowly, took a few steps toward her husband, and started rapidly hissing at him. Her voice low at first, she talked so fast, Khaled was hardly able to catch up, his Arabic as slippery as his mother's English. He knew she was saying something about Samir's mixed-up priorities, about how he cared more about what people thought of him than he did about his own son who had just— Samir tried to talk back, but every time Nagla's voice grew louder as she inched so close to him, she had to look up to maintain eye contact with her husband. Khaled, going back and forth between watching his parents fight and watching Fatima watch them, did not have time to decide what to do before they all heard a shuffle outside their front door. Samir and Nagla fell silent.

Khaled got up and walked to the window. Peering between the edge of the blinds and the glass, he saw a young reporter in a yellow blouse, black skirt, and four-inch yellow heels standing at their front door. She had her back turned to the house and was motioning to her cameraman to come closer, apparently trying to shoot a segment right there on their doorstep. Nagla saw her and, before any of them could stop her, she rushed to the door and opened it wide. The reporter barely had time to turn around before Nagla lunged at her, grabbed her by the arm, and screamed at her in Arabic.

"*Ayzeen menena eih? Mesh kefayah el ehna feih?*"

The reporter started screaming. Samir, Khaled, and Fatima all rushed outside. Nagla dragged the reporter into the front yard, still grasping her arm as the reporter frantically tried to free herself from Nagla's grip. Samir got to Nagla first and wrapped his arms around her, constricting her movement, while Khaled started prying open her fingers to release the reporter. She did, finally, but the release was so sudden that the reporter took a few hurried steps back, got her shoe stuck in the dry, cracked mud, stumbled, and fell. When Fatima made it to her, trying to help her up, the reporter, still screaming, pushed her back, knocking her down as well. Fatima got up and hurried inside while her father and brother dragged Nagla in, still yelling. By then the reporter's cameraman had made it to his colleague and helped her up. When the family was inside, before closing the door, Khaled took one more look and saw the reporters snapping pictures, both of their house and of the Bradstreets' next door. Cynthia Bradstreet was standing in her doorway, arms crossed, watching the commotion. He slammed the door shut.

An intern for the *Summerset Banner* shot the picture that graced the front page the next day. Khaled knew exactly who had taken it, because he had seen the intern climb on top of a parked Ford Fiesta, which was probably the only way anyone could have captured both houses together. Samir, on the left-hand side, pulled Nagla back into the house. Khaled waved one hand toward the reporters, and Fatima struggled to get off the ground. On the right-hand side, Cynthia Bradstreet stood in her doorway, one hand covering her mouth, the silhouette of Jim Bradstreet barely visible behind her. And to the very far left the legs of the reporter, being helped up by her cameraman, protruded low and angular while one yellow shoe could barely be seen as it stood, still stuck in the dry grass. After that picture was published, Samir did not issue any more statements.

For months afterward Khaled and Fatima had begged their father to move the family away from Summerset, to relocate them to a place where people would not stare at them whenever they walked down the street, where they could go to school each morning and disappear in the comfort of anonymity. Again and again, Samir had refused to discuss the subject. Finally, apparently weary of his children's persistence, he had relented.

"Where do you think we could go?" Samir had asked. He stood with his hands on his hips, looking down at both of his children as they sat side by side on the living room sofa. Nagla, sitting in her armchair, had remained silent.

"Anywhere but here," Khaled answered.

"And what am I supposed to do with the practice I spent almost twenty years building?"

"You could start a new one. Doctors do that all the time. Or find a hospital job. You always said doctors who are employed by hospitals have it a lot easier."

"If they start out this way, yes. But not after I've spent decades running my own practice."

"Then start a new practice somewhere else."

"Do you think it's *that* easy? Do you know how many years it takes to build a solid patient population?"

"Actually, *Baba*," Fatima started, hesitated, and then went on, "you have been complaining about how many of your patients left. You know, after what happened." She glanced at her mother. Nagla looked out the window into the darkness. "So we were thinking this might actually be a good time to move, since your practice—" she trailed off.

Samir stared at her, blushing. "So you're saying that I should move since I'm not making enough money here anymore, is that it?" he hissed.

"No, *Baba*, of course not. I didn't mean—"

"If I'm going to be discussing finances with my teenage kids, let me take this a step further. Did you ever think of the cost of such a move? Do you think I can afford to relocate my practice now? Buy a new house? Pay a double mortgage until God knows when this house is sold?"

"You can always put this house on the market first. It might sell quickly," Khaled said.

"Oh yes. Because people would race to buy our house, knowing your brother's story. Houses with tragic histories always attract buyers that way, I presume."

Khaled saw his mother fidget. Still she said nothing.

"And, while I'm waiting for this house to sell *and* paying to set up my new office, I should still be able to afford paying your tuition once you go to college in less than two years, is this correct? Do you think I own a money-printing press?"

"I could always apply for a student loan," Khaled said.

His father glowered at him. Khaled fidgeted, looked at his mother and sister. Fatima threw a quick glance his way before looking down at her feet. His mother would not turn his way, even though he stared at her, waiting for her to say something or, at least, to give him a reassuring look. When Samir started talking again, his words were quaking with subdued anger. "I have not slaved for twenty years to have my son insult me this way, tell me he would take loans because I cannot afford to pay his tuition. Tell me I am not able to provide for my own son like my father did for me and like his father did for him before that."

"I meant no insult, *Baba*. There's nothing wrong—"

"You two have the nerve to sit here and discuss my finances with me, tell me how to run my business. Tell me I should cut my losses, pack up and move before we go broke. Is this the respect you show your father?"

"We did not mean—" Fatima started.

"Enough!" Samir yelled.

They never discussed this matter again.

Lying in bed, Ehsan's and Fatima's whispers still seeping into his room, Khaled wished his father had been less stubborn, had truly considered the possibility of moving away. The angst that haunted him in the few months following his brother's death now returned with a vengeance, filling his head with images of his father drawing attention to himself again during Natalie's upcoming memorial service, promising Khaled that they were all plummeting toward a rerun of the hostilities that had plagued their lives a year earlier. Again Khaled wished they had moved away. Tossing and turning in bed, he wished he could go to a new school where Natalie's friends did not stop and glare at him in the hallways, where he did not have to listen to her former teachers speak to him without making eye contact, as if they were addressing an ethereal being floating in the air somewhere between where he sat and his teachers stood, or as if they were intent on gazing into space for fear that locking eyes with him would turn them all into stone. He wished he lived in a town where patrol cars did not occasionally trail him as he walked home from school, where he could walk down the road and fear nothing and no one, be menaced by no one, perhaps even be able to interact with people without the constant presence of his brother's memory between him and everyone else, a barrier too high for anyone to climb over. He wished, more than anything, that he could talk to Brittany about all of this. But of course he could not.

Grabbing his laptop, he sat up in bed and navigated to her Facebook page. She had posted new pictures today, and he flipped slowly through them, savoring each one, grateful, as always, for her habit of daily updates. When they first met in person a few months back, he confessed to keeping track of her photos. He had watched her as he said so, his heart pounding, afraid that she would view him as a stalker, that her eyes would mirror the panic he felt. But she had laughed, tilting her head back, and he had studied her long neck, the short black hair with its one purple streak, the many hoops that adorned her ear, and had realized that the five years separating them were an immense stretch, long enough to witness the life and death of generations of migrating monarchs, long enough to allow for a friendship only slightly marred by his obvious infatuation. He had wanted to confess more, to tell her everything he felt she needed to know about him, but he could not. Looking back, he sensed the stupidity of confessing to browsing photos she had put up for everyone's perusal but withholding other, drastically more important pieces of information. He had feared she would be scared away. Now he knew that she probably would not have been—but, after months of holding back, a late confession seemed riskier than ever.

He clicked on the message button, stared at the new window that showed her name in the recipient box. He did not know what he could possibly say to her, but he felt a need to say something, to know that he could communicate with her, if he tried. He browsed back to an article about monarch tracking he had read earlier that morning, and then copied its link in the message, sending it to her with no comment. Of all the people he knew, Brittany was the only one who would read such an article.

Closing his laptop, he turned the lights off and slid under his covers. Ehsan's and Fatima's whispers had finally abated, and, his eyes closed, he savored the anticipation of Brittany's reply and waited for sleep to come to him.

THURSDAY

4

ENGLISH: Till death do us part.

From the marriage liturgy, the Book of Common Prayer

ARABIC: Among all the permitted acts, divorce is the most hateful to God.

Saying of the prophet Muhammad, peace be upon his soul

Nagla waited in bed until she heard the garage door rise and fall, signaling Samir's departure. As soon as she was sure he was gone, she walked down to the kitchen for a cup of hot tea and then back up to her room. Today, she would clean house, starting with her bedroom. She dumped the contents of every drawer on the bed, folding everything: her underwear and Samir's, his socks, her camisoles, his pajamas, her nightshirts. Usually, this repetitiveness soothed her, and the process, like meditation, kept her mind from drifting to troublesome territories. Today, though, undershirts seemed determined to crease rather than fold, and socks remained mismatched even after she had gone through all the drawers and emptied the laundry pail on the floor, zealously looking for missing socks as if their discovery would afford the key to heaven or the power to stop all evil.

"Vexation," she murmured to herself as she stuffed the laundry back into the pail. "Just pure vexation."

She abandoned the folding and walked into the closet she shared

with Samir, examining every shirt and pair of pants for possible dona-
tions, yanking out items she decided he did not need and putting them
in a pile and then adding two of her own shirts. Years earlier, Ehsan had
told her the story of a disgruntled wife who sold her husband's favorite
razor to a traveling street vendor while her husband was at work. Ehsan
had whispered the story in a mixture of awe and disgust. "Such disre-
spect," Ehsan spat, implying that she, of course, would never have done
any such thing to *her* late husband. Nagla, in a logic she still failed to
comprehend, had despised the woman based on her hypothetical offense to Nagla's own father. Of course Ehsan never would have sold his
razor. Nagla eyed Samir's favorite shirt and walked out of the closet to
thwart temptation.

"So energetic so early in the morning?" Ehsan asked.

Nagla turned and saw her mother standing in the doorway, her own
teacup in hand.

"Good morning, Mama. Come. Sit with me."

Ehsan made her way to her daughter's bed, placing her teacup on the
bedside table before climbing up on Nagla's side of the bed, her back
resting against the headboard. Nagla continued sorting through the pile
of clothes, aware of her mother's watchful eye.

"No breakfast today?" Ehsan asked.

"Don't feel like it."

Ehsan nodded, and then she sighed. Nagla waited. When she was a
child, she used to come home and join her mother in the kitchen, help her
peel potatoes and pick through rice, and all the while Ehsan would listen
as she gushed about everything that happened in her day. Nagla wished
she could still report cut knees, spiteful playmates, and unfair teachers
who picked favorites based on fair skin and deep parental pockets.

"I don't know what this woman was thinking, walking in here yesterday," Ehsan started.

"She was just being nice, Mama."

"She only caused you to have a fight with your husband."

"She had no way of knowing this would happen."

Ehsan sucked at her lips, a long *tsssp* that Nagla understood well.

"You don't know her, Mama. She wouldn't mean ill. She's a very nice person."

"By Allah, you're the only nice one. You believe this whole speech about finding peace? I'll bet you they're only doing this to remind people of what happened. To turn them against you more and more."

Nagla let a shirt she was holding drop on the bed, looked at her mother. "Has Samir been talking to you?"

"No, of course not," Ehsan quickly answered.

Nagla searched her mother's face, her eyes narrow.

"The man means well," Ehsan went on. "He only has his family's best interest in mind."

"Best interest? You really think going to that memorial is in our *best interest?*"

Ehsan waved one hand. "I'm not talking about *what* he's trying to do, but about *why* he's doing it."

Nagla walked over to her nightstand and pulled a pack of cigarettes out of the drawer. Her mother watched her.

"Don't smoke inside, Nagla. You know how much your husband hates that."

Walking over to the window, Nagla opened it and pulled the screen out before lighting a cigarette. "I always do, Mama." She inhaled the fresh air before puffing smoke out the window. "He never notices."

"He probably does. He just doesn't want to annoy you."

Nagla snickered. "Yeah, right. Because he's so obliging. Did you ever wonder how come smoking indoors became harmful only after *he* quit smoking?"

"He's probably trying to get you to quit, too. Don't be so hard on him. He's a good man, Nagla."

"I thought I was the only nice one?"

"Don't be smart with me, girl."

Across the backyard, Nagla watched the edge of Summerset Park, the lush trees covering a plain that moved toward a gentle slope down to the park. Years ago, she heard of a woman who bought a house near a cemetery just so she could see her son's gravestone from her back porch. Back then, she had thought the idea touching. Now she was baffled at how the woman could withstand the daily reminder.

"You really shouldn't contradict him so often, Nagla. He's still the man of the house."

"Contradict him?" Nagla turned to face her mother, keeping the hand holding the cigarette dangling out the window. "I merely mentioned that going to that service was probably not the best idea—which, by the way, you agree with me on, even if you won't say so. I was being respectful and considerate. I should have said that this was the worst idea ever. Even worse than that time he went and talked to the reporters."

"You can't say stuff like that to a man. What do you think he'll do, say, *Oh, sure, honey, you're right and I'm wrong?*"

"Why shouldn't he say that?"

"Are you crazy? Your husband?" Ehsan shook her head. "You've been living in America for too long. You think our men are like theirs. Your father, *Allah yerhamoh*, would have cut me up in pieces before he would have let me challenge him so."

"No, he wouldn't have."

"You didn't know him." Ehsan shook her head. "A real man. They don't make them like that anymore." Her voice rang with pride as a faint smile curled her lips.

Turning around, Nagla leaned out the window, smoked in silence. Of course her mother would compare Samir to Nagla's father, and of course her father would win—at least in that context.

Nagla was five when her father died. The only distinct memory she had of him was of being lifted in the air and swung around the room, her hair flowing sideways as she looked down on his smiling face. Everything else she knew of him came from her mother's stories, which Nagla had found as fascinating as the Indian action movies she used to watch as a child with their exotic colors and spontaneous dance routines. Years ago, Nagla's oldest brother had deliberately and quite mercilessly cured her of the fascination she had harbored with the father that Ehsan took great pains to describe to her in the most complimentary manner. Her brother, ten years her senior, had his own memories to counter his mother's, ones that involved, among other things, a brown leather belt with a brass buckle that his father used as a disciplinary tool. But even after she had learned to doubt the accuracy of her mother's stories, Nagla still found them a welcome refuge, perhaps because they transported her back forty years, planting her in a warm bed next to her mother, a dim light the only accompaniment to Ehsan's whispers of the great and mighty Mahmoud Fuad Mansour.

The stories were endless. Among Nagla's favorites was the time he, at seventeen, had been walking alongside the Nile in Al-Fayoum when he saw a little boy being swept away by the current of the muddy water. Mahmoud, who was not the best swimmer, jumped in without a moment's hesitation and splashed his way to the boy, keeping him afloat until some bystanders found a rope to dangle from the embankment. Mahmoud tied the rope around the boy's waist, hoping the bystanders would be able to pull the boy to safety. The current, however, proved too strong: every time people tried to reel the boy in, the angry waters would rise up and push him away from safety. Exhausted, yet determined to save the boy, Mahmoud did the only thing left to do: he took a deep breath, dove down, carried the little boy on his shoulders, and, using him as weight, literally walked on the muddy bottom of the channel, holding his breath for what people later swore must have been at least five full minutes, until he finally emerged at the edge, the boy's legs dangling on each side of his head. The entire village had spoken of Mahmoud's bravery, Ehsan whispered, and to make matters even more exciting, the boy turned out to be the son of the village's *omda*, or chief. The *omda*'s gratitude was immense, and he immediately gave Mahmoud a job in his office, arguing that a man with such courage had to be a man of great integrity, as well. Ehsan herself was very impressed, and felt quite honored when Mahmoud, a year later, chose her to be his bride. For years after hearing the story for the first time, whenever Nagla passed a channel or a river, she would find herself peering through the murky water, trying to detect her father walking the muddy bottom underneath the surface.

Apart from his bravery, Nagla also learned, Mahmoud had a good singing voice, knew how to bake the best *basbousa*, was accustomed to spending hours with his sons playing soccer, had sold the watch he had inherited from his grandfather just so that he could get Ehsan a pair of crescent-shaped gold earrings, had memorized the entire Qur'an by the time he was nine, and had been the confidant and advisor of everyone living on their street when they finally moved to Alexandria: The lawyer two buildings down, the doctor occupying the sixth floor of their apartment building, and even the university professor across the street, who consulted Mahmoud on new texts he planned to assign in class. Nagla listened to all of this in awe. Most important, however, she listened with teary eyes as her mother told her how Mahmoud learned to braid his only daughter's hair by the time she was three, just so he could keep it away from Nagla's eyes as she played in the humid Alexandria weather.

Forty years had passed, and Ehsan still told stories of her husband.

"Do you still miss him, Mama?"

"Of course, *habibti*."

Nagla bit her lower lip, rubbed her eyes with the back of one hand.

"I still don't get the whole memorial service idea," Ehsan started after a pause. "But I'll tell you one thing: I do think there is some sense behind doing something to make it all better."

Nagla stubbed her cigarette against the brick of the house's outer wall and then flicked it away, watched it fall on the grass next to a dozen or so others. She would have to pick them all up before Samir saw them.

"What did you do? To make things better after *Baba* died?"

"Oh, I had no time for anything but worry." Ehsan sipped at her tea. "He left me with *koom lahm*, a heap of meat: five kids and barely enough income to afford bread and fava beans for all of us. I did not quit worrying till you got married. Worried all day, prayed and cried myself to sleep at night."

Nagla put the window screen back, stared at the warning: *Screen will not prevent a child from falling.*

"You know what you can do, though?" Ehsan asked. "You could stop torturing yourself."

"What do you mean?" Nagla turned around to face her mother.

"You think I don't see you? Up there in that attic all the time?"

Nagla crossed her arms, rested her back against the screen.

"What use is that? Keeping his stuff up there like it's some sort of shrine to *sidi* Al-Hussein?"

"That's not what it is."

"Then what is it?"

"I just—I'm not ready. I don't know what to do with his stuff." Nagla's eyes watered.

"You go through it. You keep a thing or two and give the rest away. *Sadakah garyah.* A good deed in his name to ask Allah for mercy upon his soul. Nothing better than a donation to do so." Ehsan paused, took a sip of her tea. "I've been telling you for some time, Nagla, and I'll tell you again: You cannot grieve forever. It's been a year, *habibti.* You can't go on walking around the house like a ghost, passing by your kids and husband as if you don't see them. I don't mind doing the housework, but there are things I cannot do for you. I cannot be a mother to Khaled and Fatima. They need you back, *habibti.*"

Nagla nodded, and with every nod she could hear the wire screen give a low, screeching rattle.

She waited until her mother settled in the kitchen and started preparing tonight's dinner before she ventured out in the hallway, stared at the folded-up pull-down stair.

Her mother was right. She had walked up there often. Whether this was a bad habit, though, was a matter of opinion.

She could go through her son's things. She could open the drawers, sift through the boxes, flip through the magazines, the notebooks, the leaves of paper that the police had not taken away.

She walked into Fatima's room and grabbed the chair she always used when she needed to reach the pull-down chain. She climbed on the chair, reached out, and held the chain, wrapping the cold metal around her fingers, letting her hand warm it up before she pulled.

5

ENGLISH: Birds of a feather flock together.

ARABIC: Birds fall upon those similar to them.

Garrett lay on the floor, texting Hailee. Khaled stretched out on Garrett's bed and, leaning against the headboard, browsed the Internet on Garrett's laptop. He liked sitting on Garrett's bed because it was so different from his own: bright, not encumbered by an upper bunk, not claustrophobic. The shades were drawn, yet strips of sunlight still shone directly at him, the glare making the screen flicker in dazzling stripes. He fidgeted until he found a spot where the sun would neither shine directly on the screen nor in his eyes. He was not comfortable, but stayed put. He preferred the bed to Garrett's swiveling desk chair, and he refused to resort to the floor, Garrett's new favorite spot. If Garrett's mom hadn't been home, they would have lounged on the living room sofas, watching TV. Today, however, she had come home early and brought a friend. Both women sat in the kitchen, their incomprehensible murmurs occasionally interrupted by laughter.

The computer desk hutch was buried under dozens of books. In one, Garrett had read that Buddhist monks slept on low, hard beds. In an attempt to one-up them, he had taken to lying on the floor, his back against the wooden planks. Apparently, hard surfaces were conducive to meditation since they afforded only light sleep. His devotion to meditation being less than his devotion to sleep, however, he slept in his bed, but took to the floor during daytime. "How am I supposed to stay awake at school if I only get light sleep?" he had protested when Khaled pointed out the futility of his efforts. Even on the floor, Garrett often ended up with a book in his hands: about Buddhism or Zoroastrianism, a safari travel guide, an overview of the botany of Siberia. Eventually, he ended up holding the phone, texting Hailee.

Khaled looked at the pile of books. He knew Garrett had one on lepidoptera—a booklet, in fact; Khaled had picked up two copies at a science fair a few years before, back when he still hoped to interest Garrett in entomology. From the bed, he tried to spot the booklet in the pile, too embarrassed to ask about an old gift that Garrett had probably discarded. Khaled wished he had taken his copy to school with him that morning to reference in his latest post. His blog, started to cure him of Facebook withdrawal after he abruptly closed his account, had quickly evolved from one about bugs in general to one dedicated to migrating butterflies. Today, someone had challenged one of his earlier posts, and Khaled had spent the previous hour surfing the Internet, trying to find information that he knew was on the top right-hand side of the seventh page of his booklet—at home. The Internet provided him with answers, but he felt the booklet would supply the necessary proof. He would have to wait till he got home. Or write something temporary that he could later edit.

Migration is different from dispersion. Dispersion is more random. Butterflies go from spot A to spot B and then C and so on. Migration is more direct. They know where they are going, and they fly to get there. I do have a booklet at home that explains it very well. Check again in a few hours and I'll scan the page and put it up.

"Okay." Garrett suddenly sat up, his back straight as if he were about to start a series of crunches. He looked again at the phone, chuckled, and put it on the desk. Khaled knew Hailee had a sense of humor, but he did not ask what funny thing she had written. Even though he and Garrett had been best friends since kindergarten, he could never find the right way to talk to him about Hailee. Khaled had never had a girlfriend, and any discussion of Garrett's relationship always reminded Khaled of that lack. His closest attempt at a relationship had come during his sophomore year. He had taken an interest in basketball, attending every girls' game in order to cheer for Grace, a junior he would have sworn he was in love with and would remain in love with for the rest of his life. She had long blond hair that she pulled into a ponytail and was almost as tall as Khaled. Three days before Hosaam died, Khaled had finally approached her after a game, and, the following day, he mustered the courage to walk up to her at lunchtime. Then Hosaam died, and Khaled never spoke to Grace again.

"So how come we're not at your house but here, listening to Myrtle gossip?"

Khaled shut the laptop and shoved it to his side. "How do you know your mom is gossiping?"

"She never invites anyone over unless there's a fresh scandal at work. I'll be hearing all about it over dinner tonight. You might, too, if you stay."

"What's for dinner?"

"Don't change the subject. How come you called off my interview?"

Garrett got up and slouched in his computer chair, swirling from side to side. "Did *Setto* change her mind?"

"No, no, she didn't. She's honored. Thinks it's a huge thing she'll be mentioned in a newspaper." Khaled smiled as he remembered his grandmother's earnestness in accepting the invitation to talk to Garrett.

Khaled never understood why Garrett had hit it off so well with Ehsan. Ever since Garrett was a kid Ehsan had fascinated him, swirling her incense above his head and chanting prayers to protect him from all evil because he was a good American boy who had befriended her grandson. Garrett's mother believed Ehsan was the reason Garrett had walked into her bedroom and declared he would one day tour the world—a trip he had been saving for since he was ten. Today, Garrett had planned to interview Ehsan for a piece he was writing for the school newspaper. Khaled had not asked what the piece was supposed to be about. Knowing Garrett, he was certain he could turn any subject matter into a tirade advocating multicultural understanding.

"So how come you changed your mind, then?" Garrett asked

"I just didn't think today would be a good day."

"Why not?"

"My parents had a fight yesterday. Mom is probably scrubbing bathrooms or something. I didn't think you'd be comfortable."

"Hey, man, I don't care. I just wanted to talk to *Setto,*" Garrett said, shrugging. Khaled smiled. He always liked how Garrett, too, called his grandmother *Setto,* pronouncing the Arabic nickname as if it were second nature. *Setto.*

"We can still go, if you want to."

"Nah, that's fine."

"Do you want to go to the city tomorrow?"

Garrett shook his head. "Can't. We've set up a basketball game for tomorrow." Then, after a pause, "You should come. We can go to the city together on Saturday."

Khaled reached for the laptop again, opening it. He said nothing.

"The guys all ask about you, you know," Garrett added.

Khaled nodded. He hoped his school friends truly were asking about him, though he suspected Garrett might have made this up. He still remembered the days following his brother's death, when even Khaled's closest friends would pass by him in the school's hallways and turn to look the other way. "They're just embarrassed," Garrett would reassure him. "They don't know what to say to you." Even if Khaled had believed Garrett's assertions, he was still hurt. It had taken weeks for some of his friends to nod a greeting when they saw him, for anyone other than Garrett to join him at the lunch table, for Bud Murphy to get tired of aiming a thumb-and-pointer gun at him whenever Khaled passed his way, his hand rebounding with the shock of the imaginary shot, his lips pursed as they whistled the sound of a flying bullet amid the cheer of Bud's entourage. Even now, a full year after what happened, Khaled still felt that his presence among people who had known Hosaam and Natalie increased the collective awkwardness. Garrett was the only one of his old friends he still felt comfortable around; Brittany, the only new friend he had made during the previous year. If it were not for these two, Khaled would have spent his entire previous year online, toggling back and forth between his blog and his new Facebook account, both digital portals connecting him to an outside world that rejected Khaled but seemed indifferent to his alter ego, K.A.

He had started his blog on a sleepless night a month or so after his self-imposed exile from a Facebook that had become hostile after Hosaam's crime. Sitting alone in his room, Khaled had realized he could counter the Internet's potential hostility by taking advantage of the anonymity it offered. His blog was simple: daily entries about lepidoptera and, occasionally, beetles and caterpillars he came across either on websites or on his hikes. Nothing personal. Even simpler was his signature: K.A. No way to identify him. Letters revealing no ethnicity, no identity, and no connections.

Though the signature came as an afterthought, he had used it for only a few weeks before its usefulness became clear to him. Areas of the Internet that Khaled had shut himself out of, K.A. could potentially enter, unnoticed. Suddenly, and after two months of abstinence, Facebook became a possibility again.

His new Facebook page contained a picture of him in profile, the sun shining so brightly in the background his face was visible only as a dark silhouette, the shade of his skin undecipherable, his features one dark mass. Those whom he befriended on Facebook could see a couple of other pictures in which he was recognizable but his surroundings were not: self-portraits of him out on his hikes, with backdrops of trees and open meadows. His face, a dark tan that could have easily passed for any ethnicity, from mixed to Hispanic, was not antagonistic. People did not object to his face, he learned, as much as they objected to his name. And his initials, though they were still his, could imply any name. Karlos Aguilar, with roots both in Puerto Rico and the Dominican Republic. Khristos Agathangelos, standing in the front yard of his Mediterranean villa in the Greek isles. Or, his favorite, Kevin Anderson.

Garrett was the only one of his friends who knew of his Facebook page, and even he learned of it by accident. Sitting in Garrett's room one day, Khaled had logged on to his account but forgot to log back out before letting Garrett on the laptop. On the floor, a bunch of Garrett's CDs sprawled in front of him, Khaled was taken aback when Garrett, his laptop on the desk in front of him, yelled, "Dude, you call yourself *Ka?* That's brilliant!"

Khaled, too startled to make sense of what he'd heard, blurted, "What?"

"*Ka!* Your Facebook page. Hey, how come I'm not on it?" Garrett turned to him.

"I didn't want anyone from school to find out."

"But I don't have anyone you wouldn't want on there. I unfriended Bud and his Buddies a long time ago!"

"Not just Bud," Khaled said, smiling at Garrett's name for Bud Murphy and his gang. "I just didn't want anyone to find out."

Garrett shrugged. Khaled, eager to change the subject, asked, "What did you mean it was brilliant?"

"You seriously don't know what *Ka* means? And you call yourself Egyptian?"

"They're just my initials," Khaled said, bewildered.

"*Ka*: The ancient Egyptian name for the human soul. The part of you that makes you alive. You seriously didn't know that?"

Khaled shook his head.

"Man. Your culture is wasted on you."

The blog's biggest achievement—besides allowing him hours of indulgence in entomology—was connecting him with Brittany. He logged into his Facebook account one day and found a friendship request from her. His heart pounding, he had read the unfamiliar girl's short message: Nice blog. Cool pics of the monarch. Immediately accepting her request, he spent days obsessively browsing her numerous photos, elated at the bliss of having a girl interested in insects seek his friendship. When he found out she lived in New York, he was dumbfounded. Ehsan would have deemed this fate.

Days later, he hopped on the Amtrak to New York. It took all his strength to shoot down the panic that had paralyzed him for days ever since he'd known Brittany lived close enough for them to meet. Sitting in that train, he spent the entire forty-five-minute ride assuring himself that he could do this. He could go seek out a young woman he did not know and introduce himself. Pursuing a logic that he would later remember with a mixture of fondness and embarrassment, he told himself he was, in fact, being a good Muslim. Hadn't Ehsan always told him that *Islam* shared the root of *surrender* and that a good Muslim therefore always surrendered his will to God's? Who else but God would have steered Brittany toward his blog? He truly believed that having an attractive young woman seek him out based on their mutual interest in bugs had to be an act of divine intervention.

She worked in a coffee shop a few blocks away from NYU. Inside the cramped, busy store, he stood in line, watching her, thinking that he had not known her work schedule and that she could have easily been off that day. Yet there she was, working behind the counter, placing pastries on white plates and handing cappuccinos with overflowing froth to customers. He ordered a black coffee and a slice of marble loaf, and was served by a tall, skinny young man with shining silver disk earrings and cropped black hair. The man was pale, his lips pursed, and Khaled felt too sorry for him to resent the way he had jumped ahead of Brittany to serve him, depriving Khaled of the one opportunity he had rehearsed all the way here to introduce himself. Now, sitting in a corner of the coffee shop in a large armchair, Khaled sipped at his coffee and watched Brittany work as he thought of how he could approach her.

Watching her made him uncomfortable, like he was doing something wrong or creepy, like he was intruding, spying on hapless neighbors through a telescope, for instance, or peeking into someone's private Facebook account and browsing through pictures he knew were not meant for him. There was something else, too, some other discomfort that was only his, that no one else would relate to: the discomfort of knowing Hosaam had probably done something similar to this, had probably peered through parted blinds to watch Natalie's house for any sign of her. The continuous, nagging, suffocating discomfort caused by his inability to totally dismiss Hosaam from his thoughts.

Outweighing his discomfort was the thrill of being so close to her. He had never done such a thing before. Even back when he went to watch Grace he had not felt as nervous as he did now. He feasted his eyes on Brittany's plump lips, painted a lavender that complemented the streak in her hair, and on her white, clear skin that contrasted with the black T-shirt she wore, the coffee shop's logo printed in green, stretched tight over her breasts: Claire's Coffee and Cakes. Deep dimples appeared on her cheeks whenever she smiled, which was often. Stretching her arm across the counter, rows of silver bracelets with charms hanging off of them slid back on her wrists and then forward again with each movement. He wondered what the charms were. He imagined himself picking out charms for her, maybe friendly ones, at first, a small coffee cup or a clock to remind her that time would pass each day and she would eventually get to go home, and then other charms, a small heart, a dangling Cupid's arrow, or a miniature house with smoke rising out of its chimney. He wondered if she wore anklets, too.

He saw her whisper something to a coworker before stepping outside. Through the glass front of the coffee shop he could see her smoke, the cigarette dangling between her fingers, her hand carrying it to her mouth and then back again every few seconds. In her left hand, she held her phone. She stood with her back against the glass, the sole of one heavy boot resting against the storefront, her leg covered in thick black stockings. She was wearing a gray miniskirt, but he could not tell whether she wore anklets. He imagined she did, under her boots.

She was texting, he could tell. Or typing something. Quickly, he got his phone out and checked Facebook. Yes—she was updating her status. "One more hour to go . . . too nice a day to stay in," she wrote. His hand shook, and he wiped sweaty fingers on his jeans. His heart raced as his fingers typed, "At least you get smoking breaks," followed by a winking face. He saw her look at her phone, then around. Glancing down again, she clicked something on her phone. Probably his name, he thought. Maybe trying to get a better look at his picture. She looked around her one more time, then back at the phone, typing something. He checked his phone. "Spooky" was all she added. He stared at the phone. He had to type something smart, something that would keep her interested. He didn't want to reveal his location that fast. "Not spooky. Simple," he typed. He clicked on his own picture and magnified it. The picture looked okay, enough like him for her to recognize him, he hoped.

"How?" she typed back. "Spying?" He stared at the word, squeezed the phone in his fist. Cold sweat collected on his forehead. "I don't spy," he wrote back, punching the letters through the phone's touch screen. *I don't spy,* he told himself. *I'm not a creep. I don't spy, nor do I stalk.* He got up, stared at the phone and then at her. He should leave now. He no longer felt he wanted to talk to her. How would he explain being here anyway? What kind of coincidence would that be? Of all the places in New York, for him to end up in her coffee shop? Of course she had the right to think he was a creep, spying on her, stalking her. Again Hosaam's image flashed in his mind. He looked down at his phone one more time. He would leave now. He touched the screen and saw she had replied, "Just kidding, K.A. Chill." He stared at the initials, and then sat down, touched two fingers to his forehead. Chill.

"Look behind you," he typed. His hands were not shaking. When she looked back, he lifted one arm up, waved, and smiled. She smiled back.

Later, they had walked through Washington Square Park, and he had confessed to his obsession with her pictures. Talking to her had been effortless, his words lured out of him by her ability to listen. Later, it would seem to him that he would have told her everything, had she asked the right questions. The one question she did pose he answered more honestly than he had planned for.

"So what does K.A. stand for?" she asked as they strolled through the park.

He swallowed. Minutes earlier he had reminded himself of his new moniker, the one he had settled on as he sat in the coffee shop waiting for her to finish her shift: Kevin Anderson. He had repeated the name to himself, engraving it in his memory, letting the letters roll silently on his tongue until he got used to them. Kevin Anderson. Now, walking next to her, the zeal he had felt as he clung to this name was gone. Instead, he was overcome by a desire for the extraordinary, a sudden conviction that this girl walking next to him would be more impressed by the exotic than by the common. Also, he had found neither the courage nor the desire to lie to her.

"They're my initials. *Ka* is also the ancient Egyptian name for the soul. My parents are from Egypt, originally." He glanced sideways to see her reaction. His eyes met hers, and she smiled.

"Cool," she said.

They walked across the park and waited for the traffic light to turn red before crossing, heading east on Fourth Street among a flow of pedestrians. He had not truly answered her question, yet she did not press on—and because she did not, he added, "The K is for Khaled."

"Khaled. That's nice. I don't think I've ever met a Khaled before."

He looked straight at her, scrutinizing her smile, her half-curious, half-friendly gaze. No judgment, none of the caution the mention of his name might have evoked. He would not tell her his last name, even though he knew the absurdity of fearing that she, living in New York, would recognize his brother's name in his. But he had told her his first name, and that was all that mattered. That was enough.

Sitting on Garrett's bed, Khaled sneaked a look at his friend, who had gone back to texting Hailee. Guilt consumed him again at never having told Garrett about Brittany, at never having told Brittany about Hosaam, at the secrets this past year had taught him to keep. Garrett never kept any secrets, as far as he could tell. Khaled had always envied his friend his ease with people, his ability to approach strangers and start talking with no apprehensions. The day Khaled met Brittany for the first time, he had tried to emulate Garrett, even after it was clear to him that Brittany's friendship was all he would ever be able to gain, if he was lucky enough. Almost daily, he regretted his inability to evoke the ease and frankness that came so naturally to his two friends. Then again, neither one of them had to live with his memories.

6

ENGLISH: And they lived happily ever after.

Traditional fairy tale ending

ARABIC: And the two brothers abode with their wives in all pleasance and solace of life and its delights, for that indeed Allah the Most High had changed their annoy into joy; and on this wise they continued till there took them the Destroyer of delights and the Severer of societies, the Desolator of dwelling-places and Garnerer of grave-yards, and they were translated to the ruth of Almighty Allah; their houses fell waste and their palaces lay in ruins and the Kings inherited their riches.

From the ending of The Arabian Nights

Samir used to make fun of Nagla for claiming she could smell things he could not: the new-car scent a year after they had owned the car; fresh grout months after he had remodeled a bathroom; the traces of frying oil on her kitchen apron after it had been laundered twice. He often teased her, saying that she was cursed not only with the nose of a hound but also with the ears of a cat, hearing the swish of a pin through the air before it hit the floor. Sitting cross-legged on the only carpeted area in the middle of the attic, Nagla thought that perhaps he was right, that her mother could not understand her obsession with the attic because she was never able to detect what Nagla could: Hosaam's lingering smell, a faint scent that seemed always to originate from a spot right over her shoulder, as if all she needed to do was turn around and she would find him there, a halo of aftershave mixed with traces of sweat that the attic's mustiness could not mask.

Today she carried a plastic storage bin upstairs—one larger than what her mother would have approved of, but, if she had to sort through her son's stuff, Nagla reasoned, she should at least be allowed to keep as much of it as she wanted to. She had been in the attic only half an hour and the bin was already almost full: Hosaam's collection of drumsticks; a notebook filled with doodling, notes, caricatures, and words written in block letters across full pages (*Rock Nation, Got Nothing Better to Do*); some music paper that he used back when he was getting into songwriting, the groups of five lines littered with penciled dots and sticks that Nagla stared at, marks her son had made that meant something to him but nothing to her, a coded message in a language that she never learned. His manuscript had to stay, of course, if only to honor the time he spent working on it. Sorting items by what they meant to him, not to her, made sense, at first; it gave her a gauging system that would prevent her from keeping everything, including the tossed sock that had made its way under the low cabinet and stayed hidden there for at least a year until she had pulled it out moments earlier.

Soon enough, though, she found it difficult to determine even what Hosaam would have liked to keep. The attic was his private sanctuary, and nothing seemed trivial enough to discard; his magazines, his CDs, his posters of Manchester United and AC Milan (left over from an earlier obsession with soccer), his two guitars and the music stand—*his* things. Nagla stared at the black garbage bag across from her, sitting empty and exuding disappointment. She got up and made her way to one of the guitars, standing in the corner behind Hosaam's drum set. Even in the morning the attic was so dimly lit that she had to step carefully to make sure she did not trip over some cast-off shoe or a stack of magazines. Reaching the guitar, she carried it over to the room's only window, held it up for inspection. Some kid could get pretty excited about this, even though Hosaam never really did. He had entertained the guitar idea for what—two weeks? Three? And then he was back to his drums, pounding on them at all hours of the day and forgetting all about his guitar-related plans. She wasn't even sure both guitars were his, and, glancing at the other guitar, she wondered whether one of his friends had left his there and forgotten about it. How did he end up with not one but two instruments? She put the guitar down, let it rest against the windowsill. Looking back, it seemed that she had been more excited about Hosaam's guitar prospects than her son ever was. She distinctly remembered thinking of him on a stage, guitar in hand, playing some prolonged solo in front of a hysterically enthusiastic audience. This could not have been a true memory. At the time, though, it had seemed plausible enough.

Hosaam's musical ventures had irritated Samir. At first, he had grudgingly accepted them as a phase his teenage son was passing through, but when the days stretched into weeks and months, Samir grew impatient. Every time bursts of drum solos blasted out of the attic, Samir winced.

"He's wasting his time," he complained to Nagla one evening as they both sat in the kitchen drinking their after-dinner tea while continuous, muffled drumrolls played in the background. "He'd be better off studying."

"He can't study all day long," Nagla protested.

"He can't play music all day long, either."

"He's not. He only practices in the evenings," Nagla lied.

"He already wastes a couple of evenings a week practicing with this band of his. He should spend the rest of the week studying. How does he expect to go to a good college if he can't even maintain an A average? How is he going to survive medical school if he doesn't develop good study habits?"

But Hosaam had not been interested in medical school, nor, it turned out, in higher education in general. Considering how well she believed she knew her own son, Nagla should have anticipated what came next. Yet when Hosaam walked into the living room one evening and announced to his parents that he would not be applying to college, she was thunderstruck.

Samir was furious.

"He has nothing except this band stuff on his mind," Samir had yelled the moment Nagla managed to pull him into their bedroom and away from Hosaam. "I told you we should never have let him join that band. But you wouldn't hear of it, would you? *Let him have fun!*" he mocked her. "Now look where this fun has taken him. He's going to be a total failure!" Samir took off his sweater, threw it against the wall.

"No, he's not! Maybe he's just not meant to be a doctor. Maybe he can—"

"No one is *meant* to be a doctor. You work for it! You earn it!" Samir cut her off. He was walking around the room in circles, folding up the sleeves of his shirt, tearing his tie off. "He's not going to be a doctor because he is a lazy, good-for-nothing bum who thinks he's going to be a music star!"

As if in response, a crescendo of drumbeats exploded out of the attic, right above the bedroom. Samir looked up.

"*Wallahil-azim,* if he doesn't stop that racket I will walk up there and break that thing into a million pieces," Samir hissed.

For weeks afterward, Nagla tried to reason with Samir, whose anger with Hosaam had driven him to ignore his older son, ceasing all communication with him except for the occasional remark thrown in whenever Hosaam was close enough to overhear it. "Some people have no ambition," Samir would grumble as Hosaam walked into the kitchen to grab a snack. "I wonder how long he thinks I will support him." Always speaking of his son in the third person.

"Just give him some time, Samir," Nagla would plead. She had truly hoped that time was the only thing Hosaam needed and had convinced herself that she had good reason to believe so. In the months preceding Hosaam's decision not to apply to college, he had grown closer than ever to Natalie, and Nagla knew that he dreaded the strain that distance would put on their relationship, if he and Natalie ended up going to colleges states apart. "We'd be away from each other for five whole years, Natalie!" she had heard him whisper on the phone one evening. "Five years!" Even as she regretted the year her son wasted, Nagla had hoped that he was only waiting to find out where Natalie would go so that he could apply to the same college or, at least, to a college nearby. In Nagla's mind, Hosaam's decision to postpone—not forsake, just postpone— going to college testified to nothing other than his romanticism. Samir would have balked at this theory, of course, but that's why she never mentioned her suspicion to him, reveling, instead, in the belief that she understood her son better than his father ever did.

Hosaam had been fine all the way until he graduated high school, Nagla would later tell herself again and again. But something happened during the months that followed. His bandmates all went to college, leaving him behind. And Natalie? Nagla never found out what happened between them, why or when the rift came. Perhaps she would never even have suspected anything was wrong with Hosaam, had the noise coming from the attic not stopped, the incessant practice replaced by eerie silence.

Samir had been glad. "Maybe he's finally coming to his senses," he had said.

Later, Nagla would remember that moment and shudder, wondering how things would have turned out if she had responded to Samir's statement, voicing the concern that had started gnawing at her, the fear that, whatever was happening to Hosaam, it was *not* a return to better sense. In those days, she had watched her older son become more and more withdrawn. He would walk up to the attic like he always did, but instead of the outburst of music that usually followed his ascent, nothing but silence would ensue. By the time Nagla noticed her son's change of habits, she could not pinpoint the last time she had heard him play the drums, nor could she recall having recently seen him go out with his friends or sit up with Natalie on her porch, like they always used to do.

"Something wrong, *habibi*?" she asked him one day as he passed her on his way up to the attic. He looked at her, said nothing, and then continued walking.

"Something bothering you? Tell me, Hosaam." She followed him up the stairs to the second floor, watched him climb up the pull-down ladder to the attic.

"Nothing for you to worry about," he muttered, pulling the trapdoor shut behind him. "Not for much longer, anyway."

Perhaps it was another phase, she had told herself. Perhaps he had had a fight with Natalie—his first broken heart. Perhaps he was getting bored with staying home and would soon start thinking about college; a little bit of boredom might be productive. For weeks she had waited, keeping her worries from Samir, thankful that he was beginning to grow less angry with Hosaam now that his musical aspirations seemed to have waned.

"He'll be talking about college soon, you'll see," Samir had reassured her. "He'll recognize that he needs an education, if he is to become anyone in this world."

Nagla, nodding to everything her husband said, had hoped he was right.

Standing in the attic, lost in the midst of her son's belongings, Nagla remembered how naïvely optimistic she had been, waiting as she did for her son to return, willfully and of his own accord, from whatever foreign territory he had wandered into, hoping that, any day now, he would start talking to her again, he would start going out with his friends again, he would regain his appetite, he would play music again, or, at least, he would find his way out of the attic where he seemed to have been serving a self-imposed prison sentence. Looking around her, she wondered what role that attic, so cluttered and claustrophobic, had played in her son's decline. She had to admit the room was depressing. For one thing, the attic was always dark, even in the middle of the day. The attic's only window, circular and overlooking the backyard, was coated with dust. Looking out the window, Nagla pulled the sock she had found out of her pocket and held it to her nose, sniffing. Even she could detect nothing but dankness. Why had she kept that sock in her pocket? A single, musty sock—if she kept it, it would become one more thing to care for and obsess over, one more silly thing to mourn when it got lost. She held the balled sock in one hand, hesitated, and then, deliberately avoiding further thought, used it to wipe a section of the window clean. She scrubbed the window, pushing and pulling until her upper arm hurt. When she still could not see through the glass, she reached for the latch, pushed the window open, rotating it on its horizontal axis, and then started vigorously wiping the external surface. She wiped even after the sock had turned black and she had to turn it inside out to clean the smeared dirt off the window. When she closed the window again, she could see through it well enough to detect the edge of her backyard, the border of Summerset Park, where Natalie's memorial service was to take place in only three days.

The trees seemed vexingly neutral to all that had gone on around them. In her mind, those trees should have all been burned down by now, should have burst in a willful act of spontaneous combustion, leaving an arid, gray expanse, a testimony to the horror that their branches had sheltered. She remembered Cynthia's plan to plant a tree in memory of her daughter and felt an overwhelming urge to smoke.

She searched the pocket of her sweatpants for a loose cigarette and a lighter, found the lighter but no cigarette. Probably not a good idea to smoke here anyway. Too many flammable items. Also, cigarette smoke might mask the faint scent she could still detect all over the attic, more so now that she was flipping through her son's stuff. She looked at the window, alarmed that her bout of cleaning might have let in too much fresh air. But it had not—only a few steps away from the window she could still detect his smell. She inhaled, closed her eyes. She needed a smoke. On her way out, she tossed the soiled sock in the trash bag.

Cigarette in hand, Nagla sat on the deck looking out on her backyard, which merged into the Bradstreets'. Everything was still: the grass under the blazing noon sun, the trees bordering the park at the edge of the yard, the ferns in their green plastic pots dangling in each corner of the slanted overhang. The stillness implied a peace that had been elusive of late, reminding her of how much she had loved this porch the moment she laid eyes on it, wrapping around three sides of the house, a horseshoe promising good luck. For a long time, the house seemed to fulfill what it had promised.

There used to be two swing sets out there: one in her backyard, the other in the Bradstreets'. The day they first met the Bradstreets, Hosaam had chased Natalie all around her set, and a few months later Jim had helped Samir install a similar one in their backyard. Even in picking out the swing set Samir had been conscious of what others thought: he didn't want one much bigger than the Bradstreets', lest he offend them, or smaller, because he didn't want to appear inferior. Choosing the exact same set would suggest he was copying them, which he would never do. So he had gone with one roughly the same size: one slide, three swings, and one sand box—to match theirs—but with a seesaw on the side, just to give his "a little something extra," as he put it.

The seesaw was a hit. Hosaam and Natalie put more hours on that thing than they did on both their sets combined. Hosaam, one year older and more heavily built, was almost always in control—pushing the ground to lift himself up and then squatting still, keeping Natalie up in the air as she giggled and kicked both legs, enjoying the breeze that ruffled her skirt. She always wore sundresses in the summer, even to the playground—spaghetti-strapped and floral. Natalie in her cute sundresses was the main reason Nagla and Samir decided to have one more child after Khaled, even though they had both thought two children were enough. Thinking back, Nagla also believed she wanted another child out of pity for Khaled, poor, lonesome Khaled, only two years younger than Natalie yet always left out, always alone in the sandbox while the two other kids played together. Whenever they did let him join in, trouble often ensued. Like that time on the seesaw when Natalie, trying to outweigh Hosaam, had yelled at Khaled to come join her side. She had let him sit in front of her, wrapping her arms around him to reach the handlebars, and they had both, for a few seconds, managed to lift Hosaam high up and keep him there, Natalie laughing, Khaled a bit scared but trying not to show it, and Hosaam—so angry, Nagla now realized. Later that day, he had kept Natalie up in the air until she screamed for help and then he had jumped off and let her crash, falling backward and hitting her head against the ground while he stood and watched, not even running to help her as Nagla and Cynthia did once she started crying. Why was she remembering all this now? Nagla sighed, flicked the cigarette ash on the deck, not bothering to reach for the ashtray. Everything seemed laden with meaning now, even a six-year-old's spiteful act. And Samir had overreacted, dismantling the seesaw that very day and leaving it out on the curb for the garbage collectors. Mortified, of course, that his son had done something that might make him, Samir, look bad.

Nagla got up, walked over to the wooden railing. Resting both elbows on it, she took one more puff of her cigarette before flicking it away. The stub landed on the dry grass, a couple of feet away from all the other ones she had tossed out her bedroom window in the past few days. Nagla examined it, its end still glowing a faint orange. Why had she done so? The ashtray stood on the side table behind her. The grass, tall and yellowing after weeks of drought, could catch fire. She turned around, picked the ashtray up, and walked down the few steps and over to her garden of scattered cigarette stubs. One by one, she picked them up, starting with the one that was still lit and making sure it was fully extinguished. In the pit of her stomach she felt a disappointment with herself for her carelessness, a disappointment that called up other letdowns, reminding her of all she had failed to do, all the little signs she now knew she should have paid closer attention to. All the ways she had failed herself and her son.

"What's wrong, *habibti*?"

Ehsan had walked out to the deck. Nagla looked at her mother, placed the ashtray on the ground next to her, and wiped her eyes on her sleeve.

"Nothing, Mama."

"Don't nothing me. You're crying."

Nagla shook her head. "I was just thinking—" She paused.

"What?"

"You'd be angry with me if I told you."

"Why, may Allah bring nothing but good? I can never be angry with you."

Of course she would be. For Nagla's entire life her mother had warned her against *what if?* The question that the prophet Muhammad, peace be upon his soul, said opened the door to let the devil in. The question clashed with all that Islam stood for, inviting thoughts that relinquished the total submission to God the religion encouraged and replaced it with doubt and, often, with anger.

"Tell me, *habibti*. You're worrying me," Ehsan pleaded.

Nagla looked down at the stubs, sprouting in the ashtray like the back of a childproofed porcupine. "I was thinking that perhaps I should have paid closer attention to Hosaam in his last year or so. I should've actually done something about the way he was changing, rather than wait for him to snap out of it on his own," Nagla said, carefully avoiding the use of *what if*.

Ehsan sighed. "Again, Nagla? How many times have I told you that such thoughts will only make you miserable? It's God's will, *habibti*. Nothing you could have done would have changed this."

Her mother's words, habitually tuned to help, only enhanced her feeling of guilt. Nagla bit on her lower lip, tried to hold back her tears. She longed to embrace her mother's total trust in fate, her assurance that all God did was for the good. She wished she had a fraction of Job's patience and strength, his story told in the Qur'an specifically for people cursed with unimaginable misfortunes. But, just as she could not utter the words *what if* in her mother's presence, she could not voice her thoughts in front of her. She had never told her mother that, for three months after her son's death, she had not once prayed any of the required five daily prayers. She was not only a bad mother but also a bad Muslim.

"*Al-salaamu Aleikum!*"

Nagla jumped, startled. Next to her mother, Ameena had materialized as if conjured by religious thoughts.

"*Ahlan, ahlan,*" Ehsan exclaimed, opening her arms wide.

Ameena smiled, dimpled cheeks over a pointed chin, her face framed in a white scarf. "I rang the bell but no one answered. Salaam, *khalah*." Ameena embraced Ehsan, planting a kiss on each of her cheeks. "So I thought I'd walk back here and check. I saw your car in the driveway, Nagla, and knew you had to be here somewhere."

Up on her feet again, Nagla stumbled over to the deck, ashtray in hand. She let Ameena hug her as she muttered something about washing her hands before disappearing into the kitchen, leaving her friend alone with her mother.

What was she doing here? Nagla thought as she scrubbed her fingernails under running water, peering at the two women through the kitchen window. Instantly she felt another pang of guilt. She had no reason to dislike Ameena's visits so much. The woman was an angel. Other than Ehsan, Ameena was the only one who did not leave Nagla's side for the entire previous year. After Hosaam's death, the other women from the mosque had offered prayers and support for the customary three days of mourning before retreating back into their lives, where they could resume an existence uncontaminated by bereavement. But Ameena had stayed. For the weeks prior to Ehsan's arrival, Ameena had practically taken over the care of Nagla's house, making sure her children were fed and had clean clothes to wear, even though both Khaled and Fatima were old enough to manage on their own. After Ehsan arrived and literally dragged Nagla out of the bed she had burrowed into in a weeks-long stupor, Ameena still called Nagla regularly, stopping by every couple of days to check on her, offering a shoulder for Nagla to cry on as well as the occasional dish of *basbousa* or *mehallabeyya*—Nagla's favorite desserts. Even now, a full year after what happened, Ameena still opened her house to Fatima, letting her spend more time with Maraam, Ameena's daughter, than she did at her own home. Nagla suspected that Ameena's kindness was performed more out of a love of God than out of any particular affection for Nagla herself—Ameena did have a bit of Mother Teresa in her, basking in the glory of offering help to the less fortunate, the bereaved, the sick both in body and in soul. But that suspicion was probably not fair. Nagla grabbed a towel to dry her hands and continued watching her mother and her friend, Ameena listening to Ehsan's chatter and nodding. Ameena had been her friend for a long time. Claiming that her support was motivated by religious zeal only did not do justice to the years both women spent visiting, talking on the phone, sharing tea in the mornings, running errands together. Throughout the previous two decades, no other woman had been as close to Nagla as Ameena was—except, of course, Cynthia, but that, too, was now lost. Nagla sighed, tossed the towel back on the countertop. How ridiculous it was to feel anything other than gratitude toward the only friend she had left.

Yet there was something about Ameena's continuous presence that felt claustrophobic, Nagla thought as she headed toward the deck. Perhaps Nagla wouldn't mind her visits so much if only she called ahead and announced she would stop by.

"I hope I'm not interrupting," Ameena said, reading Nagla's mind.

"No, of course not."

"I'll go make some tea," Ehsan said, heading inside.

"No need, *khalah*. I won't stay," Ameena shouted, but Ehsan had already disappeared into the kitchen.

Nagla motioned for her friend to sit and then settled down across from her. She smiled at Ameena, feeling a rush of affability toward her now that she knew the visit would not last long.

"I wanted to stop by and make sure you're okay. Also, I wanted to give you this." Fishing in her purse, Ameena pulled out a small booklet. "It's a new edition of the book of prayers I gave you a couple of months ago, remember? A friend of mine just came back from Qatar and brought some with her."

She held the booklet out to Nagla, who took it and placed it on the table.

"Thank you," Nagla said.

Ameena glanced at the table and then back at Nagla, and waited. Nagla picked up the booklet, flipped through its pages. The usual stuff, prayers that her mother knew by heart, divided by chapters: what to say when praying for forgiveness, for patience, to ward off evil, to counter the evil eye, to ask for peacefulness, to beg for health, what to say before a long trip, before going to bed, after waking up, before and after eating, when facing a tough choice, when struggling under unexpected burdens, when fighting against one's own sinning soul. A prayer for every occasion. She wondered whether her mother and Ameena had conspired to remind her of her negligence of her religion, bombarding her with suggestions designed to help her utter the words they knew would bring about healing. Then again, they probably did not need to conspire. Both women consistently relied on such words, weaving them into everything from incantations uttered during cooking to bless the food to folded talismans inscribed with prayers and tucked in clothing to provide protection. Nagla tossed the booklet back on the table, sighed.

Ameena reached out and tapped her on the hand. "We haven't seen you at the mosque in ages; we all miss you, you know."

"You're all kindness."

Nagla looked out on the yard. Ameena had let her hand rest on Nagla's palm, and Nagla felt her hand sweat. She could feel Ameena's gaze fixated on her. She should look back at her and nod. Maybe smile and make small talk. Definitely not pull her hand away before her guest did. She knew the rules very well. She pulled her hand away.

Ameena, straightening up, looked away. Nagla could see her in her peripheral vision. She waited.

A pause. Ameena cleared her throat, murmured something that Nagla could not make out. Then she turned to face Nagla again.

"I also wanted to let you know," Ameena continued, "that I'm having a lunch at my house tomorrow after Friday prayer. Just a few ladies from the mosque, and *khalah* Eishaa, the imam's wife. She's bringing a friend visiting from India who will conduct our *halakah* this week." Ameena paused. Nagla swallowed, said nothing. "You haven't been to a *halakah* in a long time, Nagla. It would be good for you."

"Thank you," Nagla said.

"So you'll come?"

"I'll try."

"Would you like me to come pick you up? Or send Ashraf?"

"I can drive, Ameena." A bit too sharply. Ameena looked down at her fingertips.

"I'm sorry. I didn't mean to sound so—"

"It's okay. I just wanted to help. I hate to see you like this, Nagla."

"Like what?"

"Locked up by yourself all the time."

"I'm not by myself. My mom is here."

"You don't come to the mosque at all anymore."

"I've been busy."

"How about the day after tomorrow? I can try to reschedule the *halakah* for then."

"I can't."

"You can't or you won't?"

Ameena tilted her head to the side, an accusatory stance that Nagla knew well.

"I can't just take off on a Saturday and leave Samir and the kids!"

"Why not? It's only for a few hours. And it's a religious lesson."

"Not even for a religious lesson." Nagla paused. "And isn't it a bit strange that, religiously speaking, we should take care of our husbands and kids first, but you all don't mind spending hours each week on these lessons, even on weekends?"

"We never do it on weekends." Ameena's face flushed. "We always hold them on weekday mornings, when the kids are at school. I only offered to try to move it to Saturday so that you could come."

Nagla looked away.

"It's not a big deal, anyway," Ameena said, getting up and grabbing her purse. "I just thought it wouldn't hurt to try. Can't make you do what you don't want to do."

Ameena turned around and knocked on the kitchen window, waved to Ehsan. Nagla watched both women gesture through the glass, Ehsan pointing at the teapot—almost ready—and Ameena putting both hands on her chest and bowing in thanks before pointing at her watch and waving—time to go. She turned around and caught Nagla's eye.

"Just think about tomorrow, okay? *Insh'Allah*, I'll see you there," Ameena said. Nagla got up. They both skipped the customary hug. "Please give my best to your mother, and my apologies for having put her through the trouble of making tea for nothing," Ameena said as she left, turning the corner of the deck and heading toward the front of the house.

Nagla watched her disappear and sighed, drawing a hand up to her head. Already she was regretting not having hugged her friend. She didn't even remember to thank her for taking Fatima in day in and day out. And that bit about the religious lessons was rude, too. She heard the car door open and close. She should at least thank her for stopping by. Running, she traced Ameena's steps and made it to the front of the house just in time to see her car pull out of the driveway. She waved but could not tell whether Ameena saw her.

Slowly, she made her way back to the deck, and off it into the backyard. The dry grass crunched under her feet as she stepped on it. She kept her head down and away from the sun. She didn't want to stay on the deck and wait for her mother, who would be walking out any moment now, inquiring about everything Ameena said and questioning why she had to leave so abruptly. Chastising Nagla for refusing to go to the *halakah*. Nagla hurried, trying to gain enough distance from the house to be able to claim she could not hear her mother, if she came out calling for her.

Reaching the edge of her backyard, Nagla headed straight for a narrow path between two tall trees and stepped into the shade, into the forest. Immediately she could feel her heart ache, literally ache, as if the branches around her with their loads of packed leaves had all directed their weight toward one spot in her chest. She kept on walking, stepping over dead branches and dry leaves, heading toward the clearing.

They had called it the enchanted forest, the kids. She didn't know who had named it, but by the time Hosaam was eight the forest was officially declared enchanted, with a range of subtitles that changed from season to season. That day it had been Ali Baba's forest—even though Ali Baba lived in the desert, according to the fable, a discrepancy that Nagla willingly ignored. The boys had run ahead of her and into the masses of trees, and she had followed, sprinting to catch up with them, panting, all the while carrying three-year-old Fatima. When she arrived, the boys had already made it to the clearing and were standing in front of a wall of trees with a tangle of trunks so dense they could not see its center.

"It's Ali Baba's cave!" Hosaam had declared.

"Let's see if it'll open!" Khaled said.

"Open Sesame!" Hosaam yelled. The boys stood in anticipation, and Fatima wiggled out of her mother's arms, jumped down, toddled over, and wedged between them, holding on to Khaled's hand.

"It's not working," Hosaam said.

"Try it in Arabic," Khaled said.

"*Eftah ya Semsem!*"

Nothing happened.

"Maybe you said it wrong," Khaled said.

"No I didn't! That's just how *Setto* says it."

"Try again, then," Khaled said.

"You try. I'm sick of this game." Hosaam headed back toward home.

Now, standing in the middle of the clearing, Nagla stared at the tangle of trees, looking at the exact spot where her sons had stood, then tracing with her eyes an imaginary line where Hosaam would have turned and walked back. He would have walked right past the spot where she now stood. Reaching out, she let one hand gently brush through the air where she thought he would have passed, twelve years earlier. She held her hand in place, at around shoulder level, a little bit lower. If time travel were possible, she would be able to go back to this same spot, and he would be right there, right where her hand now hovered, with his black wavy hair and large round eyes that so resembled her father's. He would have been just tall enough for her hand to rest on the top of his head. Carefully, she moved her palm from side to side, stroking an imaginary head. She waved her hand through this spot of air one last time, then sat down, closed her eyes, and listened for the whispers and giggles she had heard so many years ago and hoped that the air would eventually carry her way, if she waited long enough.

7

ARABIC: *Meadeddah*. A woman hired to wail at funeral
services—a professional mourner.

When the elevator door opened Samir saw Pat, Cynthia's sister, pinning a flyer to the bulletin board in the lobby of Summerset Medical
where he worked. Samir stepped out of the elevator but stopped so
abruptly that a nurse walking out behind him bumped straight into him.
He turned around and mumbled an apology. Letting the nurse pass, he
stood in place, staring at Pat. She, glancing at him, smoothed one edge
of the flyer before walking past and into the elevator, where he saw her
pull out another flyer and, Scotch tape in hand, start fastening it to the
elevator wall. She was on the lower corners when the doors closed, separating them.

Alone in the lobby, Samir felt free to examine the flyer unnoticed. He
tried not to look at Natalie's picture, though he was keenly aware of her
gaze, like a blond Mona Lisa, eyes following the beholder as long as he
was looking. The memorial was set for Sunday at the park—he knew
that much. To be held at noon—that was new. There were going to be
speakers; Reverend Fielding was presiding—good, Samir liked Reverend
Fielding. He was a moderate man, peaceful, like men of religion should
be. He would be preaching forgiveness, not calling for torches and pitch-
forks, like that guy in Florida did after 9/11. There were going to be other

speakers, not mentioned by name. He wondered who. Teachers, perhaps. They always called in teachers on occasions like these. Friends of Natalie were encouraged to attend and to share memories of her.

He heard the elevator door open and hurried out on the street. Behind him, he knew Pat would have emerged, probably watching him as he stepped out. He could feel her gaze piercing his back. She hated him, he knew; she always had. Nagla often complained that Pat's visits to Cynthia never failed to produce some awkward encounter among the three of them. Nagla was certain Pat objected to Cynthia's befriending her, even though Cynthia was too loyal to listen to her sister.

"She *hates* me," Nagla had said years ago, emphatically throwing a pan in the sink. Over dinner, she had spoken of nothing but Pat, whom she had met for the first time that morning.

"I'm sure she doesn't," Samir said. On his knees, he was busy tying Hosaam's shoelaces. The moment he was done Hosaam was out the kitchen door and in the backyard. Nagla watched him through the window as she did the dishes.

"Oh yeah? She didn't speak *two words* to me, and when she did she spoke only in slow, short sentences, like I'm an idiot."

"She probably thinks your English isn't that good."

"She heard me talk to Cynthia!" Nagla said, turning around to frown at Samir. He picked up his tea and sipped, leaning against the kitchen counter and deliberately avoiding her eyes.

"She didn't even touch the baklava I made her! I spent the entire morning slaving over this dish and she didn't even touch it! Said she was on a *diet*."

"Maybe she was."

"She had just eaten a Danish. What kind of diet is that? I saw the dish with the crumbs on the table next to her."

"Did you see her eat it?"

"*I saw the dish!*"

"That's circumstantial evidence." Samir shrugged. Nagla scowled at him again, her eyes narrowing. He had used an English word she did not understand. Hurriedly, he added, "What I mean is maybe it wasn't hers. Maybe it was Cynthia's and Pat really was on a diet. Or she might not like baklava. You're taking this too personally. Americans are not like us; she probably didn't know it was bad manners not to taste your dish. I'm sure she meant no offense."

Nagla, throwing one last angry glare at him, turned away and started vigorously scrubbing the pan. He looked at her and smiled. Back then, he had found her inability to understand American culture endearing. He accepted, as early as a few years into their lives in the United States, that Nagla would never blend in, a small price to pay considering that she would never have been able to afford the lifestyle he—and America—offered her, had they stayed in Egypt. That day, he had struggled to hold back what he truly thought: that Pat, unmarried and childless, made it back to her hometown so seldom that Nagla's presence was seen as an intrusion. Nagla was acting just like her mosque friends did whenever Ehsan came to visit: flocking to Nagla's house for tea, arms laden with homemade sweets, to welcome and entertain the mother they treated as their own, showering her with hugs and kisses that belied their superficial acquaintance. Pat's visit, rare as it was, was a chance for Nagla to show her loyalty to Cynthia by being overly kind to her sister.

But now Samir knew that Pat's actions were always calculated. No doubt she showed up at his office precisely at noon because she knew that was when he took his lunch hour. For almost two decades he had walked to the diner at the corner at noon for his usual lunch of scrambled eggs and a muffin. Everybody knew that. In a town that small, no one could maintain a habit for even a few weeks before people learned to depend on it. Even now, as he pulled open the door of the diner, Samir knew he was expected.

"Hey, Doc!" Shark yelled the moment Samir entered the diner. Samir raised a hand in greeting as he took his usual seat in the corner booth. Behind the counter, Shark was already spooning Samir's eggs onto a plate. Shark was a heavy-built man with asthma so severe Samir could hear his wheezing across the counter whenever the pollen count was high, which, in New Jersey, was the case more than half the year. He also knew Shark sometimes wheezed when nervous, though Samir would never suggest that to his face. Samir gave him free inhalers. Because Shark was his patient, Samir was also one of the few people who knew Shark's real name: Anton Tsharkovsky.

Shark called out to one of the waitresses, and she hurried to Samir's booth. She was a new girl, fresh out of high school, and Samir had seen her only a few times before. He watched as she poured his coffee, her long hair pulled back in a ponytail, just the way Fatima wore hers. He smiled. She, sensing his regard, looked at him and smiled back before trotting away. He followed her with his eyes, wondering, as he always did when he saw young people in this town, whether she knew any of his kids. When he looked away, his eyes wandered to the corkboard installed on the wall next to his booth and he saw another one of Natalie's posters.

He looked away, feeling himself blush, as if he had witnessed something he should not have, a person grieving in solitude or a private moment between lovers unaware of his presence. His awareness of his flushed face angered him, and he looked down into his coffee, chewing on his lips, trying to avoid looking at Shark, whom he could see in his peripheral vision. Of course Pat had done this. She must have come here before she came to his office building. The absurdity of imagining that she stopped in every diner and place of business to hang flyers made him certain that her choices were meant to embarrass him, to remind everyone of his disgrace. He opened sugar packets, one after another, and poured the contents into his cup, stirring. He was still looking into his cup when Shark carefully placed Samir's plate in front of him and then squeezed into the opposite side of the booth.

"Listen, Doc, let me tell you what happened," Shark started, leaning forward to whisper. Samir pulled his plate closer and took a bite of his eggs. Over the years, Shark had perfected the eggs to Samir's liking: just a little runny, made with real eggs, not out of a carton, the eggs not totally scrambled but only carefully mixed so that he could still see patches of pure white and vibrant yellow in them.

"This morning, this woman, Jim Bradstreet's sister-in-law, comes in the diner," Shark continued. "She had flyers to hang, but I wasn't here, see? The wife was here. She takes care of breakfast. Gives me a couple more hours to sleep." Shark waved a dismissive hand, as he often did when speaking of Allison, his wife of more than twenty years. Samir swallowed his food, pulled a napkin to his lips and wiped them.

"So Allison—she's known that lady since high school." Shark paused. "She told me her name just this morning. Can't believe it already slipped my mind. You know who I'm talking about, right?" He looked at Samir. He was still whispering. Behind him, Samir could see the diner filling up. When Samir first started coming here, Shark couldn't afford to hire help, and he could never leave his spot behind the counter for this long. Times have changed, Samir told himself. He sighed.

"Pat," Samir said. "Her name is Pat."

"Pat! That's it! You got it, Doc. It's driven me crazy this whole morning trying to think of her name." Shark slapped a hand on the table and the plate and utensils rattled. Samir, losing appetite, gulped down his coffee, which, as usual, was only mildly warm.

"So Pat comes in here with this flyer about that poor girl's memorial service. They're giving her a memorial service this Sunday." Shark nodded toward the flyer.

"Yes, I know."

"Good. Allison said you'd probably know about it already." Shark leaned back. He gave up whispering. "So Allison, she doesn't want to offend this woman, see? They went to high school together. Pat—can't believe I keep forgetting her name. You think I'm getting old?" He looked at Samir intently, waiting for his answer. "You know, dementia or something?"

"Not old, just fat." Samir nodded toward Shark's bulging stomach. Shark roared with laughter. People turned to look.

"You got me there, Doc," he said, slamming his hand on the table again. Samir put his coffee down, put his napkin on the table, shifted in place.

"I've been babbling, haven't I? Keeping you from your lunch. Bet your eggs are cold. You want me to make you another batch?"

"No, Shark. Thank you. I have to go back to work."

"Yes, sure." Shark got up, hovered above Samir. He put his hands in his pockets. He looked like an oversized schoolboy caught flicking paper balls at the blackboard while the teacher's back was turned. Samir waited. Shark did not move.

"What is it, Shark?" Samir finally asked. "If this is about the flyer, I've seen it before. No need to explain."

"I couldn't say no, Doc. I wanted to, but what can I do?" He lifted both hands in the air, palms facing up, and looked at Samir.

"Why is it that everyone thinks I'd object to this flyer?" Samir asked, his teeth clenched as he reached for his wallet, pulled a ten-dollar bill out, and stuck it under the saltshaker.

"I also told Allison that whole board thing was a bad idea, that people would start using it to sell stuff. But she saw it in a Starbucks and just had to put one up here." His voice was low and he was avoiding Samir's eyes. "You're one of my oldest customers, Doc, and what happened . . . I look at my own boy sometimes and wonder. You never know what goes on in their minds, you know. Just yesterday I see Brad getting out of his shirt and he has a tattoo on his side, by his rib cage. Says he'd had it for a year—and I never noticed. And it's in some sort of foreign language, too." Shark shook his head.

"It's okay, Shark. About the flyer, I mean."

Shark looked him in the eye for the first time. "You sure? Allison says the flyer is already up everywhere. Says half the town is going anyway, and it would look bad if we didn't hang the flyer up. Says the preacher at our church told people about it last Sunday. Of course they only want to remember the girl, you know. Nothing wrong with that."

"Of course not." Samir wondered how accurate Allison's estimate was. Half the town? "Actually, I'm probably going, myself." Samir got up. Shark was a good six inches taller than he was, so Samir had to look up.

"You are?" Shark's eyes were round with surprise.

"Sure, why not?"

"Well . . ." Shark looked around, as if expecting help. "Why not? You're absolutely right." He looked down at Samir. "I think it'll be very nice of you, Doc." He nodded emphatically, and Samir thought he could hear him wheeze.

Walking back into his office building, Samir saw that the flyer was gone. He stood in front of the bulletin board, staring at the empty space. He walked into the elevator, and there, too, found bare walls. He rode to his office on the third floor, walked straight into Angie's office, and looked in her trash can. Both flyers were there.

"Are you out of your mind?" he hissed, bending down and pulling the two sheets out of the trash can, waving them in Angie's face. She stared at him, then reached out and pulled down the blinds, separating them from the waiting room full of patients.

"Why'd you take those flyers down?" he asked, trying to control his voice. In the fifteen years Angie had been his secretary, she'd heard her share of his raised voice, and he knew she hated it.

"She had no business putting those flyers up here," Angie hissed back. "This is your place of business. It's not professional."

"She'll think I took them down!" he blurted.

"So what?"

"So . . . so I don't want people to think I'm that coldhearted."

Angie frowned at him. Behind her square tortoiseshell glasses, he could already see tears forming.

"I didn't mean that, Angie. But, really, you shouldn't have taken them down." He put the flyers on her desk, straightened them out. One showed only a few creases but no stains. They could probably hang that one back up. The other had fallen on top of Angie's opened tuna can. Now a big blot of grease smeared Natalie's face. The sight of the stain made Samir so sick he wanted to shred the paper, like his father used to tell him he should tear papers that held holy verses or Allah's name on them into tiny bits and pieces before throwing them away. Throwing them whole would have been sacrilege. When Samir asked how come tearing them apart was not sacrilege, his father looked at him as if he were an imbecile. "Because then they are only letters, not words. Letters alone have no meaning."

"I just didn't think it was appropriate for your patients to have to be reminded of this." Angie nodded toward the flyers. "It's been bad enough this past year without stuff like that. It's inviting trouble, if you ask me."

"No it's not, Angie."

"Not, huh? So maybe it's a coincidence you've been getting those lovely e-mails and letters again?" She opened a drawer, pulled out a stack of papers, and held it close to his face.

"Why are you keeping them?"

"Just in case. It's evidence." She shoved the letters back in and closed the drawer.

"As bad as last year?"

"Some are. Not all. There isn't exactly room for innovation here." She sniffed, a nervous habit he was used to, a period at the end of sentences she no longer wished to continue. Samir didn't need her to tell him what was in the letters—all variations of *Go Home,* he suspected, or reminders of his son's guilt. Angie had intercepted dozens of those last year before he realized they had been coming. Always the gatekeeper, always taking care of him. Nagla liked her because she sent away female drug representatives if they were too young or too provocatively dressed, only letting them leave their brochures. He liked her because she never made him feel like a foreigner.

She reached out and took the flyers from his hand. She looked at the stained one, and, uttering a soft "Oh," passed her fingers across the stain, as if her touch would erase it.

"Here," Samir said, reaching for the other flyer. "Let me hang it back up."

"No, I'll do it." She got up, headed toward the door. At it, she turned around. "It's just . . . people can get so nasty." She shook her head before walking out of her office, leaving Samir staring at the empty doorway.

In his office, Samir shut the door and walked up to his desk, let himself fall into his chair. Angie was right about Pat, who never saw him as anything but Egyptian. Egypt, to her, was a place you visited once in a lifetime to ride camels, take pictures in front of the pyramids, and walk the Khan al-Khalili street bazaar and pretend you were whisked back in time to the world of the *One Thousand and One Nights.* It was not where you went to make friends. He suspected her first reaction to what Hosaam did was some sort of variation on *I knew it.*

He glanced at the clock and saw he had fifteen minutes before his first afternoon appointment. He shouldn't have been that sharp with Angie. She was sensitive. One time, years ago, Nagla had called her at home to explain to her about Samir's temper, and he had been baffled at how both women seemed to think he had one. That was back when he did not understand Americans as well as he did today. Now he knew better than to raise his voice to any American, male or female. They always seemed in such control of their emotions. No elaborate hand gesturing. No raised voices. Memorial services held to celebrate the dead.

He rested his head in both hands, elbows on the desk, and sighed. The Americans with their well-controlled, civilized grief, their healing process, their closure. People coming together to exchange words of sympathy, to hug and whisper over canapés and diet sodas. How sophisticated it all used to seem to him, how distinguished. How polished compared with the peasants in Egypt, who hired *meadeddaat,* women dressed in black, to come to the houses of widows and orphans to wail in such loud, offensive expressions of grief. Ehsan had always been drawn to these women, though she claimed never to have actually met one. But he could easily picture her as a professional mourner, going to the homes of the bereaved to offer a spectacle of grief. For a moment, he imagined Ehsan at the Bradstreets', dressed in black from her head cover to her shoes and purse, walking into the American house under the gazes of strangers, sitting down in a chair in the corner, and doing her duty by loudly wailing while swaying from side to side and hitting her thighs and the top of her head with her open palms.

He did not understand this whole idea of memorials, this whole insistence on holding tight to a knife that was already buried deep in one's heart and then twisting. It confused him, especially because it seemed like something Ehsan would do, Ehsan who, forty years after her husband's death, still insisted on visiting his grave on every anniversary, paying the groundskeeper to sweep and dust the tiled floors around the stone monument, baking bread and distributing it to the poor who hung around cemeteries, hiring a *quaree,* a professional Qur'an reciter, to read aloud at the foot of her husband's grave, sitting across from him and listening to the melodic verses with her head bent down, nodding in approval. She believed the dead knew whenever their kin visited. Come this weekend, he was sure she would be at Hosaam's grave, reading the Qur'an and praying for Allah to forgive him his evil deeds.

Samir opened the bottom right drawer of his desk. Inside, a picture of his family lay faceup: Nagla, seated and smiling, with Hosaam, Khaled, and Fatima standing behind her, looking at a point slightly to the right of the camera lens. The photo had been Samir's idea; he saw a similar one in every doctor's office he'd been to, and he wanted one of his own to display in his office alongside his diplomas. The kids were younger, then—he remembered the picture being taken during the summer before Hosaam got to high school. At fourteen, it was evident he was not going to be too tall—Khaled had already caught up with him, even though he was three years younger. But Hosaam was stoutly built, with broad shoulders and a square face accented by a strong jawline. Later that day, he and Hosaam had played soccer in the backyard while Khaled reluctantly stood goalie. Hosaam was such a good kicker that Samir had been certain he'd make it to college on a soccer scholarship, playing center forward for whichever team was lucky enough to have him. He had imagined himself going on weekend trips to watch his son play. Four years of college, four years of medical school, three years of residency— internal medicine, like Samir—and Hosaam would have been ready to join his father's practice by the time Samir was sixty-five. Perfect timing to allow Samir to ease his son into full ownership of the practice before he retired.

Samir closed the drawer, pushing his family's picture back into hiding, where it had rested for the last year. No, making plans was not useless. For a short time after Hosaam's death he had let himself slide into that state of mind, but he refused to do so anymore. Plans *were* useful. Plans meant he would be prepared for everything that would come his way, be it hate mail or worse. He knew what those people who built nuclear bomb shelters in the fifties felt like. His responsibility toward his family meant he had to be prepared. Memorial services tended to remind people not only of their lost ones but also of their anger. He remembered every anniversary of 9/11, when he and Nagla would debate whether or not they should take the kids to Sunday school. On other weekends, Sunday school had been a must, but on this first or second weekend of September their commitment became lax, blurred with the irrational yet real fear of a retaliatory act aimed at the mosque. People became angrier with Muslims in general in September than in any other month of the year. People would become particularly angry with his family now that this anniversary was approaching.

Samir opened the drawer again, looked at Khaled and Fatima, standing behind their mother, smiling. He knew how hard it had been for them at school this past year, even though they hardly spoke to him about that. Again he felt angry with Nagla for failing to support him in his decision to attend the memorial service. Keeping herself locked up at home the whole time, of course she would never truly blend in, nor would she ever understand the workings of the community she was part of, whether she liked it or not. To think that she could bury her head in the sand and wait till the storm passed was vexingly naïve. The flyers had been out only a day or two and already everyone was talking about the upcoming service. How could she think this would not affect them? Would not whisk them back into the center of attention, the center of resentment and anger? Yes, he told himself again. This could turn ugly. But he was not going to let anything happen to his kids. Not again. He *had* to step in.

FRIDAY

8

ARABIC: *Al-maktoub.* What is written. One way to refer to fate.

And what are you going to do, *insh'Allah?*" Ehsan asked Khaled, standing in the middle of the kitchen, both hands resting on her hips. He looked at her, puzzled. He and Fatima had been dismissed from school early. A water main had burst, he told his grandmother, and the school had no running water. For a moment, he imagined her question implied he should go back and help fix the busted pipe. Never able to judge the extent of her ignorance of how things worked in the United States, Khaled hesitated before saying, in clunky Arabic, "The water company will send someone to fix it, *Setto.*"

"I'm not talking about the pipe, boy!" she said, raising both hands in exasperation. "I'm talking about Friday prayer! You get out early on a Friday, you *have* to assume God meant for it to happen so that you can go pray." She looked at him as if he had failed to understand something as simple as why a round wheel was better than a square one.

"But the mosque is half an hour away!"

"Oh, and you, poor boy, cannot drive half an hour to go fulfill your obligations toward God? Your shiny new truck cannot make it there, but can make it to hooky games?"

Khaled chuckled.

"What's so funny?"

"It's *hockey*, Setto, not *hooky*." He almost explained the difference, but seeing her eyes narrow with a familiar anger he refrained. "Sorry."

"So you will not go pray?"

"I probably won't make it there in time anyway," Khaled said, aware of a faint whimpering in his voice.

"Fine. Shows just how much trouble your parents go through to raise you a good Muslim."

"I am a good Muslim! I pray all five prayers, every day—you see me do it. And I've been fasting Ramadan since I was twelve." Her accusation was unfair, he felt, judging him based on one trivial thing. It also hurt because it confirmed his belief that nothing he could do would ever be enough to satisfy his family. They always seemed to expect more of him: more respect for his elders, better grades, more piety. He would have told her so, but the sound of his mother and Fatima, talking as they walked down the stairs, stopped him.

Nagla walked up to a cabinet, grabbed a travel mug, and started filling it with coffee. Behind her, Fatima headed toward the door to the garage. Khaled watched her place her backpack on the floor, pull a hairband out of her jeans pocket, and then swiftly toss her hair to one side, braid it, put the hairband on, and toss it back. The whole process took less than twenty seconds, and she was transformed, her long hair, which fell to the middle of her back, tamed and brought to submission. She never wore her hair down anymore, and Khaled, had he not known his father better, would have assumed the braid was a result of his parents' high expectations of Fatima, as well, of some unreasonable demands they put on her as they did with him. More piety. Less flaunting of seductive assets. More female submission. But his father would never demand that of her. That influence, he knew, had another source. Fatima, catching his eye, looked at him and raised an eyebrow.

"What?" she asked.

"Going to Maraam's?" he asked. She nodded.

"How come you don't let your hair down anymore?"

"It's too hot." She stood, hands on her hips, staring at him.

"Looks better down," he said.

"Feels better up. And who asked you, anyway?"

"Just thought I'd mention it. Just in case you're only pulling it up because you're going to Maraam's. You know, considering that she covers her hair."

Fatima scowled at him but said nothing. He looked away, uneasy, avoiding eye contact with his grandmother, who was watching both her grandkids, struggling, as she always did, to understand the English that they unfailingly reverted to when speaking with each other. He hadn't intended to annoy Fatima, but he could not help that her recent change irritated him. He suspected Maraam was behind his sister's newfound religious devotion. He would not have minded if Fatima did not, in the process, seem to shut herself away from him.

"We're leaving, Mama," Nagla said, grabbing her coffee and planting a kiss on her mother's cheek.

"Leaving now?" Ehsan asked, eyebrows raised.

"I'm going to drop Fatima off at Maraam's."

"I thought you said you'd take me to the store!" Ehsan protested.

"That was before I knew the kids would be home early. Now Fatima wants to go to Maraam's and I need to take her."

"Why can't Khaled take Fatima? It's not like he's going to Friday prayer or anything," Ehsan said, glaring at Khaled. He turned away, opened the fridge door, and pulled out a water bottle.

"No, Mama, I want to go. I want to walk in and see Ameena. But," Nagla said, looking from Ehsan to her son, "Khaled can take you to the store. Can't you?"

She looked at him, the bottle up to his lips. He held it there, swallowing, frantically trying to find a way to get out of this.

"Khaled?" his mother asked.

He put the bottle down.

"Actually . . . I was going . . ." he said, unable to find the words—his Arabic, which he was expected to stick to whenever Ehsan was around, was rusty, uncomfortable, and heavy on his tongue. Even if it were not, he did not know what he could have told her. I was . . . what? Going out? Heading in the opposite direction? Did not plan on spending the next couple of hours with my grandmother?

"Sure, Mom. Of course I can," he finally said, screwing the cap back on the bottle. In his peripheral vision, he could see Ehsan suck at her lips.

Nagla and Fatima had both stepped through the door to the garage when Fatima turned around and walked back in.

"I'll pull my hair up if I want to," she told him. "I don't care if you don't like it."

He placed his water bottle back in the fridge. She was turning around to walk out of the kitchen when he called after her.

"Do you want me to pick you up later?"

She hesitated. He watched her, waiting. "You can text me whenever you're ready to go," he added. She looked down, her hands tucked in the back pockets of her jeans, just like she used to do whenever he tried to get her to touch one of the bugs he collected out in the yard when they were both little kids.

"Sure. Fine. Thank you," she murmured before walking out.

"And your hair looks good, by the way," he shouted after her. "Even pulled up."

He listened, but she said nothing. He hoped she had heard him.

By the time they left, gray clouds hid the sun and a fine drizzle sprayed the windshield as Khaled drove down Main Street toward Foodland.

They took his truck, a used red Chevrolet Avalanche with which his father had surprised him for his seventeenth birthday only three months earlier, the kind of truck Hosaam had wished for and was never granted because Samir had deemed it too expensive. Khaled had looked at the truck and felt stunned, partly because he realized the moment he saw it that he never would have gotten such a truck if Hosaam were still alive, and the association had immediately made him resent the gift and feel alienated from it, as if the truck were tainted in a way he would rather not contemplate. Not that he hadn't liked it, of course. Still, he hated how every time he saw his vehicle, he had to remember Hosaam again.

They remained quiet the whole way except for the faint sound of Ehsan's prayers. Every time she rode with him she prayed as she tightly grabbed the handle above the passenger's window or held herself steady with one outstretched arm pushing against the glove compartment. In the winter, when he drove her through the snow, he could understand her panic, her fear of icy surfaces painting scenarios of slippery wrecks in her mind. Yet on a spring day with only a slight drizzle her attitude seemed absurd.

"You okay, *Setto*?"

She did not answer, but gave him one reprimanding look before turning away again, keeping her eyes fixed on the road. Khaled shook his head and said nothing. Ever since she'd arrived, Ehsan had been uncharacteristically sharp with him over trivial things: leaving a used glass on the countertop instead of rinsing it and putting it in the dishwasher, walking downstairs before school and heading for the coffeepot before wishing her good morning. Her criticism would have been easier to dismiss had it not always been followed by signs of tenderness, reminders of her surprisingly enduring favoritism that Khaled had expected her to transfer to Fatima, now that his sister showed deeper interest in the Qur'an and in religion than he ever had. But just as he would settle down with his cup of coffee, avoiding her eyes after her sharp rebuke, she would suddenly approach him and start murmuring prayers as her hand gently smoothed over his hair and traced his shoulders, as if her fingertips would transfuse blessings and protection from the holy words straight to his body. He, cringing under the touch that was more appropriate toward a four-year-old, often considered wriggling free, breaking away, but then he would look at her face and remain motionless.

Arriving at Foodland, he pulled in front and let her out before turning in to the parking lot. The steady drizzle, promising a late-night storm, had driven people here for provisions, and Khaled, weary of circling for spaces, parked in a spot at the far end and made his way slowly back through the rain. Walking into the store, he stood, startled to find Ehsan still in the entryway. Next to this week's newspaper deals and a poster announcing a lost Labrador retriever hung Natalie's flyer. Ehsan, shortsighted, had pulled out her glasses and was standing a few inches away, scrutinizing the poster. Khaled looked around, trying to determine whether anyone was watching her. Of all the people in his family, he felt she was the least self-conscious, though the most inviting of curious looks. Today, however, people hurrying into and out of the store paid little attention to her. Khaled pulled a shopping cart out of the dozen or so left and walked up to his grandmother, leading her by the arm. "Let's go, *Setto*," he said, pushing the cart into the store ahead of both of them.

He turned around and asked "Where to, *Setto?*" as soon as he cleared the entry's traffic. He had expected to find her right behind him, but she was still walking through the double doors, and Khaled grimaced as he realized she had fallen behind even in such a short distance. During her last visit only three years earlier he was the one who had to sprint to keep up with her whenever she took him on shopping trips. Now, watching her slowly follow him, her black leather purse hanging off one arm as she swayed slowly from side to side with every step, he suddenly realized how much she had aged. He tried to remember how old she was—seventy? Seventy-two? She had gained weight, too, or maybe he had just never noticed how heavy she was.

"Here, let me get this," he told her as he reached out and took the purse from her arm. "It's too heavy for you to carry around."

"Just watch out for thieves," she said, breathing heavily as she looked around her, scanning the customers for potential pickpockets. "Don't let it out of your sight."

"Where do you want to go first?" he asked, placing her purse in the cart.

"Don't put it in the cart, boy! It'll get stolen!"

"No it won't, *Setto*." She glared at him, then moved to pull her purse back out of the cart.

"Wait. I'll show you something." He threaded the child seat's belt through the handle, clicked it shut. "See? Now no one can snatch it." Unsatisfied, she looked from him to the purse. "Where to first?" he pressed on.

"Produce," she sighed, walking toward the fruit stands.

Khaled followed at a distance. When she moved in front of the vegetables, he watched her, and looked around to see how others watched her. Young women with squirming kids in shopping cart seats, older ones zipping through the packed grocery store, the occasional solitary man—everyone seemed to be moving at a faster pace than Ehsan, as in one of those movie sequences where the world zooms past the heroine, who moves at half speed, existing in a bubble that answers to different time laws than its surroundings. He would have to be patient. Again he scrutinized his grandmother: Ehsan looked different, he knew, with her black head cover and her loose-fitting black dress making her look stouter than she was. Meandering around, she seemed hesitant, walking up to the tomatoes, then to the rows of greens, and standing there, looking from basket to basket. Khaled waited, resisting an impulse to walk up to her, pick a few things out, and urge her to move on. She was a careful cook and a slow shopper made slower, he suspected, by age. When he was younger, he used to enjoy going to the store with her because she would always bribe him with candy to keep him quiet as she took her time selecting tomatoes, examining every single zucchini, and weighing eggplants in her hands, comparing them to determine which ones were less seedy. Her most recent visit to Summerset had lasted only three months; this one, begun only weeks after Hosaam's death, was nearing a year, her longest stay ever. Khaled assumed she would have found her bearings in American supermarkets by now, even though each one of them was large enough to hold thirty of the small produce stores she was used to shopping at in Egypt.

A woman probably her age with carefully styled silver hair, wearing khaki pants and a sky-blue sweater, stood behind her, waiting for Ehsan to clear the way. His grandmother was oblivious to the woman's patience, lost in the six or seven kinds of lettuce that Khaled knew she was eyeing in order to choose the one that most closely resembled Egyptian lettuce (romaine, he knew). The woman put her hand up to her mouth and cleared her throat. Ehsan bent down, picked up a head of lettuce, held it closer to her eyes, pulled the wire holding it together straight, and peered down to read the label. The woman coughed, louder this time, and Ehsan put the lettuce back and picked up another one. Khaled, mortified, walked up to his grandmother and pulled her aside by her arm.

"You're blocking the way, *Setto*," he whispered as he watched the woman bend down, pick up one head of Belgium endive, and trot away.

"What?" Ehsan looked from him to the woman.

"You were blocking her way," Khaled said, letting go of her arm.

"Well, she should have said something!" Ehsan said loudly in Arabic as the woman pushed her shopping cart away, moving on to the tomatoes. Khaled, blushing, stepped to their cart and waited as Ehsan went back to examining lettuce.

He watched, his fingers quickly tapping the child seat in the shopping cart, his eyes darting from her to the people around her. He knew exactly what they saw when they looked at her, knew how out of place she looked with her black attire and her exhaustive scrutiny. Everything about her seemed designed to invite disapproval: the way she picked up fruit and lifted it to her nose to sniff at it, the way she licked her fingers in order to peel the edges of the produce bags apart to open them, the way she held the green peppers in her hand, raising them to the light to examine them one by one before placing them back down, the way she seemed to wander aimlessly from stand to stand, walking around in circles in search of God knows what. Even her heaviness embarrassed him as he compared her with the elegant American ladies in their capris and flip-flops. He felt she did not belong there, and it suddenly occurred to him that she was with him, and that her misplacement reflected on him, as well. He looked around to see if anyone was looking at him, too, if anyone was thinking how he, too, did not belong, how her presence with him made him not belong.

"What's wrong, *habibi*?" Ehsan said, placing a bag filled with limes in the shopping cart. Khaled flinched. He had not seen her walk up to him.

"What's wrong?" she said again, eyes narrowing.

"Nothing, *Setto*. Nothing," he lied, reaching into the shopping cart to straighten the bags she had placed there so far, lifting them and stacking them against each other, putting them in order, waiting for her to be done.

By the time Ehsan finished, it had started pouring, and by the time Khaled pulled the truck up to the storefront and loaded the groceries, he was soaked to the bone. Back at home, he carried the bags into the kitchen and ran upstairs. He changed into dry shorts and a T-shirt, then stood looking out his bedroom window. The rain was drumming against the roof, and he could see the trees sway with the hot spring winds. His day home early was ruined, and the butterflies that an early sunshine had convinced him he would see were probably all in hiding now. Hiking would be useless.

Days like these were why he first started his blog. Sitting at his desk, Khaled logged on and scrolled through his last few entries. Earlier that day he had been thinking of the monarch butterfly. He had been interested in monarchs ever since middle school when he learned about their migration, yet his interest had piqued in the past year, with his blog taking an unintentionally obsessive turn toward them. He looked at the pictures he had posted of the different butterflies he came across while hiking, mostly grainy low-resolution photos taken on his cell phone before he developed the habit of carrying a pocket camera with him at all times. He had not seen many monarchs this spring, yet he was always on the lookout for them. The yellow, black, and earthy browns of their wings fascinated him almost as much as the royal blue of the blue morpho did, and their pedestrian status endeared them to him; unlike other, rarer butterflies, the monarchs were ever-present, dependable friends who always showed up when needed. He loved going on hikes and knowing that a monarch or two would likely cross his path. What truly interested him, though, was their migration. He scrolled up to an older blog entry and read it through again.

The monarchs migrate north to south in the fall, heading to Mexico. Sometimes a single butterfly can travel up to 3,000 miles. Their migration is different from other butterflies because it is two-way and they come back to their grounds in the north in the spring. Because their life cycle is shorter than the duration of the migration, the butterflies that return in the spring are never the same as the ones that migrated in the fall. They are their children, grandchildren, or great-grandchildren.

He read through the post again, his fascination with this aspect of monarch migration as intense as it was when he first learned about it years earlier. Of everything he knew about bugs in general and lepidoptera in particular, this one piece of information was the catalyst, he knew, the reason he had never outgrown his childish fascination with insects. Many of his friends developed that same interest for short periods of time, mostly in elementary school, walking around with squiggly bugs hidden in their pockets, ready to fling them at the closest unsuspecting girl. Yet for him the fascination never waned, and he carried it with him, first secretly as the other boys learned to scowl at such childish obsessions, then openly again after he learned to snub all those who snubbed him. His father had first encouraged the obsession, seeing it as an indication of both future machismo and future scientific inclination, a stepping-stone toward a medical career for his son. Later his father would look at an eighth-grade Khaled walking out of the house with a magnifying lens and a butterfly net with knotted eyebrows and a glare. "He's still only a boy, Samir! Let him have fun," Nagla would come to her son's defense—and, much later, Samir would walk in on Khaled, pick up one of the various entomology books that inevitably lay scattered in his room, and, lips turned downward at the corners, would comment on how biology was a good premed choice.

Once, and only once, Khaled tried to explain his fascination to his father. He was lying in bed, a book in hand, when Samir walked in and started flipping through the books that lay scattered on and around the nightstand. On the top bed, Hosaam was on his laptop, his earphones plugged into his ears, the loud and deep *thud-thud* of rhythm vibrating through the bed's frame and making Khaled's own mattress tremble. Khaled watched his father pick up one book with a large monarch on the cover and flip through it, lips pursed.

"They migrate, you know," Khaled started, putting his own book down.

"Who? Those?" Samir showed Khaled the cover. Khaled nodded.

"They migrate twice every year, from north to south in the fall and from south to north in the spring." His father looked at him, one eyebrow raised. "I thought you'd be interested in that."

"In what? Butterfly migration?"

"Yeah."

"Are you serious?"

Samir looked down on him with a smirk. Khaled blushed, picked up his book, and stared at a random page. He could feel his father's gaze on him as well as his own regret for having tried to communicate, for having subjected a topic so dear to him to his father's unfailing sarcasm. He stared at the open book, unblinking, until his eyes watered and his father eventually walked out, tossing the book he had held back on the floor.

Looking at his blog post, Khaled remembered what he had originally intended to tell his father, what he had hoped his father would recognize: the fascinating possibility of finding the way back to a home that one has never known. No one knew how the second- or third-generation monarchs found their way back north when they had never been there before. Even now, when he was too old to believe in any of Ehsan's fables, Khaled would sometimes remember her stories of lost boys following unseen clues home and imagine that the butterflies, like those boys, had an inner compass that directed them to where they were supposed to be, and the idea of a home that one carried within filled him with hope and peace. His father's inability to appreciate such ties flabbergasted him.

Still staring at his weeks-old blog post, Khaled noticed a new entry from Brittany. Heart thumping, he focused on the date, afraid he had missed an old communication—but he had not. She had been on his blog this morning. Check out this link, her post said, followed by a hyperlink to a travel website. Quickly, he clicked on her link and saw an advertisement for a monarch-tracking trip to Mexico, a companion to the article he had sent her earlier. So she had read his article. She had also been interested enough to look up the topic further and send him a link in return. He grinned.

"You want to come and drink a cup of coffee with me?"

Khaled jumped. Turning around, he saw Ehsan standing in his doorway. "It's only me, boy. You look like you've just seen the *Jinn*."

"Sorry, *Setto*. Didn't hear you coming."

"So how about that coffee?"

"Not right now, thank you."

"Come on. It's one cup of Turkish coffee, and I've already prepared it," she said, walking away from his door and heading down the stairs. Khaled stared at the empty doorway, his head bent to one side, his eyes narrowing. What was the point of asking a question if it was really an order? His father did this—*Why don't you give up this bug nonsense and go to medical school?* Ehsan certainly did it. His mother, too—*Can you take your grandmother to the store?* For a few seconds he considered staying where he was, ignoring Ehsan, pretending she was not sitting downstairs in the kitchen waiting for him. Then he got up, sighing, and closed his laptop before heading down himself.

Two small cups stood in the middle of the breakfast table, filled to the brim with steaming Turkish coffee. Ehsan sat down and reached for hers, started sipping at it as she looked out on the pouring rain. Khaled pulled out a chair and sat across from her, sniffing the rising aroma of dark roast coffee spiced with cardamom.

"I haven't had this since the last time you were here," he said. She nodded, still looking out the window. He knew she could remember it as well as he did, the way she used to make coffee for him and Hosaam and have them sit down and drink it with her in the mornings. He remembered how bitter the coffee tasted when he first tried it, how its coarse grounds felt like fine sand on his tongue, but he was so happy to be included, so proud he was finally old enough to try the favorite drink of his mother and grandmother, that he did not mind the taste. He even grew to like it, by the time she left. Not as much as Hosaam, who continued making it for himself for months after she was gone. To Khaled, the ritual was always associated with Hosaam. He thought that was perhaps why Ehsan had not once made the coffee for him in the months she had been here.

"It's good coffee," he said, trying to get his thoughts off Hosaam. He had sipped at it a bit too eagerly in an attempt to finish it quickly and rush back to his room, and now his tongue burned and prickled. He looked up at her, wondered how come she could slurp the scorching liquid with such ease. She was still looking out the window. Waiting for her to talk, Khaled became aware of the drumming rain, the monotonous sound soothing. He tried his coffee again, took a small sip and let it swirl around in his mouth.

"So, tell me what happened." She turned her empty cup over in its saucer.

Khaled swallowed, almost choking on his coffee. He coughed. "What?"

"What happened to your brother. Tell me what happened."

"You know, *Setto*," he said. She shook her head.

"I know what they told me. I want to know what *you* know. What you saw."

Khaled's heart raced and he grew dizzy, seeing her image sway in front of him. He waited for a moment to regain his bearings. She had been here almost a full year and not once had she talked to him directly of his brother. Why start now?

"What do you mean?" he asked, his voice hoarse. The coffee grains clung to his throat and almost made him gag.

"How was he, the last few months? How did he behave? Your mother used to call and tell me stuff, but . . . I want to hear it from you," she said as she turned her cup upright again, straightening it and looking at the lines the coffee grounds had drawn on the inside surface of the delicate china.

Khaled watched her turn the cup around in her hand, hold its inside surface to the light and look at the lines, biting on her lower lip. She was trying to decipher the future, he knew, to read clues from God or angels or someone, he didn't know who, someone who knew what was going to happen to her next and who she believed would send her encoded messages. She had done the same with his cup, before, as well as Hosaam's. Khaled had held Hosaam's cup in his hand on the last day she was there, three years earlier, and had stared inside, had seen a dark line squiggled on the side of the cup, its end bifurcated. *I see a snake,* Khaled had said. Hosaam had snatched the cup from his hand, *That's my cup,* he had said. Then the cup fell to the floor, shattering just as Ehsan hurried to grab it from the fighting boys. For the rest of the day, the last day she had with them, she had followed Khaled around asking, *What did you see, exactly? What did you see?*

He watched her turn the cup in her hands and waited. Her face was contoured with concentration, and for a moment he wished she'd see something good, something bright and happy that would come through just because she said so.

"What do you see?" he asked.

"Oh, nothing," she said, putting the cup down. "The usual stuff. Nothing new. Now, tell me."

"I don't know, *Setto.* What do you want to know?"

"How was he during the last year or so? Your mother kept complaining about him but never really told me what he was doing. What happened to him, do you know?"

Khaled shook his head, as if the motion would hurl away the images that came flowing into his mind with her questions: Hosaam's calm face as Samir handed him a couple of college applications, followed by his brows knitted in concentration as he sat at his desk and, as soon as his father was out of the room, took a pair of shears and cut each application in hair-thin strips, then, holding the strips in bunches, cut those again, until the bundle of applications turned into a pile of fine strands that he then flushed. Hosaam's disappearance into the attic, that space that he had claimed years earlier and that Khaled had envied him, and the onset of unnerving silence—no outbursts of loud music, no crescendos of drumbeats. When his grandmother asked what had changed, Khaled remembered the distance in Hosaam's eyes whenever he looked at him, a new vacancy behind them that implied anything could now move in.

He didn't want to remember, and he loathed talking about his brother. It reminded him of the police interrogations the days after the murder. *Did you see anything suspicious? Was he in contact with anyone new? Did he develop any new religious affiliations? Did he pray more often?* And of him, trying to refrain from asking why on earth they thought it made sense that Hosaam did what he did out of religiousness. Really? Killing his ex-girlfriend and himself because Allah told him to do so? But he knew better than to question the police, so he just told them all he knew. Almost all he knew. Everything he thought would be relevant, anyway.

"I really don't want to talk about this, *Setto,*" he murmured, gulping the last of his coffee. His grandmother nodded.

"I know, *habibi,* I know. I didn't mean to open old wounds." She lifted his empty cup and turned it, laying it upside down on its saucer.

"How do you know what the patterns mean?" Khaled asked, nodding toward the upturned cup.

"My grandmother taught me how to read the coffee grounds. She was famous for her ability to find things out. People eventually grew scared of her," she said, smiling and shaking her head. "One time she read the cup of one of her sons in front of a dozen or so people. They said she looked down, peered inside the cup, then reached for her slipper and flung it at the poor man." She laughed. "She had seen in the pattern that he'd taken a second wife in secret. Called him a coward, and he, a grown man, stood shaking, humiliated in front of the entire family. They say women would smuggle their husbands' cups to her after that incident."

"Was she right? About the second wife?"

"Of course she was!"

"But that's more like finding a secret out, right? Not exactly foretelling the future."

Ehsan shrugged. "Sometimes. Sometimes you can do both."

"But *Baba* always said it is *haram* to foretell the future. Called it a sin. *Kazab almonagemoon wa law sadafu,*" he said in slow Arabic. His father had repeated the popular saying so often in his presence that he had memorized it. *Fortune-tellers lie even if they accidentally tell a truth.* Always repeated in association with Ehsan, Khaled now remembered.

"That saying speaks of reading the stars, like the Arabs of old used to do. Not of reading the coffee," Ehsan retorted. She was being literal, Khaled knew, hanging on to her interpretation of one word. He considered saying that, just to keep the conversation going and to insure that she did not speak of Hosaam again, but he decided against it.

"So why do you do it, *Setto*?"

"Old habits," she said, taking his cup and peering inside. He fixed his eyes on her face, felt his heart racing. Nonsense, of course. Nonsense and superstition.

"But didn't you always say there was no way to avoid God's fate? That what was written on the forehead had to be seen?"

"Sometimes," she said, still peering into his cup, turning it toward the light.

"How come sometimes? You think you can change the future if you see it in that cup?" He pointed toward the cup in her hand but noted his own hand trembling. He put it down, resting it against his thigh.

Ehsan put his cup down, sighed, and looked at him. "Why are you being so difficult, *habibi*? Why is it always questions, questions, questions? Can't you let an old woman have her—"

"I'm not being difficult!"

"See? You won't even let me finish my sentence."

"I just don't see why you waste your time on this stuff."

Ehsan sighed again, shaking her head. Khaled pushed on. "What do you think you'd do? I mean, if you looked here and saw that something was about to happen to me, for instance—"

"*Baad elshar!*" she retorted, reaching out and grabbing his arm across the table.

"Relax, *Setto*—I was just talking hypothetically. But even if you saw something good. Anything. What good would it do to know?"

He looked at her, and she, still holding on to his arm, squeezed it in her hand. He looked down at her fingers and was struck by a sudden, vivid memory of her hand brushing aside wet strands of hair that clung to his forehead as he lay sick in bed.

"Knowing might do no good. But praying could. Praying always helps. And knowing might help you decide what to pray for." Her words were whispered, her eyes fixated on him yet soft. Slowly, she released him, and he jumped up. He took a step toward the kitchen door before stopping and turning around. She, standing, had picked up both her cup and his, and headed toward the sink. He followed, took both cups from her hands, and carried them there himself, placing them carefully on the countertop. Running warm water, he picked up his cup and held it to the light, looking inside. His grandmother, standing beside him, took the cup from his hand and patted him on the back, her large presence squeezing him away from her sink, her territory.

Khaled stood to the side, resting his arm on the counter. He did not know why he had been so persistent in challenging her. But, no matter what he did, she never became truly angry with him. And then, out of the blue, he would do something harmless, forget a pair of socks where they did not belong, and she would lash out at him. Still, he regretted having been defiant. He looked at her as she slowly ran her fingers inside the cup, rinsing it.

"So, *Setto*?" he asked. She looked up at him. "What did you see?" He pointed toward his cup, empty now, white inside with all traces of coffee grounds washed down the drain.

"Your cup, you mean?" She smiled. "All good. With you, *habibi*, it's all good." She placed the cup on the draining tray, grabbed a dishcloth, and dried her hands, turning to face him. "I knew that from the moment I held you in my arms, when you were just a few minutes old," she said, smiling tenderly and reaching out to hold one of his hands in hers. "You're a good boy, Khaled. Always remember that."

He looked down, resenting how he had led her to believe he cared what patterns the coffee grains drew on the walls of his cup. All nonsense and superstition, of course. But her hand was warm and tender as she pressed his in hers, and he felt good letting her do it, just like she used to grab and hug him every time he walked by her when he was young, just like she used to let him sit in her lap before that. Still, he wished he had gotten a chance to take a better look at his own cup. The one glance he had taken had shown him something that looked like a tree with branches and roots that mirrored each other, the top branches reaching the edge of the cup while the bottom ones disappeared into the moist coffee grounds in the bottom. He wondered what that meant, but he didn't want to ask. He didn't want to know. All superstition anyway, he reminded himself again.

She was still holding his hand. Gently, he pulled it away from her.

"I think I'll go upstairs now, *Setto*, if you don't mind."

Ehsan nodded.

"Of course, *habibi*. Sorry I took so much of your time today," she said, looking up at him. She looked exhausted, he felt, or maybe sick—he wasn't sure. He turned to go up the stairs, but then he stopped.

"*Setto*," he said.

"Yes, *habibi*?"

"I'm . . . I'm sorry," he said, blushing. He hoped she'd understand what he meant.

Ehsan nodded, and, to his surprise, he thought he saw tears forming in her eyes.

"No, *habibi*. No. I'm sorry. I'm really sorry. May Allah forgive us all," she said, looking away from him. He took one step toward her, reached one hand to touch her shoulder, and then changed his mind. She was so old, he felt, so old and seemed so tired, and he was sick of all of this, sick of the sadness and the apologies and the condolences. He did not want to do this anymore. Yet even as he stepped back he wished he could come close to her, lean down by her side just like she had done for the months he was sick such a long, long time ago, and offer her healing, a sip of holy Zamzam water, maybe, or a murmured prayer powerful enough to banish whatever it was that was making her shake with sobs. But he had nothing to offer, and he was sick of his helplessness. He ran upstairs and into his room, shutting the door behind him.

Sitting at his desk, Khaled gave himself a few moments to calm down before flipping open his laptop and getting on his Facebook page. He let his fingers rest on the keyboard, drawing comfort from the touch of technology at his fingertips, from his rooted presence in the modern world and away from prophecies drawn in coffee grounds and obsessions with both an unchangeable past and an unknown future. This was what he had now: keys at his fingertips, pictures on his screen. More important: he had Brittany.

He glanced at the clock and saw it was hardly past three in the afternoon. She got off work at five on Fridays, and, if she had no other plans, she might be willing to meet with him. He had not seen her in weeks, had been avoiding her, in fact. The last time they had met, he had had a close brush with disaster—a slip of the tongue about Hosaam. He had hated the pressure of that slip more than he had feared the exposure. Still he was not sure whether a meeting with her would be wise. But he missed her. Considering what this weekend might bring, he also needed to talk to her. Even if he would never be able to discuss his brother with her, her presence might still help.

He sent her a message, then closed the laptop without waiting for her reply. He would change and go to the city anyway, hope that she would meet him there. That much he knew: he was not going to stay home alone with Ehsan, whose faint sobs seeped through the floor and the walls and dropped throughout his room, nudging him out.

9

ARABIC: *Ekra'*. Read.

*The first word the archangel Gabriel spoke to Muhammad,
peace be upon his soul*

Fatima ran upstairs the moment she walked into Maraam's house, and Nagla followed Ameena into the kitchen. Food was cooking on the stove, the scent of spiced beef and onions mixed with a sweet aroma drifting from the oven. Nagla sat at the counter as Ameena stirred the beef stew and said, "Trying to get dinner ready before I leave. Can you believe they were out of goulash at Zidan's?" Nagla nodded automatically to everything her friend said and made a mental note to walk upstairs to Maraam's room and bid Fatima goodbye before she left. The ritual did not matter as much as the words did: *La ilaha illa Allah*, to which Fatima would answer, *Muhammad rasool Allah;* the *shahada*, or testimony of faith, broken in two: There is no god except God, and Muhammad is his messenger. When Nagla was a little girl, her mother would say the first phrase and instruct her to answer with the second whenever mother and daughter were to separate, even before going to bed at night. It would be years before Nagla understood the logic behind the strange greeting, the recitation of the testimony that is the first pillar of Islam in lieu of a goodbye. "That way we always know we'll meet again," Ehsan had explained. "Just like you cannot be a Muslim without

believing in God *and* his prophet. The phrases belong together, insepa-
rable. You say one and I say the other, and we each carry half of this
testimony, and, like it, we become one. The two parts have to meet
again." Years later, during one of their visits to Egypt, Nagla had bought
two silver pendants with each of the phrases engraved on a half circle
with a jagged edge, the edges, when put together, completing each other.
She had given one to Fatima to wear and had kept the other for herself.
Now, sitting in Ameena's kitchen, Nagla tried to remember whether she
had seen Fatima put the pendant on that morning. Again she reminded
herself to go bid her daughter goodbye before she left, utter the words
that, she hoped, might offer her protection.

Ameena's house was filled with words. Walls were covered with
calligraphy—the art of Islam. One wall in the family room was half-
covered with a wall hanging of the ninety-nine names of God embroi-
dered in gold over black velvet. Placed in concentric circles around a
central Allah in decorative letters, the names went through each of God's
attributes. Nagla searched through the circle and found the Compassionate, the Merciful, the Forgiving. She liked the Forgiving. She used to
like the All-Just, too, but now it scared her. She searched again: the
Loving, the Resurrecter, the Patron, the Giver of Life. Behind Ameena,
on three staggered shelves, stood other words: *Allhamdu Lellah,* or
Thank God, in gold letters on a blue ceramic square that stood on miniature legs resembling a painter's easel; a phrase from the Qur'an evoking God's protection and painted on a white plate in blue letters; two
entire suras on a free-standing plaque—Al-Nas and Al-Falaq, evoking
God's protection from the evils within and without. The upper shelf held
a wooden engraving of the testimony: *La ilaha illa Allah, Muhammad
rasool Allah.* For all Ameena's obsession with quotations from the
Qur'an and evocations of God, she never approved of the use of the
testimony in greeting. "All hocus pocus; and a bit blasphemous, if you
ask me," she had once chided Nagla on hearing her use the greeting with

her children, on witnessing what, to her, was a use of God's words out of context. Again, Nagla reminded herself to see Fatima before she left. She would have to make sure Ameena did not hear her.

"So you think you'll be able to make it to our *halakah* this afternoon?" Ameena asked.

"No—but that's why I'm here. I wanted to thank you for inviting me. And to apologize. For being—" Nagla paused, looking for words. Ameena nodded.

"No need to apologize for anything. I was still hoping you'd come, though. This week of all weeks."

"Why?"

"Because of the anniversary, of course." Ameena banged a wooden spoon against the edge of the large pot. Nagla watched her. She tried to say something, but her throat felt lumpy, so she did not.

"Speaking of that, I'm assuming you know of the memorial service," Ameena said, running her finger around the edge of the spoon and licking it before tossing the spoon in the sink.

Nagla nodded. "Samir wants us to go."

Ameena froze, staring at Nagla. "That's a horrible idea. You really think people would want you there?"

Nagla looked at her friend, eyes narrow. She could feel her ears growing hot.

"I don't mean to offend you, Nagla," Ameena added. "But—think about it. Aren't you afraid people might bother you?"

Nagla paused. Of course she was. "I hope they won't. Anyway, we are still part of this community." She put one hand up, rested her forehead on the heel of her hand, and snickered. "*Ya rabby.* I'm starting to sound like Samir."

Ameena, washing her hands, turned around and looked at Nagla. "I'm sorry to hear that."

Nagla smiled despite the sting of her friend's words. She was often at a loss as to what to make of Ameena's remarks. Sarcasm seemed too evasive for her to resort to, but, sometimes, Nagla wasn't sure.

"How's Zayd?" Nagla asked.

"Late for prayer, as usual." Ameena looked up, as if able to see her husband on the upper floor through the ceiling. "Zayd!" she screamed at the top of her lungs. "We're going to miss Friday prayer because of you, *ya ragel!*"

Upstairs, Nagla heard shuffling feet.

"You want to come with us?"

Nagla shook her head. "No, thanks."

"You really should start coming to prayer. It'll be good for you."

"I'm not used to it, Ameena. I never went to Friday prayer, not even in Egypt. I'm just fine praying at home. Why do you feel like you have to go all the time, anyway?"

"I don't *have* to; I want to!" Ameena glared at her, half offended, half reprimanding. Nagla looked down at her hands. In Egypt, women had never gone to Friday prayer, and now here, in the United States, her friend of all people was making her feel deficient because she was not volunteering to attend a service only men were obliged to observe. She remembered one of Khaled's favorite phrases of late: "Nothing I do is ever good enough, is it?"

Ameena slipped on oven mitts to pull out a tray of baklava, placing it on the stovetop before pouring a stream of cool syrup from a small pan, the smell of rosewater filling the air as the hot baklava soaked up the sticky sauce. Nagla watched her and tried to fend off the feeling of discomfort that had crept up on her sometime during the last few minutes. The feeling was not new; recently, being around Ameena never failed to remind Nagla of her shortcomings: Nagla prepared dessert only on special occasions, such as the elaborate dinner parties she and Samir used to give for the mosque families. Her walls were not bedecked in protective verses from the Qur'an. She never voluntarily went to prayer at the mosque. She did not attend, let alone organize, weekly religious gatherings. Unlike Ameena, she did not devote hours out of each week to teaching her kids Arabic and the Qur'an, and, as a result, Ameena's kids were twice as fluent in the language as Nagla's were. It was impossible to avoid adding all of these shortcomings together and wondering what role they had played in Hosaam's fate. Nagla fidgeted and glanced at the wall clock, pondering whether it would be rude to make a run for it and flee only moments after she had arrived. But if she did, she would only feel guilty afterward. She watched her friend rinse a baking sheet she had just washed. Ameena—the evoker of guilt.

Yet it was impossible to feel resentful toward a woman who, even now, was fishing out one of the disposable aluminum foil containers that Nagla suspected she bought in bulk specifically for her, scooping up a generous portion of baklava and sliding it carefully into the container, pushing it around with the spatula in order to make room for one or two more diamonds of the crunchy dessert. Nagla knew for whom her friend prepared the container. Over the past year, Ameena had sent her countless meals packaged in disposable trays so that Nagla would not have to return the favor and send back a tray full of her own cooking, as custom dictated. For the weeks preceding Ehsan's arrival, the only home-cooked meals Nagla's kids ate originated in Ameena's kitchen. Even after Ehsan took over the care of the house, Ameena still pitched in, supplementing Ehsan's cooking with trays of her own food while Nagla roamed the house, smoking, drinking coffee, staring at the trees on the edge of Summerset Park, and forsaking her share of the housework. Letting her elderly mother clean and cook for her and her kids. Right now, Ehsan was probably walking around the grocery store doing her daughter's shopping, her knees cracking with arthritis. Nagla added that image to the list of her guilt-inducing failings. She sighed.

"I'll have to bake you a full tray one day, but this should be okay for now. I know how much Khaled loves my baklava." Ameena pushed the tray aside, placing the transparent cover next to it. "Just wait a few minutes till it cools down before you cover it."

"*Teslam edeiky,*" Nagla said, reaching out for a piece, holding the diamond with forefinger and thumb and pulling it, streaks of sticky syrup marking its upward path. She placed the piece in her mouth, listened to the crunch of the baked filo dough with its walnut filling. Glancing at one of the plaques decorated with verses from the Qur'an, Nagla realized that her reflexive reply was a prayer—May your hands remain safe—a compliment for a cook, a maker, a woman who creates things with her hands. For a moment she suspected this was the result of being around Ameena, but it was not; it was the customary reply. She wondered how come the compliment did not offer thanks but, instead, offered a prayer. Did she need to thank her, too? She licked her fingers, sucking on the sweet syrup. Why was this question bugging her now? Dozens of gifts from her friend and she had never thought of how to put her gratitude into words.

"Ameena—" Nagla paused. Ameena looked up from her cooking. "Did you ever notice how everything we say has to do with prayer? *Doaa,* I mean—something we ask God to do? Everyday things, like offering thanks for something or wishing someone good health. It's almost—" she paused, looking for words "—like we don't talk directly to people. We talk to God and ask Him to do something for them. We just let them overhear what we say to God."

Ameena looked at her, one eyebrow raised.

"Like just now," Nagla went on. "I said *teslam edeiky,* which is what I've always said, but I was just thinking that nowadays people don't even say that. They say *jazakee Allah khairan,* right? May Allah reward you in good? Do people say 'Thank you' anymore?"

"*Jazakee Allah khairan* is a very good way to thank someone."

"Why?"

"Because you're praying for them, of course!"

"But why not say 'Thank you'? *Shokran?*"

"*Alshokr lellah wahdoh.*" Only God is to be thanked. "It's better to offer a prayer."

"They don't do this here, do they?"

"We're more religious."

"Are we?" Nagla paused. "Actually, just the other day a lady at the grocery store said 'God bless you' to the checkout girl. Is that the same?"

"Probably. I don't know." Ameena turned the stove off, wiped her hands on a kitchen towel before settling down across from Nagla.

"So Samir really wants to go to that service on Sunday?" Ameena asked.

"Yes. He thinks the community needs to know where we stand on this subject, that we are as sorry about it as they are."

"Bad idea. You should tell him so."

Nagla sighed. "My mom disagrees. She thinks it's a bad idea to keep on 'contradicting' my husband."

"*Contradicting him?* You?" Ameena laughed. "That's funny."

"What do you mean?"

"I mean you never do!"

"Of course I do! I don't agree with everything he says."

"You don't agree, but you don't disagree either, do you? Not openly, at least."

Ameena got up, grabbed a headscarf that she had draped on a chair, and started wrapping it around her head, turning away from Nagla in order to look at her reflection in a small mirror that hung on the wall. Nagla examined the mirror's frame—even that was decorated with verses from the Qur'an etched in copper, Ameena's face a bright pink enclosed in a halo of words.

Nagla's hands started shaking, so she placed them under her thighs to steady them—her newfound remedy to this recent yet quite frequent ailment. But Ameena's wooden counter chairs were less forgiving than

Nagla's upholstered ones; her wedding ring dug into her finger. She pulled her hands out from under her, placed them flat on the counter's cool surface. Her arms, bent at the elbows and outstretched in front of her, reminded her of the sphinx, the looming symbol of muteness. *Abu El-Hool hayntak,* her mother often said whenever she witnessed something so outrageous that it defied silence. *Even the sphinx would speak in protest.*

"This is what I don't get," Nagla started, struggling to keep her voice calm. "My mom thinks I'm wrong because I don't agree with my husband. You think I'm wrong because I don't oppose him. You both agree that I'm not handling this situation as I should, but which one of you should I listen to?"

"Your mom is old-fashioned, Nagla. I'm sure she means well, but you can't behave the way she was expected to fifty years ago." She was pinning the last strip of the oblong scarf, tucking loose strands of hair under its upper edge.

"But wouldn't contradicting my husband be considered a sin?" Nagla asked, emphasizing the word *sin,* hoping her voice did not betray too much sarcasm as her eyes darted to the religious verses surrounding her. *"Al-rijaallu qawamoona ala al-nisai?"* she quoted the Qur'an.

Ameena turned to look at her. *"Bima anfaqoo.* It's really not authority men have as much as a responsibility to protect their women and maintain them financially. Besides, even if he has authority as a man, this doesn't mean you cannot tell him if he's about to plunge you all into disaster. I'm not asking you to be disrespectful of your husband. I'm just saying you need to point things out to him, if he's too blind to see them."

"Samir would die before he'd let me push him to change his mind on something he is so bent on doing."

"How do you know if you never try?"

"I do try! But when did I ever succeed?"

"So you'll just give up?" Ameena took her place opposite Nagla again, speaking in a low, urgent whisper. "For years all you've done is complain about him. I'm not trying to turn you against him, I'm just saying that you should stand up to him. *Inna Allah la yughayyiru ma beqauwmin hatta yughayiroo ma bianfusihim*," Ameena said, quoting the Qur'an again. Surely Allah changes not the condition of a people until they change their own condition.

Nagla sat back in her chair. Her hands, resting on the counter, had resumed their shaking despite the constant pressure she kept on them. Both her mother and Ameena had an uncanny ability to quote the Qur'an in support of their arguments, even if their views opposed each other, even, she now realized, using the same verse to support two different sides of an argument, their interpretations as flexible as Nagla's ignorance of such tactics was vexing. She rummaged through her brain for a religious retort but found none. More infuriating than Ameena's tactics was the implication of her words: she was blaming Nagla again, this time for Samir's stubbornness. As if all she needed to do was say the words and he would fall to his knees and start following her commands. Which is probably exactly what Zayd did.

"That's easy for you to say, considering how much Zayd lets you get away with," Nagla said.

Ameena sat straight up. "He doesn't let me get away with anything—he listens to what I have to say. Nothing wrong with having your husband respect you."

"So now my husband doesn't respect me?"

"Ease up, Nagla. I'm just trying to help."

"Blaming me for what my husband does is not helping."

"I'm not blaming you for what he does. I'm talking about what you don't do. Like how you never try to change things before they happen. Even when you can see that things will not turn out right, you just wait for disaster and then you're miserable about it. Just like—" Ameena stopped.

Nagla got up, backed away from her chair. She took a deep breath and asked, "Just like what?"

"Like now. When you were talking about prayer, that is. Maybe if you pray a bit more—"

"That's not what you meant."

"Yes, it is."

"Liar."

Ameena shot up and stood staring at Nagla, mouth gaping. Nagla stayed put, lips pursed, her heartbeat throbbing in her ears. In the fifteen years they had known each other, Nagla had not once called her friend a name. Everything Nagla had ever learned about Egyptian notions of civility flashed in her mind. Ehsan would be mortified if she knew her daughter had been so impolite. She fought an instinctive urge to apologize, to run over and hug Ameena, to explain how stressed out, how depressed she was.

But she would not apologize.

"I'm sick and tired of all of you blaming me for everything," Nagla hissed.

"I'm not blaming—"

"You, my mom, Samir. Why does everything have to be my fault?" Nagla's eyes teared up. "You don't think I blame myself enough? You have any idea what goes on in my mind every day?"

Ameena walked around the kitchen island and over toward her. "I know, *habibti*. But I swear to Allah I never meant to imply any of what happened was your fault."

"You're lying again. Isn't that a sin, Ameena?"

Ameena took one step back, hesitated.

Nagla went on, "And what exactly do you think you know? I stay up every night wondering what I did wrong, why this has happened to me. Why God did this to me."

"Astaghfiru Allah." Ameena put one hand up to her mouth. "Don't let

the devil get hold of you, Nagla. Such blasphemy. *La yukallifu Allah nafsan illa wusaaha."* God burdens each soul with only as much as it can handle.

"Well, you know what? Perhaps He has miscalculated this time. Because He has certainly given me much more than I can handle."

Ameena gasped. *"Astaghfiru Allah Al-Azim,"* she murmured, asking God for forgiveness on behalf of Nagla. *"Astaghfiru Allah Al-Azim."*

Nagla threw both hands up, squeezed her temples. Her words, true expressions of what had boiled up inside her for so long, sounded blasphemous even to her, and the sting of her own irreverence burned her. She groaned. Again she could see her mother's face and imagine what she would do if she knew her daughter had such thoughts lurking in her head. She would be just as shocked and disappointed in her as Ameena was. Right now, standing in Ameena's kitchen, her hands still pressed against her temples, her feet firm against the cold tile, Nagla felt that everyone judged her: her mother, her friend, her husband—and, after she uttered those words, even God.

She walked out of the kitchen, leaving Ameena there, her prayers a whisper that still reached Nagla's ears even as she ran up the stairs to Maraam's room. In the hallway, she slowed down, letting her breath steady and wiping her eyes before she went on. She would bid her daughter goodbye and then go, leave this house, stay away from everyone. A few feet ahead of her, Maraam's open door emanated soft words that oozed comfort, the whispers of young girls. Nagla stood transfixed, listening. The words were too low to comprehend, even for her. Softly, her bare feet sinking in the plush carpet—she had remembered to take her shoes off at the door, the way Ameena preferred—she walked up to the room, stood by the door watching both girls. Maraam was sitting Indian-style on her bed, already dressed for going out, her head covered in a blue scarf woven with occasional silver strings that complemented the embroidery on her jeans. On her bed lay a pile of scarves that she was folding. At her dresser, Fatima stood, trying to tie a white scarf with penny-sized pink polka dots around her face.

"You're doing it wrong," Maraam said, jumping up, pulling a pin out of her own head scarf and using it to fasten Fatima's in place.

"It's okay, Maraam, I was only trying it on anyway. I love how soft it is," Fatima said, tracing both hands along the top of her head.

"You can keep it, if you want to."

"Really?" Fatima said as Maraam plopped back on her bed.

"Sure. Mom brought a whole bunch home last time she went to Syria. I keep telling her she doesn't need to, there are perfectly good scarves here. They don't have to be labeled *head scarf* to work, you know. Here, this one is from Banana Republic," she said, pulling a yellow oblong out of the pile.

But Fatima was not listening. Nagla watched her daughter look at herself in the mirror, patting the head scarf, pulling at its corners to adjust it around her face. Fatima's smile glowed with a serenity that Nagla had not witnessed in a long time.

"Oh, hi, Aunt Nagla," Maraam said, finally glancing toward the door. Fatima turned around. Nagla's eyes met her daughter's, and the smile turned into an embarrassed one, as if Nagla had caught Fatima holding some boy's hand.

"Hi, Mama," Fatima said. Swiftly, she tugged at the head scarf, but the pin caught on some of her hair, and the scarf dangled off one side of her head.

"Wait," Maraam said, rushing toward her and finding the pin, pulling it and the scarf off.

"You could keep it on, *habibti*," Nagla said.

"No, it's okay. I was just trying it on," Fatima said, blushing. Nagla bit at her lips. She had never imagined Fatima would consider covering her hair. Samir would have a fit if he found out, would probably blame it all on Ameena and her family, and, by extension, on Nagla, for letting

Fatima spend so much time at Maraam's. Never an advocate of women's covering up, Samir's attitude toward the head scarf had changed from indifference to rejection after 9/11. "Who'd want to draw that kind of attention to herself anyway?" Nagla herself had never worn a head scarf, the sign of modesty, the symbol that unites all Muslim women, a group from which Nagla was, at least by appearance, excluded—one more deficiency, one more way Ameena was better than she was, one more reason God was probably angry with her.

"You can take it to the mosque; wear it there," Maraam said, stuffing the rest of the scarves in the drawer, unfolded.

"You're leaving?" Fatima asked her mother, holding the scarf in both hands.

"Yes. So are you. Maraam's parents are getting ready to go, so you better hurry."

The girls ran past her, Fatima stopping only to plant a quick peck on her mother's cheek. In the kitchen, Ameena sat with her arms crossed, her eyes cast down. She looked up just in time to catch Nagla's eyes before Nagla looked away.

"Ready, everyone?" Zayd's voice boomed before he dashed into the kitchen, followed by Ashraf.

"May I drive, *please?*" Ashraf begged his father.

"Not on your life. Not when we're late," Ameena said.

"You can go start the car, though," Zayd said. "Pull it out of the garage." Ameena glared at him, and Zayd, smiling, leaned over Nagla, mock-whispering, "Now I'll probably not have any dinner." Nagla attempted a smile and failed.

"That's all I get from you: mockery," Ameena said.

Nagla watched Zayd smile at his wife, then saw his smile change to an inquisitive look that Ameena responded to with a subtle shake of the head and a downcast look.

"I'll go make sure Ashraf doesn't wreck that car," Zayd said, still smiling but avoiding Nagla's eyes. "Come with me, girls." He motioned to Fatima and Maraam, who followed him, all three of them disappearing through the door to the garage, their chatter trailing behind them.

He had understood. Maybe not everything, but from one look at his wife he had understood enough to leave her alone with her friend. Nagla bit at her lip, fought back tears.

"Come, let's sit down for a few moments," Ameena said, motioning toward the chair next to her. "Please?"

Nagla shook her head. "Not now."

She walked out of the kitchen before Ameena could hold her back. Outside, the sky that had been cloudy when Nagla walked in was now overcast, a solid gray. She got in her car and watched Zayd get in the driver's seat of his Accord while Maraam squeezed in the back between her brother and Fatima. Ameena, the last one to walk out of the house, made her way slowly to the car, stopping once to glance toward Nagla before getting in the passenger seat. They had already started moving when Nagla jumped out of her car and ran toward them.

"Wait!" she yelled. Zayd stepped on the brake and the car jolted to a stop. She ran up to Fatima's side and waited for the window to roll down.

"What, Mama?"

Everyone in the car looked at Nagla. She hesitated for a moment and then rested one hand on the Accord, and a drop of rain fell on her forearm.

"Will . . . will you need me to pick you up?" she asked Fatima.

"No, Mama. Khaled will."

"Okay. Just checking." She backed up, let her daughter roll the window halfway up before stepping back up and tapping on it.

"*What,* Mama?"

"*La ilaha illa Allah,*" Nagla whispered, leaning close to her daughter. "*Muhammad rasool Allah.*"

Stepping back, Nagla saw Ameena look at her. Again she felt the accusation of being superstitious, the ridiculousness of the ritual, of the hope that words would ensure reuniting. For weeks after Hosaam's death she had obsessed, trying to remember whether or not she had used the testimony to bid him goodbye on that last morning, but she never could remember. Still, she had to do it, and she watched the car roll away, enduring Ameena's gaze. In the backseat, she saw Fatima tugging the polka-dot scarf from her pocket and draping it loosely over her head. She looked like the Virgin Mary.

10

ENGLISH: Today's news is tomorrow's history.

ARABIC: The news you pay for today, you get tomorrow for free.

Khaled watched Brittany walk down Bleecker Street and waited till she joined him, her hand casually touching his for a greeting before they both headed toward the park. He walked next to her in silence. She, keeping her head low, did not glance his way but walked, hands in the pockets of her jeans, one arm covered with bangles that, surprisingly, looked similar to the ones Ehsan always wore, only Ehsan's were gold and Brittany's were a mixture of silver and green hues. For months now he and Brittany had followed the same routine every time they met: they walked up to the park and strolled down a path or sat on a bench, watching people and talking. Their meetings were never long—he always showed up after her shifts; she always hung around with him before going home. He was her interlude, he knew, a way for her to transition from the hectic coffee shop to her busy nights. Still, he was flattered, because not only did she never refuse to meet him, she also sought him out, sometimes. He hoped she felt as close to him as he did to her, that he, perhaps, provided her with a degree of comfort, as she did him. He feared she hung around with him only out of pity.

"How come you're here this early on a Friday?" she asked as they headed into the park.

"School got called off," he said, resenting the need to refer to school and remind her that he was still a high school junior while she was a college senior. Quickly, he added, "I saw the link you sent me."

She smiled. "Did you like that?"

"Sure!" A trip to observe monarch nesting grounds in Mexico sounded perfect. He had imagined they would one day take the trip together, but he did not tell her that.

"I thought you would."

"How about you? Would you ever want to go on a trip like that?"

She shook her head. "I'd never be able to afford it."

"How do you know? You're graduating in less than a year!"

"And then what?" They had reached a bench and she flung herself on it, looking up at him as he stood, puzzled. "What happens after I graduate?"

"You work?"

She laughed. Khaled felt his face blush so quickly that he had to turn away from her to hide it.

"I'm sorry, Khaled." She reached out and grabbed his hand, pulling him to sit next to her. "That was cruel."

They stayed silent, watching people pass them by. He did not want to risk another comment.

"I've been thinking about college a lot, lately. About what's next, that is."

He waited for her to continue. Instead, she turned to him and, her eyes flashing, asked, "You know what? Why don't you tell me about *your* plans?"

"What plans?"

"Anything! I just want to hear you talk."

Again he looked down and said nothing. She was making him self-conscious, which she never did. She sighed. "I can't do anything right today, can I?"

"Bad day?"

"Bad year. I really don't know what I was thinking, studying art."

"But you're so good at it!"

"Good doesn't pay. Business pays."

"You can't study business! I have a better chance becoming a doctor than you do going into business."

She laughed. "Does your father know you're not applying to any of his top five picks?"

He shook his head. "He hasn't asked, and I didn't say anything."

"Good for you." She looked away, and he watched her, wondering how he had managed to tell her everything about his life except for the most important event.

"That's what I meant, when I asked you to tell me about your plans. You know what you want, all the time. I really like that."

"Not all the time."

"The times that matter, at least. The big stuff."

"I make plans, yes. But that doesn't mean they will all come true." The image of Hosaam tearing up the college applications flashed before his eyes and he had to look up to see something else, a bird flying from one tree to the next or the glaring sun shining through the branches overhead. Ehsan, of course, would know what he meant. All her prayers and rituals, the swirling incense and the pats on the head accompanied by incantations, everything she did was aimed at making the real future match the imagined one as closely as possible.

"My grandmother tried to predict my future today," he said.

"How?"

"Reading coffee grounds."

"Very appropriate. I should tell Claire about that, maybe she'd like to add a coffee grounds reading service. This would definitely lure people in. Here's a business idea for you."

"Would not work with regular coffee, though. She reads Turkish coffee. Thicker grounds. They leave traces on the inside of the cups."

"So what did she see?"

"Nothing important, I guess."

She sighed. "I'd like to see my future." She turned to him. "Has she ever predicted something that came true?"

"Kind of. Once, I guess. I don't know." His heart raced as he remembered Hosaam's broken cup. He stared at his feet but could feel Brittany look at him, waiting. All she needed to do was ask one more question, and he would blurt it all out. *She predicted something bad would happen to my brother. He shot himself and his girlfriend. I saw the bloodstained grass.*

She waited, and when he said nothing, she looked away. He could see her in his peripheral vision, her head turning from him, respecting his privacy, perhaps, or giving him the same freedom she did when she had not pushed him to reveal what his initials stood for. He wished he could let it all spill. Instead, he said, "It's all nonsense, anyway."

She nodded. "I know."

She folded her arms and slid down in her seat, letting her head rest on the back of the bench. Seeing her stare up at the tree branches above, he knew he had missed his chance. He wanted to reach out and hold her arm, say *listen,* and then tell her everything about Hosaam *and* confess that he did, perhaps, believe in Ehsan's fortune-telling capabilities. Instead, he looked up as well and, watching the birds hop from branch to branch, remembered Ehsan's stories about how Arabs of old used to watch bird movements for divinations. Beside him, he could feel Brittany fidget. He feared she might be getting ready to get up and go home already.

"So what would you like to see?" he blurted out.

"What?" she asked.

"Your future, I mean. What would you like to see, if you could see your future?"

She sighed, still looking up in the trees, her arms crossed. Then, slowly, she started, "An art gallery. Something small, not garish like those huge empty ones that make you feel like you're visiting the dentist. I'd like to work with painters no one knows, the people I know spend days locked up in a tiny room drawing. I'd make just enough money to take a whole week off every month. Then I'd go out to the woods, somewhere new every time, camp out somewhere, and paint. In the winter, I'd stay home; I'd have a small loft in the village—that'd be cool; or I'd go down somewhere warm. Georgia, maybe. I'd like to go to Georgia. I saw a picture of a canyon there once," she said, turning to face him. "Providence Canyon. The picture showed this big cliff with sides that went from snow white to yellow to orange to a dark rusty ocher to Tuscan brown—all in one cliff. And the top of the cliff was covered with trees— not all bare like the Grand Canyon, but green." She leaned back again. "I'd like to paint that."

The colors of the monarch, he thought, imagining the cliff like a color chart of the wings of a butterfly. "Sounds beautiful. I'd like to see this painting, one day."

She laughed. "Sure. I'll even dedicate it to you. I'll also give you shares of my nonexisting studio and my never-to-exist loft."

"You're not in a very good mood today, are you?" She had never been sarcastic before. Straightforward, yes. But not sarcastic.

She lifted one hand to her face. "No. No, I'm not."

He waited. Her fingers, nails painted a dark violet, touched her brow so he could not see her eyes. He focused on her eyebrow ring, two bright yellow dots that accented the sharp point of her brow. "Yellow contrasts with purple," she had once explained to him, showing him a color wheel. "See?" He had thought only of how the piercing must have hurt, which reminded him of Natalie. Now, whenever he looked at the eyebrow ring, he tried not to think of Natalie.

"Sebastian dropped in at work, today," she went on, slowly. She let her hand fall down to her lap, and he saw she had been crying.

"What did he want?" He spoke softly so she would not hear the quiver in his voice.

"I don't know," she groaned, her shoulders drooping. "I really don't know. He says he wants to get back with me, but I *know* he doesn't."

"Why not?" He could never imagine how Sebastian had let her go, even though he knew she'd dumped him, not vice versa. Still, he had blamed the rich boyfriend for breaking her heart. He should have been able to keep her.

"Because I know it would never work out, and he does, too. His parents would kill him, for one thing. I should show you his apartment, one day. The rent his father pays for that thing is more than what I make in six months at the coffee shop." She sniffed, snickering. "Maybe that's where I got the loft wish from. Bad influence, hanging around with him for so long."

Khaled had seen Sebastian only once, during one of his and Brittany's on-again periods. He had looked like a Polo ad, complete with side-parted blond hair. Based on race alone, Khaled felt he would have no chance competing with Sebastian; age and wealth drove the point further in. Still, Khaled had seen Sebastian kiss her goodbye. He had seen him grab her hand as he walked away, letting go only when he was too far from her to keep holding on.

"But he does love you, Brit. And if he keeps asking you to come back—"

"He doesn't love me," she spat. "He loves *the idea* of being with me. It makes him feel special, different from his friends. I'm just one more show-and-tell thing."

She lifted both hands to her face, letting one sob escape before she held herself still, her entire body rigid. Khaled waited. If he had Garrett's courage, he would have hugged her now.

"Miracles don't happen, Khaled," she murmured through her fingers. "Rich boys don't sweep poor girls off their feet and take them to live happily ever after in their castles."

Khaled knotted his brows, looking away from her. He could not contest the idea—if miracles did happen, Hosaam and Natalie would have been alive and happy. His family would have been intact. The town would have embraced them, like he had believed they did his whole life, up to last year. If miracles did happen, he would have had a chance with Brittany.

Again Ehsan forced herself into his thoughts. She would disagree, of course. *Eldoaa yarodd al-qkadar,* she always said. Prayer thwarts fate. He had heard the phrase so often, it had become one of her staples, like her prayers for his safe return whenever he left home, or her mumblings during the day, asking God for forgiveness and blessings. Never before had he truly contemplated what her words meant. Now, looking away from Brittany but still hearing her occasional faint sob, he considered what Ehsan had told him, how her obsession with foretelling the future was a manifestation of her constant search for the right prayer. If she knew what fate had in store, she could pray for a reversal of misfortunes, and if she prayed long enough and sincerely enough, God would intervene. Perhaps she saw Hosaam's end as a failure of prayer on her part.

He wished he could truly believe in that, as well. He felt he once did, but could not recall when. At some point, he remembered prostrating himself and praying fervently for something—what? A good grade on a test he had not prepared for? A new butterfly habitat that his father would not buy him? A day without being bullied at school? The prayer escaped him, but the sensation did not—he could feel it now, overcoming him like it must have years ago, the desperation gingerly kept from crushing him by a hope of being heard, of being noticed, of being deemed good enough to deserve divine intervention. He almost groaned. Not once this past year had he asked God for anything, even though he had dutifully performed his five prayers every day. Almost every day. Now he wished he could still pray with the belief of a ten-year-old or that of his aging grandmother. If he could, he would ask God for happiness for Brittany, for peace of mind for him, for a coming weekend devoid of humiliation for his family. He would ask God to intervene and thwart whatever other misfortunes fate had in store for him. He would, at the very least, ask God to let him stay seated here, next to Brittany, for the rest of the day.

"I'm sorry, Khaled. I didn't mean to be such a bore," Brittany said.

"You're not. You never are." He looked at her and saw her smile at him. Her eyes, though still red, were dry.

"You're so sweet, you know that?" she asked. He blushed, tried to mumble something, and she laughed. Pulling closer to him, she put one arm around him and placed her head on his shoulder. He stayed perfectly still. Then, slowly, he wrapped his arm around her waist. She was looking up, away from the crowds of runners and stroller-pushing mothers that passed them, and he lifted his head up, too, toward the trees, and, closing his eyes, prayed that she would remain like this for as long as possible.

11

ENGLISH: Like father, like son / Like mother, like daughter.

ARABIC: This cub is that lion's offspring / Turn the carafe upside down, and the daughter will resemble her mother.

So you'd rather hide?"

Samir's voice, calm as it was, had an edge that Nagla recognized. She paced her bedroom as she spoke to him on the phone, trying to keep her voice low so her mother would not hear. As a precaution, she closed her bedroom door.

"I'm not saying that. I just don't think going there would work out well."

Samir sighed. "Of course it would. We can show them we're a family, still together despite what happened. We can show them we care enough to offer our condolences and are brave enough to do it *despite* their resistance. We'll look courageous. Americans like this kind of stuff. Trust me. I know them better than you do."

"I've been living with them for as long as you have, remember?"

"Yes. But you're home alone all the time. I'm interacting with them every day. I know what I'm talking about. We need a public act of solidarity. It's the only way we can get them to forget what happened."

"Can't we offer this public act of solidarity some other time?"

"Like when? Do you want me to call a town hall meeting just for our sake? When on earth will we have all those people gathered in the same place again?"

"There has to be another way to do this."

"There is no other way." He paused. "Why are you so bent against this? You're the only one who thinks it's a bad idea."

"I'm not. The kids don't like it, either."

"Since when do we listen to advice from children? They're just too self-conscious. They don't want that many eyes on them."

"They're not children anymore."

He sighed again. "Okay, so Khaled's seventeen years of existence make him see things clearer than I do."

"I didn't say that."

"I'm telling you, it's all in your head. Even your mom agrees with me."

Nagla paused. "You spoke to my mom about this?"

"She's living with us, isn't she? She was here when Cynthia came visiting. What's wrong with discussing things with her?"

"And she agreed with you?"

"Yes."

Of course. Why was she even surprised?

"You're making too big a deal out of this, Nagla. Trust me—it will work out."

He waited. She paced the room and said nothing. She should tell him that Ameena thought it was a horrible idea, but he would only belittle her opinion, then be angry with Nagla for discussing family affairs with strangers. She would respond that he had discussed it with her mother, but he would argue that her mother was not a stranger and defy her to contradict that. The entire conversation was heading toward a dead end.

"I have patients waiting." He hung up before she could protest. She stared at the phone in her hand and then flung it onto her bed.

Not until she was on her second cigarette did she realize she had forgotten to open the windows. She cranked them both then opened the door as well, hoping the draft would help disperse the smoke before it clung to her bed linens.

The rain had stopped and the day turned calm, with only a gentle breeze, not even enough to make the trees sway, a change in weather that contradicted earlier forecasts and seemed to banish—or, at least, postpone—the expected storm. She rested one arm on the side of the window, looking out, and inhaled the warm, moist air, surprisingly soothing, a reminder of spring days in Egypt when the air would blow from the sea, filling her lungs with the smell of salty iodine, so fresh and clean. Pulling the screen off and placing it on the floor, she wiped the windowsill dry and then leaned out, flicking cigarette ash on her deck below. In the distance, she traced the tops of the trees, a wavy line bordered by the sky. To her right, a cluster of trees formed a large hump that protruded from the mass forming Summerset Park—how had she never noticed that before? How could she have lived in this house for close to twenty years and yet never noticed the shape of the trees that greeted her every morning?

She cranked the casement window fully open. Holding on to the edge and biting on the cigarette to keep it in place, she carefully lifted one leg out the window and slowly raised herself until she sat straddling the windowsill, her back pushed against the frame, one foot in her room and the other dangling out of it. She held on to the frame with both hands before she looked down to see what her foot was hitting and realized that she could reach the roof of the living room's bay window. She let her foot rest on it and settled in place.

The windowsill did not make for comfortable seating. A small pillow would have probably spared her tailbone the nudging pain, and the moisture that she had apparently not fully wiped away was already seeping through her pant leg, but she was reluctant to move after she had found her balance. She grabbed the cigarette, brushing off the ash that had fallen on her jeans. From where she was seated, she could see the trees clear ahead, and she examined them, feeling a strange satisfaction in knowing that she, in her late forties, could still wear skinny jeans and maneuver her way out a window—or, at least, halfway out. The breeze tickled her ankle, whisking her back to when she was nine, riding her bike along the Alexandria shore. She had to take a deep breath to steady herself again and to control the shiver that went through her.

She regretted having called Samir. Waiting until he came home would have been better, but, then again, she didn't want to risk having the kids overhear their conversation, which, considering Samir's tendency to yell, would have been inevitable. She wondered whether he had always been so loud; when they first got married, she used to like listening to his voice, especially with her eyes closed. He would be talking and she would simply close her eyes—that much she remembered. His voice, so deep it seemed suited to a man twice his breadth and a foot taller, had soothed her, and keeping her eyes closed allowed her to dissect its tone until she found the one layer that she knew affected her so, giving her a feeling of home that even the snow outside—so foreign, at first—could not disprove. When he asked why she did it and heard her explanation, he laughed, teasing her about her sharp hearing—an inside joke threading its way throughout their marriage. At least once, she was certain, he had stopped talking as her eyes were closed and tiptoed around her, then, coming up from behind, he had yelled in her ear, causing her to jump. He had doubled over in laughter in response. But that had been long ago. If she were to close her eyes while he talked now, he would probably ask whether he was boring her to sleep.

It hit her, now, that his voice had changed. She took another puff of her cigarette, blew the smoke into the air, and watched it dissipate. She could not be certain, of course, but it seemed that his voice had gained another layer of impatient, dissatisfied edginess that she had not sensed before. Or perhaps it had always been there and she had failed to hear it. Whatever the reason, she could not remember the last time his voice had soothed her.

She heard a branch crack in the distance, and, behind her, her mother's slow step climbing the stairs. Her senses had become increasingly sharp—perhaps Samir was right and she *was* cursed with the hearing of a cat. But she was noticing things that she had never noticed before, like that hump of trees far ahead, or the words on Ameena's walls and the prayers that sprinkled her own talk as well as her friends'. She remembered her encounter with Ameena and winced. Why was she dissecting everything today? A few months ago, Khaled had tried to explain to her how evolution happened when animals were subjected to external stress: a new predator, perhaps, or an environmental threat to their existence. She had listened and nodded, grateful for what she had seen as an uncharacteristic attempt at intimacy on Khaled's part, but she had not really paid attention to what he was saying. She wondered whether her newfound perception was a sort of evolutionary leap, too; whether the stress of this past year, and now this past week, had made her see things she never recognized before.

"What are you doing?" Ehsan stood in the doorway, as she always did. Why did she have to pause at the door before she walked into any room? Was this, too, something Nagla should add to her list of new observations? She watched her mother, pondering when Samir had had time to talk to her in private. Nagla drew on the last puff of her cigarette and then flicked it away.

"I was smoking."

"Like this?" Ehsan raised an arm as she walked toward her. "Are you out of your mind?"

"I needed the fresh air."

"You're half naked!"

Nagla looked down at herself. She was in her camisole, the edge of her black bra showing under the camisole's lace. She stumbled into the room, got her foot caught on the windowsill, and fell down, headfirst. Both arms outstretched, she caught herself and jumped to her feet and then walked away from the window, her heart throbbing. When had she taken her top off? She had it on when she first called Samir, she was certain. She walked up and down her room, perplexed at how she had noticed the shape of the trees and the breeze brushing against her ankle but not her naked shoulders and arms, slightly moist—she now saw—from resting against the window.

"What were you doing dangling out the window like this anyway? You could have fallen! *And* people probably saw you, naked as you are." Ehsan followed her into the bathroom, where Nagla found her top bunched up on the vanity. She grabbed it, pulling it over her head.

"And what would have been worse, do you think—falling off the window, or having people see me half naked?" she asked her mother. In the mirror, she could see Ehsan's pursed lips, her incredulous look.

"What kind of stupid question is this?"

"It's a question of priorities. Which is more important? My life or how people perceive my decency?"

"I don't know what's gotten into you, lately." Ehsan walked out of the bathroom. Nagla looked at her own reflection. She had often heard of grief-stricken people who woke up one morning with grayed hair, the discoloring a testament to their shock at what life had thrown their way. Her hair, despite all that she had gone through, was still jet black. She ran her fingers through it, ruffling it, looking for any gray strands. Her hair's resistance to graying felt like a betrayal of her son.

Perhaps this was one more thing she had failed at.

She turned around and saw her mother sitting on the edge of the bed. Ehsan's hair was a dark salt and pepper, not the silvery gray that most people of her age wear. She, too, had managed to go through life seemingly unfazed—at least as far as her hair color testified. Nagla walked back into her bedroom, stood across from her mother, examining her hair.

"What's wrong with you, girl?"

"I'm noticing the strangest things today. Like your hair color." Nagla paused. "You know, I'm starting to think I'm more like you than I ever thought I was."

Ehsan looked at her, her head tilted to the side, her brow knotted.

"My hair won't turn gray, just like yours." Nagla walked closer to her mother, looking her in the eyes. "Another thing I've noticed: how much Samir likes to talk to you."

"What—"

"I don't know how I never thought about that before. He used to call you in Egypt, didn't he? Whenever he and I had a fight over something, he would call to get you to convince me of his point of view."

"Only once or twice—"

"And then, in the middle of our argument, he'd throw it at me: *even your mother agrees with me.* How come you always take his side? Did you ever think that this is a betrayal of me?"

"Betrayal?" Ehsan slid off the bed and stood in front of her daughter. "You truly are an ungrateful child. Is this the thanks I get for slaving in your house for the entire past year?"

"Didn't you tell me just yesterday that you thought going to that service was a bad idea? Distasteful, right? Why didn't you tell him so when he asked you? Or had he already spoken to you then?"

"It's his house and his family. I'm only a guest—"

"So you lied to him."

"Nagla!"

"And you lied to me, saying he never spoke to you."

"*Bent!*"

"Just like you used to lie to *Baba*, right?"

"Mind your manners, *ya bent!*"

"Don't think I don't know. Don't think I believe all those stories you tell about how great *Baba* was. You lie about him just like you lied *to* him. I know. Your sons told me."

"*Eh ellet eladab di?*"

Nagla ignored the accusation of ill-breeding and yanked her bedside table's drawer open, rummaging through it, her heart pounding. If her feelings had layers similar to those of Samir's voice, only one deeply buried layer would house the thread of guilt she felt at calling her mother names to her face—another first. Twice in one day she had called those closest to her liars, she noticed as she found an empty cigarette pack and squished it, balling it up and tossing it back in the drawer. She could not claim the accusations felt good, but they felt necessary. Fair. Her recent attention to detail seemed to have clarified things for her, and she argued that this clarity led to a degree of honesty—because that was what her words must have been: honest—that was utterly justified. The only reason she was unable to feel good about her scrupulousness was that crack in her mother's voice as she spluttered something behind her. Nagla looked for cigarettes—there had to be another pack in one of those drawers—perfectly aware of her mother's manipulative attempt at making her feel guilty. She was not taking any more of this.

"Don't walk out on me while I talk to you, girl!" Ehsan's shrill voice boomed behind her. Nagla ignored her, ran down the stairs and into the kitchen, where she kept a stash of cigarettes in one of the drawers. She had already lit one and was walking up and down the length of the breakfast table when her mother caught up with her.

"You think you can get away with being disrespectful to me? You think now that you're all grown up I won't know how to teach you manners?" Ehsan banged one hand on the table, and Nagla jumped.

"Stop yelling." Nagla's voice was calm, though her words caused a funny, minuscule ring in her own ears. She paused, trying to detect it again. It was gone.

"Is this what I get for trying to keep the peace between you and your husband? For leaving my home and traveling halfway across the earth to be with you? *Saheeh: men kharag men daroh etall me'daroh.*"

Nagla snickered at the saying. "Leaving your home did *not* result in any loss of status or dignity. Don't try to make me feel guilty, Mama. I'm onto all of that."

"No loss of dignity? Then what do you call your attitude?"

"Being honest." Nagla rested both hands on the table across from her mother. Her cigarette dripped ash on the tabletop, and Ehsan glanced at it.

Nagla went on. "For once in my life, I'm trying to be honest."

"There is a difference between honesty and ill manners."

"I was not ill-mannered."

"Calling me a liar is not ill manners? Accusing me of lying to your father, may Allah have mercy on his soul? Insulting him, too?"

"I did not—"

"And which one of my ingrate sons has spoken to you about him, anyway?" Ehsan interrupted her, her voice getting edgier by the moment. "What lies have they told you?"

Nagla hesitated. Honesty dictated that she say what she knew: her father's temper, his string of professional failures, his anger that often bordered on cruelty directed at his wife and sons, his abusiveness. She knew the stories. She could still remember Waleed's face, the way he winced when he told her of the thrashings he and her other brothers endured, of the way their mother would throw herself between her husband and children to shield them from his belt. Nagla could recount those stories, one by one, and point out the not-so-subtle discrepancies between them and her mother's versions. Perhaps then Ehsan would recognize this thing that Nagla was trying to get at, this string of habitual, perpetually justified, allegedly harmless lies, these "embellishments," as her mother would probably call them, just as Waleed had done when trying to justify Ehsan's lies. *Because we do not air our dirty laundry for everyone to gawk at,* Nagla could imagine her mother saying. We do not even stare at it ourselves, the reasoning would follow, because, after all, this would not be decent. Better pretend all is well. Better justify abuse, cover up failures, keep on praying that God will not expose our nakedness like he did Adam and Eve's, will not withdraw his protection and subject us to the judgment of others.

Nagla struggled to find the words. There had to be a way to explain this to her mother, to get her to see what she now saw. But before Nagla could speak, Ehsan let herself drop onto one of the chairs. Resting her head on one hand, she started rocking from side to side, faint sobs emanating rhythmically, as if initiated by the pendulum-like motion.

"Why do you do this to me, *ya Allah*? What have I done to deserve such ingratitude from my own children in my old age?"

Nagla sighed, pressing the balls of her thumbs against her eye sockets, trying to steady her hands. Her mother's reaction did not surprise her. This was a signature Ehsan maneuver, as Samir called it, a staple of her arsenal reserved for unwanted conversations. Look at *me*, she seemed to say. Feel sorry for me. Forget about this other, unpleasant thing you wanted to talk about.

"Please don't cry, Mama."

Ehsan sobbed louder.

Nagla pulled up a chair and sat down. As she smoked, she watched her mother and tapped her fingernails on the glass top of the breakfast table.

"This isn't going to work, you know. Not this time." Nagla puffed a cloud of smoke in the space between her and her mother.

Ehsan looked up. She was no longer crying. "I truly failed to raise you well."

Nagla pushed her palm against the tabletop. Although pressed firm against the cold surface, her hand was still shaking.

"I am not going to be drawn into this fight." Nagla kept her voice as calm as she could. "I'm trying to explain something—to understand something."

"*Astaghfiru Allah Al-Azim,*" Ehsan sighed, covering her face with her hands.

Nagla went on. "I'm trying to explain to you that agreeing with everything my husband tells you will *not* bring me any peace. I know you mean well, but you are not helping."

"So next time I should call him an idiot to his face—is this what you want? Will this bring you peace?"

"I never said that." Nagla's cigarette was almost gone. She pulled a new one from the pack that lay on the table, used her old one to light it, and then tossed the stub into a half-empty glass of water that stood on the counter next to her. The cigarette fizzled and then went out, turning the water a murky gray. The color reminded Nagla of her treacherous jet-black hair.

"All I said," Nagla went on, "is that you should not let him use you to get to me. He always tries to do so. Don't make it so easy on him. At least give me a chance to have a say in my own life."

"I'm not preventing you from having any say in your life. Not that I've ever seen you try."

The sarcastic tone pinched Nagla, and she jumped. "What do you mean?" She paused, narrowed her eyes. "Have you been speaking to Ameena, too?"

"What?" Ehsan looked puzzled. "What has she got to do with any of this?"

"Are you all ganging up against me, now? Is that it?" She walked up and down the kitchen again.

"I'm only saying that my opinion does not matter one way or the other. If you want to take charge of things, *you* need to talk to your own husband. Don't blame it on me if you can't get him to do anything your way."

"I *do* talk to him!" Nagla yelled. "Do you know how difficult it is to get him to change his mind on anything?"

"Oh, that's more like it. *Aywah kedah*." Ehsan got up. The last trace of self-pity was gone from her voice, replaced with a tone that Nagla struggled to identify, placing it somewhere between anger and self-satisfaction. "So your husband can be difficult, huh? You can try to get him to change things but fail, correct? And what do you do when you fail? What do you do when he looks you in the eyes and tells you he will do what he pleases because he is the man of the house, because he is putting a roof over your head and your children's?"

"Samir never—"

"What do you do when you reach a dead end? Tell me, Miss Stand-Your-Ground."

Nagla paced the kitchen.

"I'll tell you what you do," Ehsan went on. "You tell him it's okay. You tell him, *Whatever you say, Samir.* You tell him you have nothing more to say." She paused. "You lie."

"I don't—"

"You lie to protect your family. It's what we do, Nagla. Because we are women, and there is nothing else we *can* do. So take a close look at yourself before you start judging me."

At the head of the table, Nagla stood rooted in place, staring at her mother. Again a hurricane of minute details flooded her senses: how her mother's eyes kept darting to her cigarette as she spoke; how a strand of her hair had fallen away from her tight bun and was hanging loose at the side of her face; how the lighting had changed, with rays of sunlight reaching the edge of the countertop, illuminating the glass with its ash-infused gray water. Nagla tried to push the details away, to focus on the unfairness of it all, on the cruelty of having both her mother and her friend blame her for things that were beyond her control.

"*Erhamoony ba'a,*" she whimpered. Her call for mercy did not seem to faze her mother, who stood in place, watching her. Nagla rested both palms on the table and let her head hang down.

Ehsan walked out of the kitchen, only to walk straight back in. Before Nagla could lift her head to see where her mother had gone, she heard the click of glass against glass and saw a crystal ashtray that her mother placed on the kitchen table, right under Nagla's face.

"Here," Ehsan said. "You're dripping filth all over the place. If you have to smoke inside, at least use an ashtray."

Nagla stared at the large circular object, one of the many relics from Egypt. This one her mother had carried here over a decade ago, after a previous visit to her daughter's house had revealed an unsatisfactory lack of crystals. Samir had nicknamed it "the ten-kilogram ashtray," marveling at how her mother had managed to bring it all the way from Egypt without breaking it or violating the airline's baggage allowance policy.

Nagla straightened up, still staring at the ashtray. Its very existence in her house seemed trivial and perplexing. She took another puff of her cigarette, struggled to concentrate. Another chunk of ash fell to the floor.

Ehsan sighed. "You just won't listen, will you?" She picked the ashtray up and shoved it into her daughter's hand. Nagla looked from the ashtray to her mother.

"How can you care about something like that right now?" she whispered. "I'm trying to talk to you. I'm trying to understand things, and all you care about is whether or not I get ash on my floor?" She tossed the ashtray onto the table. It landed with a loud clunk.

"Careful!" Ehsan shrieked. "You'll break your table!" She walked up to the table, pushed the ashtray aside, and started inspecting the tabletop.

Nagla's hand shook. Of course she should not have tossed that ashtray. Such carelessness. She walked up closer to her mother, lifted the ashtray, and flipped it, checking its underside for scratches. Even the ashtray's weight in her hand could not steady it. She bent down and checked the breakfast table, too, scrutinizing it for unevenness or flaws.

When she straightened up again, she saw the edge of the ashtray sparkle in the sun that shone through the window behind her. On the tabletop, the light broke into a prism of yellow, red, and blue.

She stared at the colors, looking from them to the ashtray in her hand.

"Nagla?"

She, like her mother, had been concerned—even if only for a moment— with this piece of crystal, with the furniture that should not be allowed to wear down with use or age.

When had she learned that? Why was it so important that the furniture not break or tarnish?

She looked up at her mother. The air grew cooler, and her head started spinning. She focused, her brows knotted in concentration.

"Nagla? What's wrong, *ya benti?*"

Again she thought of the shape of the trees, of the words on Ameena's walls, of all the little things that had recently started to crowd her brain, fighting for space, pushing other thoughts out.

Like her mother, she, too, was more superstitious than she cared to admit.

She had gone back and used the *shahada* to bid Fatima goodbye. Even now that thought comforted her.

Like her mother, she, too, had lied to her husband. Habitually. Had never mustered the courage to criticize him to his face.

She groaned.

"Nagla?"

Like her mother, she, too, allowed men their imperfections. Their little quirks.

Such as Samir's constant pride in his own judgment. The way he gloated whenever something he foresaw happened. The silly little things. The car trouble he would diagnose, insisting that the brake fluid was leaking. She would take the car for repair and back, and, when he would ask, she would tell him he was right. She would *lie,* deliberately. Because, after all, he was a man, and he should not be proven wrong in front of his wife and children.

Stupid things. Such as how Samir would belittle Hosaam's opinions in front of everyone, arguing that boys needed a firm hand. That, too, she had accepted.

She had allowed other things as well.

Such as when Hosaam started spending more and more time in the attic. The never-ending drumbeat, and, later, the eerie silence.

Such as that time he inflated dozens of balloons and hung them in front of Natalie's window, then spent the night sitting on her porch, watching the dark window, waiting for her to wake up. Nagla had seen him and told no one. When Cynthia, the next day, had seemed alarmed to find him asleep on her deck, Nagla had scoffed at her friend's failure to see the romance in the boy's gesture.

Such as when he stopped answering her when she spoke to him. She had told herself that she was giving him the distance he needed, when, she now saw, she had been too cowardly to do otherwise.

It was, of course, all her fault. She had known that for a long time.

Behind her, a sudden blast of wind rushed through the trees, and the branches shivered. Even across her backyard, she could hear them. She turned around, facing the window.

Ahead, the line of trees bordering Summerset Park called her, the swish of wind through branches a language she understood as well as any other she knew. She squinted. From where she stood, she could see the trunks of the first row of trees, could even detect the shape of the rows behind it, the checkered patches of light and dark that the shadows of the branches above formed on the bark and on the ground. She looked closer. Around her, everything fell silent, her mother's voice retreating into the background together with everything other than those trees. A sense of sudden urgency overcame her, a conviction that, if she looked closely enough, she would detect something of major significance.

Perhaps Samir was right and she did possess supernatural eyesight as well as hearing.

Perhaps, if she looked closely enough, she could see through the depth of the woods and all the way to that clearing where, a year ago, her son and her friend's daughter stood, talking. Perhaps she could even freeze time, eternally watching this one moment, preventing it from progressing to the next, sparing herself the pain of *what if.*

But she could not see that far. She shifted her focus, and now all she saw was her reflection in the glass and the reflection of her mother behind her.

She groaned. With the most force she could muster she lifted the ashtray up and flung it at those trees, at the window that she had often spent hours so futilely scrubbing, at her own reflection as well as at her mother's. The ashtray hit the windowpane with such force that the crystal went right through it, shattering it on impact, the shards falling onto the deck in a cascade that chimed and twinkled, a downpour of glass.

12

ENGLISH: The truth shall prevail.

ARABIC: Lies have no legs.

They lied to him about the broken window, of course. Samir knew they were lying the moment Ehsan told him how *she* broke it while mopping. She even demonstrated the alleged accident to him, showing him how she was vigorously working on a spot where some spilled marmalade had stuck to the floor when the top of the mop's wooden handle struck the glass. Seriously? The one-inch diameter of the handle making an eight-inch-diameter hole? And was Ehsan really as strong as she wished him to believe? Sure, the windows were as old as the house, and he and Nagla had talked about replacing them for years, but still—no glass was so weak as to shatter on the impact of Ehsan's accidental stroke, enthusiastic though her mopping might have been. And if logic alone was not enough to prove her deception, one look at Nagla convinced him that her mother was lying. He knew that expression very well, the incredulous look his wife threw at her mother whenever she spun one of her stories. The deception would, perhaps, not have bothered him so much if Nagla had acknowledged it, as she often did. He waited for Ehsan to turn her back and tried to make eye contact with his wife, anticipating a roll of the eyes or a mouthed word that would place her firmly on his side, not her mother's—but Nagla avoided his eyes, gazing instead out the window and, minutes later, stepping out for a smoke and leaving him to face Ehsan alone. His mother-in-law ranted endlessly about cheap windows that broke on touch, about paying him for it, *paying him,* as if he would take her money, even if she had broken it, as if she did not know what kind of an insult that was, to offer him *awad,* compensation for something she, his guest, had accidentally broken. Which, of course, she had not. Because she was lying.

What she and her daughter did not know, however, was that he knew perfectly well what had happened. He was certain of it, could picture it as if he were there. The whole incident played in his mind's eye as if it had been captured on film for posterity, like those videos about Hosaam that surfaced on YouTube after he died, or like those photos of Samir, his family, and his home that Angie had shown him only this morning.

Walking into his office, Angie had pushed him aside unapologetically and taken over his spot by the computer before he had a chance to object.

"I need to show you something," she whispered. On her Facebook news feed he saw a picture of his family. They were walking up to their car in a parking lot—probably by the movie theater complex, which was the last time he remembered they had all gone out together. When was that—three months ago? Four? In the photo, he and Nagla walked in front, talking, while Fatima and Khaled trailed behind, Fatima glancing to her right, Khaled checking his phone. The photo was a close-up, a clear shot of their faces and torsos. A nice picture, actually, Samir thought—until Angie scrolled down and pointed at the screen.

Under the picture stood a question—a poll: Do you think the family should be held accountable when a teenager commits a crime? The two options—Yes, they never taught him better, and No, it's not their fault— showed growing bars indicating the number of people voting for each. As of right then, both bars were almost equal in length.

"Wow," Samir muttered.

"That's not the worst of it." Angie clicked on an icon and a seemingly endless column of comments rolled down.

"What is this?" he said, his voice so hoarse he could hardly hear it.

"It's a poll someone posted on Summerset's Facebook page."

"Summerset has a Facebook page?"

"Yes, of course it does." Angie muttered. "That's not the point. Read those comments."

Samir started reading through them, grateful every time he read a compassionate one (Will you all leave the poor family alone?), nervous whenever he read the others—and there were so many. He had seen it all before, of course: the ethnic slurs, the insistence that *those people* were all inherently violent, the self-satisfied assurance that Islam was the real threat, the suggestion that, for their own sake, they should pack up and move somewhere else where they could *blend in* more easily. He reminded himself that he had grown a thick skin over the last year, that he had promised himself to pay no attention to such hate. Still, the sheer number of comments seemed to snuff the last breath out of his chest. All those people—talking about him and his family. He reached up and loosened his tie, took a deep breath. Told himself to calm down.

"Look, this is what's scaring me." Angie scrolled farther down. In one of the comments, someone had posted a link. Angie clicked it and Samir saw a picture of his own house spring up in front of him, the yard littered with unrolled toilet paper, the garage door colorful with sprayed graffiti. For a moment, his heart sank with fear, but then he realized he had seen all this before.

"This was last year!" he exclaimed, pointing toward the screen. "I reported it to the police then. It was even on the news—that's probably how they got this picture. It's all gone now."

"I know it's old, but why are people bringing it up again now? That's what's scaring me. Look." She pointed at the minuscule profile picture of the person who posted the link. Samir squinted but could not make out his face. "I know this guy. The son-of-a-bitch used to go to school with my brother." Samir stared at his secretary, his eyebrows raised. She looked back at him. "Oh, shush—like you've never heard me curse before." She waved an impatient hand at him. He managed a smile.

"This guy is trouble. And look at the comments he got—people are encouraging him! I'm scared, Sam." She turned to look at him. "This is not good. You and your family—you need to be careful." She paused. "I know you don't like to hear this, but maybe you should rethink your decision to stay in Summerset," she whispered.

Samir blushed.

"You don't have to go too far. You wouldn't even have to leave New Jersey. Perhaps a larger town—"

"For God's sake, Angie," Samir blurted out. "We've been through this already. I'm fifty-six. Do you really expect me to overhaul my entire life now?"

"It doesn't have to be that radical a change."

"Not radical? A new house? A new town? A new practice?"

"Many doctors relocate their practices. Your patients will follow you."

"Yeah, right. Because they are so loyal. You know how many have dropped me over the past year, Angie."

"And I know how many have not. You're a good doctor. One of the best around here. People know that."

"Then I shouldn't have to move, should I?"

Samir got up and walked away from the computer, turning his back to Angie, certain that, if she took a close look at his face, she would see the veins he now felt throbbing at his temples. He stepped up to the window, looked out, focused on his breathing. Behind him, he could hear Angie move.

"Do you need me to cancel the rest of today's appointments?" she asked. He glanced behind him and saw she was standing by the door.

"No."

He waited. She did not move.

"You're not mad at me, are you? For suggesting you move away?"

Samir shook his head.

"You know I mean well. I'm only worried about your wife and kids. I know you thought people would forget, given time, but they haven't, have they? Someone might hurt your family, Sam. You should keep that in mind."

Samir had to bite down on his tongue to keep from speaking. He waited till she left the room, and then he walked up to the door, closed it behind her. Placing both hands on the door, he pushed hard, trying to keep his hands from shaking, breathing heavily, waiting. He was not sure what stung him more: having his family paraded all over the Internet or hearing his secretary suggest he run away, exiled by shame. The insinuation that he was failing, as head of the family, to keep his wife and kids from harm was bad enough—but the suggestion, again, that he should move away in defeat was more than he could bear. He remembered one of his father's old neighbors, a loud, heavyset man who, after years of lavish success, had made headlines when it turned out he was involved in one of the Ponzi schemes that ravaged Egypt in the eighties like a swarm of hungry locusts. Unable to muddle through the scandal, the man had left the apartment building in the middle of the night, dragging his family behind him to God knows where, the FOR SALE sign surfacing later a constant reminder of his disgrace. Samir would never succumb to such humiliation, such a dishonorable exodus, moving away from the Promised Land rather than traveling in search of it. His entire life had been a constant labor aimed at providing a good home for his family, a stable practice for himself, a superior education for his children. This was why he had moved to America, why he had endured the uprooting of immigration. And now, when he was only a decade away from retirement, his secretary had felt the need to suggest he start all over somewhere else, just as Khaled had had the audacity to propose before her. Samir pressed harder against the closed door, his head bent down. They could offer sugarcoated advice from now till Judgment Day—he was not going to let anyone coerce him out of the life he had spent decades building. He would rather see his practice crumble and his wife and kids become imprisoned in their own home than leave the town in disgrace.

Back home, the broken window fulfilled the morning's prophecies. Considering how the upcoming memorial service was resurrecting the town's anger, it was only natural that the ripples such anger generated would find their way to Samir's property, as was frequently the case in the first couple of months following his son's crime. Ehsan's attempts to pass the vandalism off as an accident were almost amusing. Still, he listened to her explanations, let her play her story out.

"Are you sure, *ya haggah*, this was what happened?" he asked Ehsan once she stopped talking, loud enough for Nagla to hear through the hole in the window as she sat on the deck, smoking.

"Of course I am! What kind of question is that?"

"I was just wondering, because, you know, I heard something else. I *was told* something else," he revised himself, walking up to the table and leaning across it toward Ehsan, who backed up against the wall, holding the mop in one hand like a medieval spear.

"What do you mean?" Her voice was shrill, and she threw a rapid glance toward Nagla, who, interestingly enough, seemed to snicker as she lit yet another cigarette. Samir pressed on.

"I mean that what I heard was different. A guy I know passed by here earlier today, and he said he saw someone in the yard, someone standing across from the deck, looking at the window." Ehsan looked puzzled, and Samir held her gaze. He was determined to break through her lies, this time. It was one thing to allow her to rave on about her own life and superstitious nonsense, and a totally different thing to let her lie about what happened in his house. Under his roof.

"He said he thought that person seemed about to throw something at the house. For a moment he thought he'd seen a large object—a rock, maybe?—fly in the air and in the direction of the house, but he thought nothing of it. He drove off, but then he decided to call and let me know. Just in case someone had tried to deface the house. It wouldn't be the first time, you know," he said, his teeth clenched, remembering the spray-painted vulgarities on his driveway and garage door, the insults shouted from passing cars, remnants of the days and weeks after Hosaam died that still clung like leeches to his memory. Ehsan seemed puzzled, and he was satisfied to see her look outside at Nagla for what he assumed was help or a beckoning for her daughter to walk back in and shield her. He had cornered Ehsan, and now she had dug herself in so deeply she could not turn back. Nagla, extinguishing her cigarette, did not acknowledge her mother. He had driven both her and Ehsan to silence, which was a rare feat in and of its own. There was no need to humiliate them further.

From his bedroom window he could see Nagla, still sitting on the deck, the ashtray filled to the brim with cigarette stubs. Her refusal to acknowledge her mother's lies, even indirectly, stung him as a dismissal, another crack in their alliance as husband and wife.

She used to come to him first. "I am your family now," he had whispered in her ear one night when they first moved to the United States, trying to ease the pain of homesickness that had driven her to bed, crying. For a long time his assertion had held true—he still remembered days when Ehsan would call *him* to try to coax out news that Nagla had denied her: where Cynthia had taken Nagla and the kids the weekend before; why she never tried to use her degree in pharmacy and work, at least part-time, not even after the kids had grown. Talking to Ehsan on the phone, Samir would then choose how much information he wanted to provide to her: he wasn't sure where Cynthia and Nagla went (a lie); Nagla still felt the kids needed her at home, even though they were old enough for her to work, if she wanted to (true); Nagla didn't need to work anyway because he was providing for them well enough (a semi-truth). Though he had not noticed it at the time, his control over how much information Ehsan had about her own daughter had cemented his position as Nagla's husband and closest ally. This, too, had changed. Now Nagla spent the entire day with her mother, confiding in her, collaborating with her when she chose to lie to him.

But blaming her withdrawal exclusively on her mother's presence was not fair. He had started losing her years ago. He could feel her inch away from him with every argument, every fight. He saw her hardened look whenever he insisted she spoiled Hosaam too much, and felt her anger when she retorted, as she never failed to do, that she did it only because he was too hard on his firstborn. She blamed him for Hosaam's death—he was certain of that.

But the unfairness of her accusations did not hurt as much as her distance did. Sitting on his bed, he resisted an urge to go and look out the window one more time. He did not need to see her to feel her presence, only yards away from him yet separated by wood and glass that made it seem as if she existed in a world detached from his own. He had felt this distance the moment he walked in and saw the broken window, saw her sitting there with her head resting on her arms—she had been crying. Had her mother not been there, he probably would have reached out to her, walked up and held her tight as he had so many years ago when she burned her hand in that cramped apartment in New York. For a moment, he had been tempted to ignore her mother's presence and run to his wife anyway, throwing his dignity together with decorum into the air—but she had lifted her head and looked at him, and he had frozen in place. Even now he still could not understand her look. All he knew was that it had pushed him away as surely as any physical shove would have.

And now all of Summerset was against them—again. He had felt the hostility in the air the entire week, had seen the renewed looks of curiosity in people's eyes wherever he went, from Shark's diner to his own office building. Angie's warning had bothered him, but it had not surprised him. Inevitably, someone was going to make an appearance at his doorstep just as so many had a year earlier, from lawyers wanting him to sue the newspapers for defamation to teenagers driving by to shout insults. This time, someone had hurled something at his window. Someone probably familiar with the house, too, since the kitchen windows were the only ones with no screens. He was as sure of this as he would have been if he had seen the kitchen floor covered in shards—there were none, neither inside the house (to confirm his theory) nor outside (to bolster theirs). Ehsan had picked them all up before he arrived, doubtless to cover up her fabrication. Her nervousness surely confirmed this theory. In the two decades he had known her, he had never seen her flinch when she told a lie. Today, she had. And Nagla's refusal to acknowledge her mother's lies? For this past year he had almost welcomed Ehsan's fabrications and superstitions—his and Nagla's mutual ridicule of them seemed to be one of the last semblances of intimacy they had. Even during this past year, Nagla's withdrawal from him was not complete because she never failed to share a conspiratorial glance with him behind Ehsan's back. Today, she had not. Today he felt he had, perhaps, lost her for good.

He got up from the bed, paced his room. This would not do. He would not allow for such total loss, such total failure. Now more than ever he believed in the necessity of action, and the memorial service provided him with an opportunity that might never come again. Nagla would have him hide and wait it out, like an ostrich burying its head in the sand. If he had once considered her argument, today's incidents convinced him that she was wrong. Today they had targeted his house—who knew what they would do tomorrow? Go after Khaled? Fatima? He was not going to wait for that to happen.

The hum of the moving garage door signaled his children's arrival. He heard Nagla's hurried footsteps—she was coming upstairs. Quickly, he slipped into his bed, pulled the covers to shield his eyes from the faint dusk light still seeping through the windows. He heard his bedroom door open but remained motionless. She would not bother him if she thought he was asleep.

"Samir?"

He did not budge. He heard her close the door and walk up to the bed, reach out and touch his shoulder.

"Samir?"

He pushed the covers away from his face, squinted. "What?"

"I broke that window."

He sat up in bed, staring at her. "What?"

"I broke it. I threw an ashtray at it and broke it."

She stood a few feet away, her arms crossed. A bit pale, he thought—or perhaps it was the early evening light.

"You used an ashtray to break the window. I see. Must have been a steel ashtray." He should not be sarcastic. But this was ridiculous. And slightly insulting.

"It was the crystal one. The heavy one. I broke it, too."

He nodded. "Hmm."

He waited. She sat down on the floor, hugged both knees to her chest, and stared at her feet.

He took a deep breath in. "And why did you break the window?"

"I was upset. I didn't mean to do it. It just happened."

He nodded again. Her distance had been bad enough, but this—this was something else. To think that he would buy such an audacious tale.

All one hundred pounds of her, hurling an ashtray—an ashtray!—at the window and breaking it. Preposterous. Even more preposterous was her conviction that he would be that easily fooled. He took another deep breath, tried to steady himself. At least she was not supporting her mother's story any longer.

"So why didn't you say anything when your mother lied to me?"

She grimaced. "I—didn't want to embarrass her. Also—" She paused. "I had a fight with her."

"What about?"

She lifted one hand to her forehead, touching it, as if checking for a fever. He wondered whether she was trying to get him to believe she was sick.

"About several things. Mostly about lying."

"You fought with her about lying, but you said nothing when she lied to me?"

"I told you: I didn't want to embarrass her." She sighed. "I'm just trying to be honest." Her voice broke.

He got up and walked to the window, looked out into the darkening mass of trees. He had to admit it was clever, making up a story and pretending it was the truth, shooting down her mother's lie with another lie and hoping he would be satisfied with her admission of her mother's guilt and not question her own. That she could have truly done it was out of the question, of course: sure, she did have occasional outbursts of temper—like the time she flung herself at that reporter, or the several times she had charged him in the middle of a heated argument—but he knew the extent of her strength. He knew the most force her delicate fists could carry. Besides, the few times she did show signs of a temper were truly exceptional circumstances, not a result of something as pedestrian as a fight with her mother.

No. She had a motive for lying. He lifted one hand and scratched his chin.

"You've never broken anything in anger before," he said without turning to look at her. "Perhaps it's all the stress."

She said nothing, but he heard one soft sob. He went on. "Perhaps you still think I should reconsider going to that memorial?"

Silence.

"I still think going is a bad idea, yes." Her voice was fainter than usual.

He turned to look at her. "So when you could not convince me not to go, you decided to pretend to be losing it, is that it?" He walked closer to her, bent down to look her in the eyes. "You think that making up such a story will get me to back down?"

"I'm not making anything up!"

"You expect me to believe you broke that window?" he hissed.

"I *did* break it!"

"You think I'm an idiot?"

He stared at her eyes, wide with what he hoped was fear. He went on. "You think you and your mother can spin tales and get me to swallow them? You think you can trick me into giving up our best chance yet at beating this thing? At fighting back?"

"Fighting what back?"

He straightened up, walked away from her, his hands on his waist. "You need to get your head straight, Nagla. You need to snap out of it. This is ridiculous, what you're trying to do."

"I'm trying to be honest!" She jumped up, walked toward him. "For once in my life, I'm trying to be honest!"

He turned to look at her, his eyes narrow. "Really? And who taught you this honesty in your old age? Your mother?"

She glared at him, then walked out of the room. He stood in place, listening to her footsteps as she ran down the stairs. Doubtless to her mother. To complain about him.

Let her go, he thought as he walked up to his bed and sat down. Let her think about his words. Perhaps she would finally come to her senses.

He lay in bed, closed his eyes. Too much interference; too much trouble. He needed to concentrate. He needed to think about what had happened and decide what he would do on Sunday. He was not going to accept today's attack on his house—and he knew it was a hate crime—or the comments and invitations to violence that Angie had shown him on Facebook. He would fight back. He would protect his family, as he should, even if they resisted his efforts. Eventually, they would know he had done the right thing.

13

ENGLISH: Ignorance is bliss.

Saying

ARABIC: Ignorance is light.

Often used as a sarcastic twist on the traditional saying:
Knowledge is light and ignorance is darkness.

Khaled sat on the floor in his bedroom, his back pushed against the wall, the moonlight shining through the window by his shoulder and painting checkers on the floor. For the previous hour he had crawled from wall to wall, restless, trying to find a comforting spot but failing to do so. He could not stay in bed, the upper bunk more claustrophobic than ever. He tried sitting at his desk, but that faced the wall that separated his room from his parents', where Nagla's and Samir's muffled voices had ebbed and flowed the whole evening. He did not want to listen—not out of respect, but out of an aversion that added guilt to his torments. He had walked over to the opposing wall, only to hear Fatima's and Ehsan's whispers through the Sheetrock, their voices low, stifled, and invading his space even though they never rose in the sharp whispered outbursts that peppered his parents' conversation. From there he had crawled to the outer wall, taking his laptop with him, getting up only once to grab his iPod and shove the earplugs in, letting them scream the music of Matchbox 20 and Jay-Z as loud as he could bear. He sat, his legs stretched out before him, his laptop by his side and opened to Brittany's Facebook page.

Facebook had turned against him again. For one thing, he had not known Summerset had its own page. How a page devoted to a town as small as Summerset ended up with 1,736 likes was beyond him. How he had missed it for so long was equally puzzling, considering that news of Natalie's planned memorial service had dominated the page for the previous week, a copy of the flyer serving as the page's cover photo, Natalie's eyes peering through the upper banner. Now a picture of him and his family took center stage, a trail of comments multiplying underneath it like some out-of-control bacterial strain. News of this renewed interest in his family had reached him through Garrett, whose text message he received sitting on the train back from the city, and who, he found out, was one of the 1,736 people who liked Summerset's page. He wondered when he would have found out, had Garrett not told him. Would he have walked around his town not knowing that half its inhabitants had logged on to their computers today and taken the time to voice their thoughts on his family's accountability for what Hosaam had done?

His ignorance sparked a revelation. How had he never realized how little he knew about his own life? He counted the things he had not known, limiting his survey to the previous year:

He had not known his brother left home that day with a gun in his backpack, a gun that must have been hidden in this very room for at least one night, if not longer.

He had never imagined his brother had stolen that gun from Ned Taylor's home, even though the news of the missing gun had spread through the town the day after Hosaam had visited Ned.

He had not known his brother was *that* sick. Sick, yes. But not *that* sick.

He never knew who would bring up the subject of his brother. He counted the times he had walked into the school cafeteria, his eyes downcast, fearing that someone would comment on his brother's crime but having no one challenge him, and compared these times with all the other instances when he had walked into a store or down the road and had been assaulted with a reference, a shouted name, a fake gunshot, a racial slur, or, on at least three different occasions, a flying object (a baseball, a notebook, and, of all things, a can of tuna that hit him on the shoulder and left a crescent-shaped bruise).

He had never considered the possibility of a memorial service for Natalie. He had stood in front of that flyer in utter bewilderment, even though, in retrospect, he felt he should have anticipated that.

He never imagined his father would insist on attending the service. That, also, should have been predictable, considering Samir's character, which Khaled prided himself on having figured out years ago.

He was stupid enough to think that his trips to New York took him away from all this.

He was even more stupid to think that he could conceal it all from Brittany, that he could be honest with her about everything but exclude his brother, as if he had never existed.

He was an idiot to think that creating a Facebook page with his initials instead of his full name provided him with anonymity.

Thinking of the Internet and anonymity as synonymous proved his idiocy.

He was apparently the last one in Summerset to know that the town had its own Facebook page.

He had never considered that telling Brittany so much about himself, including where he lived, would inevitably lead her to find out about his brother.

He had browsed Brittany's page daily for months now, and not once had he noticed that she, too, was one of the 1,736 people who *liked* Summerset's page.

He glanced at the screen, waiting for a comment, a message, or, to his utter panic, the moment when Brittany would unfriend him in punishment for his deceit. He calculated the possibilities: she could see the post about his family and recognize him at once, read the comments underneath and learn of his brother. If she did so, she would probably never speak to him again—and he wouldn't blame her. She would know his brother had killed a girl. She already knew Khaled was infatuated with her; even if she did not take him seriously, she knew of his crush. He was certain of that. Learning about Hosaam would doubtless make her fear him. Anyway, who wants the attentions of a young man whose older brother killed his beloved in cold blood?

Then again, she might not visit that page—she was a digital hoarder, accumulating Facebook friend after friend and liking page after page, and chances were she had subscribed to this particular page only after finding out that Summerset was his hometown and had forgotten about it ever since. On the other hand, Facebook sometimes pushed such high-traffic posts right up to your face, and she might be alerted one way or the other.

Even if she did find out—would she blame him? She might not. She was too understanding, too kind to ostracize him. She might understand. Then again, she might not.

No one was to blame except him.

He read through some of the comments, sighed, and closed the laptop, too weary of waiting for the one misfortune he now saw coming, for the moment when he would lose her friendship. His head throbbed and, getting up, he pulled the earplugs out, only to be assaulted with one of his mother's louder outbursts, incomprehensible and angry. He groaned, looking up to the ceiling. He was trapped in his own room. He would go downstairs, but the broken window (one more thing he didn't anticipate, know about, or understand) was depressing, and the living room held the constant threat of unwanted company, if Ehsan or Fatima chose to walk downstairs. He was angry with both of them, but more with Fatima, who had walked in with him and, seeing the broken window, had directly shut herself up with their grandmother, shutting him out, not even bothering to exchange a few words or to convey whatever information she got from their grandmother to him. He did not want to talk to her now. There was nowhere to go except leave the house, but he did not know where he could go at midnight. There was nowhere to go. Except— he suddenly realized, staring at the ceiling—up.

Carefully, he opened his door and looked out. Both Fatima's and his parents' doors were closed. He tiptoed into the hallway, reaching up to grab the pull-down chain that released the stairs to the attic. Someone had looped the chain up, attaching its end to a hook on the ceiling to get it out of the way. Failing to reach it, he walked into his room and back out a moment later, a clothes hanger in hand. Threading the loop of the hanger into the metal link, he released it from the hook, and the chain came rattling down. He looked around, waited, and when the constant hum from both rooms continued uninterrupted, he slowly pulled the hatch down and released the ladder.

He had not been in the attic for more than a year. Reaching the top of the ladder, he put one hand on his mouth, muffling his cough, waiting to get accustomed to the stale air. Stepping up and into the attic, he grabbed around for the light chain, turning the single bulb on. The light, a hazy yellow, combined with the moonlight that the attic's one circular window let in and showed him his way. Turning around, he knelt down and tried to pull the ladder back up, but managed to do so only halfway. He considered tugging harder, but feared the metal might creak, alerting everyone to his whereabouts. He let it be. After all, no one was likely to step out again tonight.

He made his way past plastic containers, a discarded floor lamp, a few black garbage bags, filled and tied, and stood in the only clear spot, in the center of the attic. His brother's drum set still stood with its back to the window, its silver rims glistening in the low light. On one side of the drum set stood Hosaam's old boom box, a black monster of a machine surrounded by piles of CDs. On the other side stood a large easel that Hosaam had used to support a tackboard. On the rare occasions when Hosaam had allowed him in the attic, Khaled had stood by the board, marveling at the staff paper covered in music, at the various posters ripped out of magazines, at the verses that Hosaam or one of his bandmates had composed for a song. By the time the police had made it up to the attic, the only pictures covering the board were of Natalie. Now the board was bare.

The silence unnerved him. Having climbed up here to shut out the rumblings of his family, Khaled found his head buzzing with echoes of his brother's sounds. Stretches of drumbeats. Music booming so loudly it made his entire bedroom underneath vibrate, the ceiling fan shuddering in rhythmic outbursts. Khaled was almost never allowed up here, and, years ago, he had stopped pleading his case for the unfairness of devoting such a large space to his brother when he had no similar place of his own. Once, during the last year, his mother had sent him up to try to coax Hosaam down after an alarmingly long stay in the attic. He had made it only halfway up the ladder before Hosaam looked down through the rectangular opening: *Stay the fuck away from my attic.*

His presence here felt like an invasion of his dead brother's privacy—and the feeling thrilled him. Perhaps he could add this to the list of things he did not know: how vindictive he could be, how angry. Perhaps he had been angry for a long time, or perhaps he had found his anger the moment he saw the picture of his family on Facebook. He liked this new version of himself, his anger implying a power he had never claimed before. Looking around, he imagined what he could do to the place. He could clean it up and take it over. He could have it all to himself, set up a lab or fill it with his own music. He wondered whether he could use any of his brother's CDs. Walking up to the table, he shuffled through them, his heart racing, as if touching his brother's belongings were sinful.

Almost a year earlier, he had felt the same way when Ehsan, summoned by tragedy, had arrived and questioned, on her first day there, why no one had cleared his room of his brother's belongings. She had stood, hands on her hips, and looked over the room, her lips twisted in silent disapproval. Hosaam's things had lain scattered, as if he were away on a short trip and would return and make his bed, organize the CDs on his desk, pick up the clothes he had taken off and thrown on the back of his chair. Nagla would not enter the room, but Khaled had seen her pause by the door, one hand resting on the frame, and look in. For her sake, he would not move any of his brother's stuff, not until enough time had passed.

As far as Ehsan was concerned, enough time was exactly two weeks into her visit. On her third week in Summerset, she had locked Khaled up with her in the room and gone through everything, separating his things from his brother's and sorting all of Hosaam's belongings into two piles: give away and throw away. As far as Khaled could tell, there was no "keep" pile.

"Mama might want some of this stuff, *Setto*," Khaled had said, watching her stuff clothes and shoes into garbage bags, throw the contents of all the desk drawers into cartons. He looked at the cartons, feeling guilty, almost blasphemous. On top of one of the boxes sat a letter, handwritten, bearing Natalie's signature. An actual letter, not an e-mail or a note, written in blue ink on sepia paper. He looked away.

"If she wanted something, she would have taken it by now." Ehsan did not look at him. He watched her take each shirt, each pair of pants in her hands, and look at it for a moment before tossing it in one of the piles. He would have thought she did not care for any of this stuff, had he not heard her prayers, a constant hum under her breath, only occasionally interrupted by a sniffle.

"Maybe she's not ready yet."

"She'll never be ready. No one ever is."

In only a few hours she had cleared the room of all of Hosaam's belongings. Even the desk she had made Khaled pull out to the hallway; he and his father would later carry it downstairs for the Salvation Army to pick up. She told Khaled the room was now his, not "a shrine to your brother, may Allah have mercy on him." She wanted nothing to remind Khaled of Hosaam.

Standing in the attic, Khaled wondered at himself for having been so reluctant to part with his brother's belongings. Now, shuffling through the CDs, he savored the thrill of knowing he could not only claim the ones he wanted, but also break them into pieces, if he chose. Give them away. Sell them on e-Bay. He turned to look at the drum set, his eyes narrowing. The seven-hundred-dollar Ludwig kit could fetch him a fortune. Instantly he felt a pang of guilt as he imagined how his mother would react if he tried to sell it. He walked over, ran his hand across the taut skin of one drum. His brother had cared for this set, cleaning it obsessively, rubbing the cymbals with some sort of cream, keeping it covered whenever he knew he would not use it.

He had cared for those drums more than he had cared for anyone in his family.

Khaled placed his palm on one of the drums. He arched his fingers, touching his fingernails to the cool surface. The moonlight combined with the dim lightbulb, giving his fingers multiple shadows, drawing intersecting spiders that stood, waiting. Khaled pulled his hand away and looked around. In a corner of the room he saw an old toolbox of his father's. Rummaging through it, he found a box cutter. He grabbed it and walked back to the drum set. Pushing its blade out, he stared, trying to keep his hand from shaking.

"What are you doing?" Ehsan's whisper was urgent, an alarmed hiss. He jumped, dropping the box cutter and narrowly missing his own foot.

"*Setto!* You scared me!" He walked up to the attic doorway, trying to compose himself. In the hallway, he saw his grandmother, hands holding on to the halfway pulled ladder.

"Have you lost your mind?" she hissed.

He looked at her, puzzled. "What?"

"What are you doing up there?"

"Nothing! I was just . . ." He looked around, angry with himself for feeling like he had been caught misbehaving. He spotted the pile of CDs. "I wanted to grab some CDs."

"What CDs? His?" His grandmother never used Hosaam's name anymore.

"Yes."

"What for?"

"Just to look through them."

"Come down here."

He turned the light off and climbed down, pushing the ladder back in place so violently it shrieked.

"Don't ever go up there." Ehsan's voice was trembling with something he could not identify. Anger? Fear?

"Why not?" He faced her, looking her in the eyes. "Is he going to claim the attic even after he's dead?" His own words made his skin crawl.

"So now you want to lock yourself up there, too?"

"I didn't say that. I was just up looking for music. It's no big deal."

"No big deal? Going into *his* space? You see nothing wrong with *that*?"

"It's just a room, *Setto*." He knew where she was going with this: jinxes and bad luck, ill omens and traces of the evil eye, witchcraft, sorcery, and jinn walking among us that we cannot see. All nonsense. He stared at her, prepared to tell it to her as it was if she started preaching.

She did not. Instead, she looked at him, and then asked, "Do you want more?"

"More what?"

"Music CDs. Do you want more? Is that it?"

"No," he cried. "No, no. I was just curious. Just looking around, that's all."

She stared at him, saying nothing, then turned around and hurried into her room. Khaled went back to his room and sat on the bed, trying to steady himself. His hands were sweaty, and he rubbed them on his pants. Ridiculous, how his heart was racing, as if he had been caught stealing. Ehsan, storming into the room, extended her hand to him, holding a stack of twenty-dollar bills, carefully folded in half.

"What's that?" He got up.

"Here. You want music CDs, you go buy music CDs." She stuffed the money in his hand and backed up into his chair, panting. Khaled unfolded the bills—a hundred dollars, total. Six hundred Egyptian pounds, that is, if the exchange rate was still the same as the last time he was there. His throat tightened, his eyes burned, and, to his utter humiliation, he felt an almost uncontrollable urge to cry.

"I can't take this, *Setto*," he said, walking up to her, sitting on his knees on the floor, gently placing the money in her lap.

"Why not? Is it not enough?"

"Of course it is. It's plenty. I just can't take it. I don't need any more CDs."

"I already gave you the money. If you don't want to buy music, then go get something else."

"But I don't need anything, *Setto*!" He placed the money in her palm.

"Don't give me back my gift, boy! Do you have no manners at all?" She pushed his hand back.

"But I can't take this, *Setto*! It's too much!"

Bending down, Ehsan kissed his forehead. *"Mateghlaash aleik ya habibi,"* she said. Nothing is too precious for you, my love.

She patted his head, the way she used to do when he was a boy, as she still occasionally did, even though he was almost a man, and Khaled realized that the house had fallen utterly silent again, the stillness interrupted only by his grandmother's prayers, murmured under her breath.

He opened his laptop and checked Facebook again. Nothing. The confrontation with his grandmother weighed on him and merged with his fear of losing Brittany's friendship. He had to pant to keep himself from crying. There might be many things he did not know, but one thing was getting clearer by the day: he could not keep this up, this constant fear of backlash, of humiliation, of solitude, of losing the one person he cared about.

He navigated to Brittany's page, clicked to send her a message. He had to see her again. He hoped she would let him. He knew he had to try.

SATURDAY

14

ENGLISH: Breaking bread.

ARABIC: Eating bread and salt.

Nagla woke up to the smell of baking. Staring at the ceiling, she remained motionless, sniffed the air. The smell was unmistakable, instantly recognizable even though it had not greeted her nose in decades. She closed her eyes and she was eight again, standing by her mother in the kitchen, helping her knead the sweet bread and then roll it into sticks, every three sticks pinched together at the ends to make a boat-shaped pretzel that she would then brush with an egg wash and sprinkle with crystals of brown sugar. Her mother was baking *shoreik*—or, as she would sometimes call them, *fetir el-rahmah*—Pastries of Mercy.

In the kitchen Ehsan kneaded bread as Fatima stood by her side, elbows on the countertop. Both ovens burned hot with batches of *shoreik*, already golden brown. Verses of the Qur'an resonated in the kitchen, coming from the iPod that Ehsan had finally learned how to place on the round speaker, how to navigate to the precise sura she wanted to hear. Today, her choice was Al-Rahman—the All-Merciful. Nagla stood at the bottom of the stairs, watching. Fatima looked just like her mother, could have been her on any one of the many anniversaries of Mahmoud's death, when Ehsan would spend the day preparing for the annual visit to the cemetery, sacred as pilgrimage. Freshly baked *shoreik* placed in wicker baskets lined with and covered by clean white cloth, they would head to the cemetery together, where her mother would distribute the pastries among barefoot children and mothers carrying babies, all roaming the cemeteries in anticipation of charity, aware that no one gave alms more heartily than the bereaved. "Pray for my husband's soul, may Allah have mercy on him," Ehsan would whisper, and the recipients of her gifts would readily oblige, their prayers pouring with a generosity that outdid Ehsan's gifts.

Nagla used to love those visits. Her father was buried in his family's plot, its entrance flanked by two rooms, one for the men, another for the women, joined by a tiled, covered courtyard. To the side stood a kitchenette, where her mother would make tea and coffee, offering them to the cemetery keeper and to the Qur'an reciters who would come, each in turn, and sit by her husband's grave, reading the verses in slow, humming tones in return for a few pounds, a hot cup of tea, and, perhaps, some of the *shoreik* to take home to their families. The day always seemed like a trip to the park; Nagla would be allowed to run around the two rooms, play with the children of other visitors, even have her own cup of hot minted black tea to sip in the shade. Her mother let her help the cemetery keeper splash water around the graves, causing the dusty ground to settle. Nagla would watch as the wet mud dried and cracked under the sun, and then she would water the cacti that her mother had planted all around the graveyard, the only plants that survived the summer heat. Even the *shoreik* felt like a treat, its coating of baked crystalized sugar crunchy in her mouth, the sweet bread filling, warm.

"The dead boast of their visitors," her mother used to tell her. "They like to know their loved ones still remember them." Her mother would sit in a wooden chair by her husband's grave and talk to him, speak as if he could hear her through the ground, and Nagla, watching from a distance, would picture her father, smiling, boasting to relatives buried close by: "See? My wife and daughter have come. My wife and daughter still love me." She had seen burial chambers in movies, knew that the dead were placed, side by side, in the underground room, whose entrance would then be sealed with a heavy stone, not to be opened for forty days after each death. No caskets, no clothing, just bodies wrapped in white burial shrouds, lying flat on the dirt, their faces turned toward Mecca and God's house that Ibrahim, peace be upon his soul, built so many years ago. She wondered how her father would be able to talk through the shroud that, she knew, covered his face. He couldn't move, of course—but he could talk. Her mother said he could. So she would picture him supine, wrapped in white cloth, speaking to others lying flat around him, dead as well but still listening, nodding in approval and envy as he boasted of his visitors.

"Come and try this," Ehsan said. Nagla slowly walked toward the baking sheet that Ehsan had pulled out of the oven. "They're still hot, though, so watch out." With two fingers Ehsan lifted one of the pastries off the sheet, swiftly wrapping it in a paper napkin before handing it to Nagla.

"*Shoreik?*" Nagla asked. What did her mother expect to do with the pastries? Did she think she'd run into beggars at the Summerset cemetery? Her mother, unaware of Nagla's incredulous tone, smiled.

"Just like the old days, huh? Try it!"

Nagla stared at the pastry, a sort of birthday cake for the dead. She bit into it, and steam rose from the part that she pulled off. Instantly the sweet and chewy pretzel filled her with a nostalgia that made her gag, her eyes watering.

"You don't like it?" her mother asked, alarmed.

"It's hot," Nagla said as soon as she could swallow.

"Careful, then," Ehsan told Fatima as she handed her another pastry wrapped in a napkin.

Fatima tore off a piece with forefinger and thumb, blew on it before placing it in her mouth. "Oh, it's good!" she said, her mouth full.

Ehsan laughed. "Your mother and I used to bake these together and take them to your grandfather's grave, may Allah have mercy on all our dead."

"What for?" Fatima asked, pulling another piece out and placing it in her mouth.

"*Sadakah.*" Ehsan pushed the baking sheet aside and went back to kneading the rest of the dough. "Only three things can benefit a person after his death: a good son or daughter's prayers; knowledge that he left behind for others to benefit from—you know, like a scientific discovery or something; and *sadakah garyah,* an act of charity that keeps on giving after his death. These"—she nodded toward the pastries—"are a form of *sadakah,* charity given out in hopes of mercy for the soul of the dead person."

Fatima nodded. "Kind of like people who set up charitable organizations here. Only you probably have to be rich to do that."

"No money required for those pastries, except enough to pay for flour and sugar. And there are always enough poor people who'd appreciate fresh-baked bread."

"Not here, though," Fatima murmured. Her grandmother looked up at her. "I mean, it's not like you'll find beggars on the streets here, *Setto!*" she stammered, voicing her mother's thoughts. "Not like in Egypt, that is."

"I know that, girl. I'm not an idiot!"

"Sorry, *Setto,*" Fatima murmured, glancing at her mother for help.

"She didn't mean it, Mama." Nagla pulled out a chair and sat down.

"A tradition is a tradition. Even if we end up eating all of it. It's the intention that counts. *Alaamalu belneyyat.*" Ehsan punched the dough as she spoke.

"Sure, *Setto.* We'll take it to the cemetery tomorrow, when we go visit Hosaam," Fatima said.

"We? Who said you're coming?" Nagla asked.

"I want to come! *Setto* said I could come!" Fatima's eyes instantly teared up.

"Let her go visit her brother!" Ehsan said.

Nagla glared at her. "I don't think a cemetery is a good place for a young girl."

"I'm not that young anymore, Mama!"

Ehsan sucked at her lips. "I took you with me all the time, and you were younger then than she is now. Don't see how that's harmed you."

Nagla ignored her mother. "I said you're not coming, and that's it. I don't care how old you think you are—you're still too young for this."

"Fine." Fatima picked up the baking sheet, dumping the still-hot *shoreik* onto a cooling rack before tossing the sheet in the sink. Nagla watched her, trying to decide whether to call her out on this edginess that bordered on anger.

Behind her, Khaled walked in, heading straight to the coffeepot.

"*Sabah el-kheir,*" Ehsan said.

"*Sabah el-kheir, Setto.*" He walked over and gave his grandmother a one-armed hug. "I'm sorry; I'm still not fully awake." He looked at his mother, a nervous glance that puzzled her. "Hey, Mama."

"Here, try this." Fatima handed her brother a pastry. "It's *shoreik.*"

Khaled bit at it. "It's good." He grabbed his coffee and dipped the edge of the pastry in it, took another bite. "Good."

"It's called *shoreik,*" Ehsan explained, watching him with a smile. "*Sheen-waw-rah-yeh-kaaf,*" she spelled in Arabic. "You should write it down. Do you still do that? Write down new words?"

Khaled nodded. "Yeah, sure."

"Haven't seen you do it in a while."

"I still do it."

"It's a special kind of pastry that we bake on anniversaries. To bring mercy to the dead."

Khaled looked at the piece of pastry still in his hand, swallowed.

"Also called *fetir el-rahmah*." Ehsan went on.

"Pastries of Mercy," Fatima translated.

"Mercy is good. I'll take that." Khaled stuffed the rest of the pastry into his mouth and reached for another one.

"All gathered up, huh?" Samir's voice came. Nagla, not looking, put her pastry down. She could not have swallowed another bite.

"May Allah always bring us together in good times and spare us bad ones," Ehsan murmured. Her voice was lower than usual, and she leaned down, meticulously shaping the dough.

Samir stood still, staring at the pastries.

"Is that . . . *shoreik*?" he asked, looking from Ehsan to Nagla.

"Of course it is!" Ehsan replied, still avoiding his eyes.

"What on earth are you baking that for?"

"Why do you think? What kind of a question is that?" Ehsan asked, pinching three sticks of dough together at the ends.

"Seriously, *haggah*? Who's going to eat all of this?"

"I'm sure we can find people to give it out to. Or are you, too, going to claim you don't have poor people in America?" she asked, finally looking up at him. "And if we find no one, I'll eat it all."

"Don't worry, *Setto*. I'll help." Khaled reached out for another pastry even as he still held a half-finished one in his hand. Samir glared at him. Khaled examined his pastries, avoiding eye contact with his father.

Samir looked down at Nagla, his eyes narrow. She got up and headed to the deck. He followed.

"I can't believe you're letting her do this," he hissed as soon as he caught up with her outside. Nagla turned around and looked into the kitchen, noticed, for the first time, that the hole in the glass had been clumsily patched using duct tape.

"Do what?" she asked.

"This! *Shoreik*? Seriously? What is she going to do—walk around the cemetery with a basket on her head, giving out homemade bread?"

Nagla frowned at him. Of course he would never understand. His own family would never have done so, even if his mother had outlived his father. They would have deemed it beneath them, a habit of the commoners, an embarrassment. All anger Nagla still felt toward her mother evaporated now, replaced by a wrath at her husband for his self-perceived superiority, his insensitivity, his failure, again and again, to feel any empathy. Not with her mother, not with her children, and certainly not with her.

"You know what?" she said, slowly, inching closer to him until his face was so near she could hardly focus on it. "She can do with it whatever she wants. She can walk around that cemetery, dressed in her black *galabeyyah*, carrying the basket on top of her head and yell out loud for the *shoreik*, if she wants to."

"Why do you always have to be so stubborn?"

"Why do you have to make such a big deal of everything? She's baking; let her bake."

"She's teaching my children superstitions and nonsense. No one does this anymore; no one makes a party out of a death anniversary."

"Oh. But they can have a memorial service, can't they? If it's in English it's somehow—what? Classier?"

"Careful, Nagla." He clenched his teeth, and she grinned.

"You know what? I have an excellent idea," she went on, speaking softly, pronouncing each word deliberately, like she used to do when she would teach her children how to speak Arabic. "Why don't you go to the memorial service tomorrow, and let me take my peasant, commoner mother to the cemetery to visit your son's grave and pray for him? That would suit you better, wouldn't it?"

"I told you to be careful, Nagla. I don't want to fight with you."

"Because if you think I will actually go with you to that service, you're crazy; crazy and stupid," she went on, her heart drumming with the excitement of knowing she was crossing a line. "I'm not going with you.

In fact, I'm going to spend the whole day by your son's grave, eating *shoreik*."

She saw his fists clench, saw him blush. She watched, almost dizzy with satisfaction, as he stepped closer to her, whispered through his teeth, "Well, you know what? You *are* coming with me to the memorial service tomorrow. You *are* going to offer the Bradstreets your condolences. You *are* going to support me in front of those people as I try to undo some of the damage your son has done. Because if you don't, you can pack your bags and go back to Egypt with your mother, eat that *shoreik* on the airplane. I will do it, Nagla. I will send you packing if I have to." He was panting with anger. She stood still, her eyes wide, watching as he walked back in, his footsteps resonating as he ran up the stairs. In the kitchen, her mother and children looked away when they saw her glance at them.

Nagla sat in one of the patio chairs, lit a cigarette, and glanced toward the Bradstreets' house just in time to see the blinds on Cynthia's bedroom window fall. Minutes later, she heard her husband's car speed away, tires screeching.

She was alone.

15

ENGLISH: God helps those who help themselves.

ARABIC: The worshipper is to think and God is to find the means.

The *shoreik* sat heavy in Khaled's stomach as he walked out of Penn Station and headed downtown. Walking the New York streets, Khaled felt Ehsan's wad of money in his pocket, poking him with every step. He was grateful for one thing: the money gave him the pretense he needed to get out of the house—he told his grandmother he was going shopping for CDs, going to spend her money. He was not grateful for the way each step he took reminded him of Ehsan, as if the wad of money were her representative, an accidental chaperone.

He met Brittany at Claire's and walked with her to the park, as they always did. He could hardly speak, responding to Brittany's remarks with monosyllables or low hums. He knew that she was waiting for him to reveal the reason behind the urgency of his appeal to meet her; in his confusion the night before, he had practically implored her to meet with him, his language, he now realized, tinged with uncalled-for panic. Sitting next to her, a soft breeze blowing her scent his way and making him feel he sat in an open meadow instead of the city park teaming with walkers, he became speechless. How could he even broach the subject?

And was telling her about Hosaam truly necessary? She had not found out. She might never find out on her own.

"I met Sebastian again yesterday," she told him. He nodded, grateful for the time her words bought him but reluctant to discuss Sebastian. Khaled still disliked him, and the mention of his name always reminded him of how Brittany would one day find a boyfriend and slip away from him, her free time devoted to a man she loved instead of the boy she had befriended.

Brittany looked at him, her eyes inquisitive. He had drifted away. Quickly, he asked, "What happened?"

"I told him to stay away." She watched passersby, her eyes following a young jogger: tall, slim, with a blond ponytail, a pink tank top, and neon-yellow shorts. Khaled glanced toward the jogger then looked at Brittany, traced her short black hair with his eyes, counted her hoop earrings, and was seized with a terror that he might never see her again if he told her about his brother. She was going to hate him for having withheld this for so long. She was going to fear him.

"I think he got it, this time," she sighed. "Or I hope he did. I'm just sick of the whole thing. He comes and goes all the time, and every time he shows up he messes up my day. I don't need this." She looked at him, caught him staring at her ear, and smiled. He blushed, looking away.

"I'm sorry it didn't work out," he lied.

"I'm not. Not anymore. It was eating me up. Every day I would obsess over whether or not he would contact me, what I would do if he did, whether or not I should go back to him. And I realized I was letting him control my life. He was doing everything, and I was just reacting. You don't know how hard it is, having one person dominate your life this way." She came closer, resting her head on his shoulder, yawning. "God, I'm tired."

He stayed motionless. The top of her head brushed against his cheek, and a wave of emotion rushed through him, reducing him to a disjointed heap of sympathy, panic, and love, all dwarfed by an overwhelming desire to hold her tight, to bury his nose in her hair and sniff the aroma of flowers and grass. His words came out before he could think them over.

"Actually, I do. I know what it feels like to have someone control your life."

She raised her head and looked at him, smiling. She had misunderstood him, and he blushed. "No, Brit. I didn't mean that." She thought he was about to confess his love like the infatuated teenage boy that she knew he was. She looked away, blushing, too, and his embarrassment was replaced by his ache at having dismissed her.

"I have something I have to tell you," he blurted out. There was no time to think this through and, he became convinced, no use in doing so. "I—my family—" How could he say this? He sighed. "I had a brother. He did something horrible."

She looked at him, curious, no longer embarrassed. He went on. "Exactly one year ago, my older brother—he killed himself and his girlfriend." He looked away, unable to bear her look of mixed horror and sympathy, terrified that she would inch away from him, get up and walk off. He waited for her to do so, and when she didn't, he went on. "They had been friends their entire lives." His voice was breaking. He swallowed, paused. "She lived next door to us. They were in love for a long time, and then she broke up with him." Just like Brittany broke up with Sebastian, he realized, and he turned to look at her, the association filling him with irrational fear for her safety. "He had her meet him at the park—" Just like he was meeting with Brittany. He sat back, groaned, covering his face with his hands. "Oh, God."

"What happened?" Her hand, small and warm, held on to his wrist, not pulling it away from his face but holding it, supporting it. Her touch made him shudder—how come she was not scared of him?

"He shot her, and then he shot himself." He was speaking through tears, mortified at his own weakness. He had not cried in public since he was ten. Then again, he had never told anyone what had happened. This was his first time telling this story that everyone knew through the media, through Facebook and YouTube and the news stations and blogs. Everyone except Brittany. She let go of his hand. He dared not look her way, not even to see if her horror had overtaken her sympathy.

"I'm sorry I never told you." He wiped his eyes on his sleeves. "It's just that—" She was the only person who knew him and not his brother. She made him feel untainted. "I was afraid."

He darted a glance her way, expecting to see the familiar: a look of fear, of disdain, or maybe of curiosity, a head tilted to the side and examining the foreign creature that he was with his tainted blood that drove people to murder. Instead, he saw her hand covering her mouth, her eyes watering.

"I'm so sorry, Khaled."

He took a deep breath and looked away. Ahead of them, three squirrels chased one another up a tree. He stared at them, collecting his thoughts. Was it too soon to assume she'd forgiven him for lying to her for so long, for concealing his brother the way people bandaged up an infected wound? He dared not look at her. Perhaps she would be angry with him for his dishonesty. Perhaps—his heart sank again—she would not be angry, because she did not value their relationship as he did. She would have taken offense if Sebastian had concealed something as monumental from her, but not if he did. He was nobody.

"What do you do?" she asked.

"About what?" He clung to her question, signaling interest in his story, elevating him from insignificance.

"Everything. How do you cope?"

No one had ever asked him that, not even Garrett. He looked at her again, finally able to meet her eyes. He could not believe that, after hearing his story, her first thoughts focused on him, not his brother.

"You just cope," he said. Then, after a pause, "Actually, that's bullshit.

You don't. At least I never did." She was still looking at him, listening, waiting. He went on, the words spilling out of him uncensored. "Everywhere I go, I think people are looking at me and thinking of what he did. Thinking I must be like him. It's almost like a branding or something— a scarlet letter of sorts."

"But you didn't do it!"

"It doesn't really matter. It's a sort of weird association game, I guess. They see me, they think of him. They think of him, they think murder. And it works the other way around, too: I see people, I think they recognize me as his brother, and then I think of him. It's like he's gone but he really isn't—he's attached to me now." He turned to look at her, held on to her wrist. "You know how you don't want Sebastian controlling your life? My brother has been controlling mine for the entire past year. And the worst part is—I can't shake him off. I can't drive him away, because he's not even here anymore."

She was listening. He stared at her—and she was listening. Thoughts and feelings that had been spinning in his head for a year came rushing out, chasing one another. "The worst part is, half the time I'm angry with him, and the other half I feel guilty. Guilty because I don't miss him like my mom and sister do, and guilty because I can't even remember whether or not I ever loved him. Can you believe that?"

She tugged her hand away from him, gingerly, and he let go of her wrist, sliding away from her. He had been squeezing too hard. He looked at her, dizzy. "I'm sorry," he mumbled.

"It's okay."

She moved closer to him, put her arm around his shoulder. He hid his face in his hands. He had hurt her. "Oh, God," he mumbled.

"It's okay."

"No, it's not."

"Yes, it is. You're being too hard on yourself. And, chances are, you did love him—you're just angry, right now. And I'm sure he loved you, too."

He shook his head, both to dismiss her remark and to shake away the fear that had gotten hold of him. "He never loved me. We were never close. He even—" His throat tingled and ached, as if his words were shards of glass that wedged themselves in his flesh. "He hated me."

"I'm sure he didn't—"

"He hated me," he spat, feeling angrier with his brother than he ever had, the image of his hand squeezing Brittany's wrist making him wish he could purge his own blood of everything that tied him to Hosaam. "You know what he did before he died? You know what the last thing he told me was?" He turned to face her. "He tried to get me involved in what he did. He even—" He hesitated, stammering, his words refusing to acknowledge thoughts that he had tried hard to suppress for so long. "He even—I think he tried to frame me. I think he tried to make it look like I knew what he was going to do and I helped him do it." His voice broke. "He had to drag me into this, and now I'll never be able to shake this thing off."

Brittany stared at him, horrified, her eyes wide. She pulled her arm away and hugged herself, her shoulders hunched. She did not ask him to go on—but she did not need to. She was still sitting next to him. She was still listening.

Khaled had walked into his room in the evening to find his brother sitting on his bed. Hosaam, seeing him enter, grinned and patted Khaled's bed next to him, inviting his brother to sit by his side. Khaled became instantly suspicious. For the previous year, ever since Hosaam graduated high school, Khaled had hardly seen him, and never at bedtime, partly because Hosaam had been staying up all night and sleeping all day. Khaled would wake up in the morning and find him lying in his bed, fast asleep, but would never actually see him climb in. He had started suspecting Hosaam had developed powers that let him slide from the attic, through the floor, and directly onto his own bed, without having to come by the door. Perhaps he'd found out how to turn himself into some sort of gas, Khaled would think, half in jest. Only half in jest.

"What do you want?" Khaled asked as he stood in front of his bed. He was tired. He wanted to go to sleep. He had a physics test the next day he had not prepared for, and he was nervous. He did not feel ready to indulge in one of Hosaam's games.

"What do you want? Is that how you talk to your big brother?" Hosaam's eyes were red and a bit hazy. Doubtless from spending so much time in that attic.

"I need to go to bed, Hosaam." Khaled squeezed past his brother and onto his bed. Hosaam let him get under the covers before leaning sideways and hovering over him, one hand holding the covers in place on each side of Khaled, his face close to his brother's. He was smiling, but Khaled, the covers holding him tightly in place, had felt choked. Ever since they were little kids, Hosaam had scared him, and now that Khaled was taller than Hosaam, he was upset to find his brother could still intimidate him.

"Fuck off, Hosaam!"

"Do I scare you, bro?"

"Of course not."

"Do you love me, Khaled?"

"What?" That was new.

"I'm your older brother, right? You're supposed to love me. And since you do everything you're supposed to do, then you must really love me, right?" Hosaam was smiling, and Khaled, accustomed to the *good brother* sarcasm, said nothing.

"Would you do me a favor?" Hosaam asked.

"What?"

"I need you to help me out." Hosaam finally let go of the sheets and sat straight up. Khaled moved his legs away from his brother.

"I need you to get a message to Natalie."

"Why don't you get it to her yourself?"

"I . . . I said something stupid, last time we spoke, and now she won't talk to me." Hosaam was not grinning anymore, and Khaled could not quite understand the look on his face.

"Text her, then," Khaled said. Hosaam shook his head.

"She won't answer that, either. I tried."

"So maybe she doesn't want to talk to you."

Hosaam grinned again. "Always the smart boy, aren't you?"

Khaled blushed. "What do you want, Hosaam?"

"I want you to send her a text message. I want you to tell her something, but don't mention my name." Hosaam leaned forward again. He had started talking rapidly and Khaled felt his speech was a bit jumbled. "Tell her to come and meet you at the park tomorrow at three, after school, at that spot next to the Visitors' Center. She'll know which spot. We used to go there together. Tell her you have something to give her. Something that you can't bring to school. Tell her you can't do it at home because you don't want anyone to see you. Tell her you don't want *me* to see you. She'll like that." He smirked again. Khaled felt his fear return.

"I won't do that! What would I want to go meet her for? Whatever you have to give her you can give her right here. Just walk up to her door." Khaled nodded in the direction of the Bradstreets' house.

Hosaam shook his head. "You don't understand," he said, his voice low, the words still coming out a bit too close together. "You won't have to go meet her. I will. I'll go talk to her. She won't listen to me here, but there she will. And then you can be the one who brought us together, right? You'd be the one who made it all happen, who made sure we'd be together forever, right?"

"I don't know, Hosaam. I don't want to get involved—"

"Just send her a text. Or give me your phone and I'll do it. Just don't say you didn't send it if she sees you at school tomorrow and asks, okay?" Hosaam reached out to get Khaled's phone from his bedside table.

"No, I'll do it." Khaled got to his phone first and held on to it. "Tomorrow morning, though. I can't text her now; it's almost midnight. She'll be asleep."

Hosaam looked at him, his eyes narrow. He was not smiling anymore.

"Promise you'll do it?" he finally asked.

"Sure, I will."

"You're a good boy, right? You won't go back on your promise, will you?"

"No, I won't, Hosaam. I'll tell her tomorrow."

"Don't tell her. Text her."

"I might see her at school and tell her instead."

"No, don't tell her. Text her." Hosaam held Khaled's arm as he looked him straight in the eyes. Khaled pulled back, hit the headboard. "Do it for me, will you?" Hosaam smiled again.

"Okay, okay. I'll text her."

"Good." Hosaam got up. "Good night, bro." He leaned down and planted a kiss on Khaled's forehead. Khaled pulled away, and Hosaam laughed.

Heading to the door, Hosaam turned around one last time, looked at Khaled, and said, "You know what? Tomorrow evening, before you go to bed, I want you to remember one thing: I want you to remember that you're my little brother, that you'll always be my little brother, and that we're just alike, you and I. We're just alike. Remember how you used to copy all I did when we were young? Well, that's your fate, bro. To always follow in my footsteps."

He had laughed as he turned around and walked away, and Khaled remembered feeling angry with him, not because he had scared him, but because he was, again, trying to manipulate him to do things he did not want to do.

He did not text Natalie. In the morning, before Khaled left for school, when his surprisingly still awake brother asked if he had texted her, Khaled lied and said he had. Lying to Hosaam had made him feel good. For once he had refused to do something Hosaam's way. For the entirety of the following year Khaled wondered, every day, what would have happened if he had left it at that, if he had not looked for Natalie between classes and told her what had happened.

"Why does he want to meet me?" Natalie had asked. They were both standing in front of her locker, where she had been looking in a mirror and adjusting a stray strand of hair when Khaled approached her.

"I don't know." Khaled shrugged. "He didn't even want me to tell you that much. He wanted me to text you and pretend you'd be meeting me there, not him."

"Your brother!" Natalie's eyes narrowed, as if this description encompassed all the obscenities she was thinking of, and as if Khaled would somehow know exactly what she meant. Which, in fact, he did.

"Listen, Natalie. I don't want to be a part of this, whatever he's doing. I just thought I'd let you know, just in case."

"Just in case what?"

"In case you guys still had something going on."

"Huh. You know what we have going on, now?" Natalie stepped closer to him so that no one else could hear. "You know why your crazy brother wanted *you* to text me?" Khaled shook his head. "Because he thinks you and I are together." Khaled stared at her. He could feel his face get ready to blush, the blood running up his neck and to his ears. "Your idiot of a brother barged in on me at Friendly's the other day, just as I sat down with my friends, and totally freaked out on me. Told me I've been seeing you behind his back. He went on so much that Audrey had her cell phone out and was about to call the cops."

"Where'd he get that idea from?"

"I don't know." She turned to get her books out of the locker. "I guess he saw us talk that day when we walked home together."

"But we walk home together all the time!" Khaled exclaimed. "Or, at least, we've done it a lot before."

"Don't ask me." She closed the locker and turned to head to class. "But you know what? I think I'm going to go meet him. I think I need to tell him to fuck off, once and for all. I mean, jeez! He used to be so sweet!" Natalie looked at Khaled as if it were his fault that Hosaam had changed.

"Do you want me to tell him I never told you? That way you don't have to go?" he called out to her as she turned around. She, without turning back, just raised one hand in the air and waved him off.

Sitting next to Brittany, Khaled remembered how he had spent that entire morning feeling a strange glee at having tricked Hosaam.

"I kept thinking how cool it was that I had told him I texted her when I had not, as if this one detail made all the difference." He sighed. "Afterward, I kept thinking why he had insisted I text her. It sounds crazy, I know—but I couldn't help but think that perhaps he had wanted the cops to find my message and somehow think I was involved." He had lain in bed one night, shivering, as he imagined his brother killing Natalie and then disappearing, leaving her with her phone lying by her side. His paranoia had gotten such a strong hold of him that he felt he was slowly turning into his father. "But then I think he just wanted me to feel guilty. Or—" He hesitated, searching for words. "He wanted to control me, like he always did. Either way, he succeeded."

"No, he did not." Brittany was sitting with both knees pulled up to her chest, her arms wrapped around them. On the path across from their bench, people were hurrying past, and Khaled wondered whether any of them could have guessed what he and Brittany were talking about.

"Think about it, Brit. This whole past year has been about him. To-morrow, Natalie's family is holding a memorial service, and that, too, is because of him. My mom, my dad, my sister—everything we're doing is shaped by what he did. And how can I not feel guilty? If I had not given Natalie his message, she might be alive today." He paused. "Every single day I wonder what could have happened if I had not gone looking for her."

"You can't think that way, Khaled. You can't second-guess yourself after the fact. How could you have known?"

"I should have known better than to do anything he told me to do."

"Monday morning quarterback."

He stared at the ground, his brows knotted. "Wow."

"What?"

"You just reminded me of my grandmother. Only she always tells me never to say *what if.*"

"She's right."

"She often is, surprisingly." Khaled smiled. In his pocket, he felt Ehsan's money nudge him.

Brittany looked around, her eyes resting on an older woman who walked toward them, hand in hand with a little girl. The woman was too old to be the girl's mother, but Khaled had trouble imagining her as the girl's grandmother. He remembered the first time he had seen Garrett's grandmother. "She can't be your grandma! She's—she's so young!" he had objected. She also did not wear long, flowing robes, was obviously fit, did not smell of homemade cakes and incense, and did not, for the entire duration of her visit to Garrett's house, insist on feeding the boys anything. To the then-ten-year-old Khaled, she could not have been a grandmother. Later, he would find out she was two years older than Ehsan.

"You know, my mom lost a brother when she was young. Vietnam,"

Brittany said as she watched the woman and the girl pass by them. "He was a good decade older than she was." Khaled listened, curious. She had never mentioned her family before. "My grandmother, the poor soul—she became so religious. Some priest told her that it was God's will and that she had to accept it. Her whole life she pounded my mom with this stuff. I think that's why my mom never believed. She says it only made my grandmother superstitious, believing in angels and miracles, all to cope with the fact that her son was blown to pieces in some fucked-up war."

Khaled looked away. Ehsan believed in miracles. His whole life he had believed, too: that the Zamzam water had healed him, that Moses had split the sea, that Jesus had raised the dead. He could still hear Ehsan's voice telling him the stories, could still remember verses from the Qur'an she had explained to him, telling of how Moses threw his cane and it turned into a serpent, how he took his hand out of his pocket and it shone a bright white, how Jesus had spoken as a newborn, defending his mother's honor. Even now, this whole past year, he had believed in the possibility of miracles: that he would wake up one day and find that his brother was still alive, that Natalie was still alive, or, if not that, that the town would somehow forget the entire fiasco, that people would not glance toward him in fear or loathing.

"You don't believe that miracles can happen?" He tried to sound casual, his tone dismissive of the question's naïveté.

She laughed. "Yeah, right."

But he *knew* they could.

His certainty struck him, for the first time, as ridiculous. Considering how many things he did not know, how could he be that sure about this, of all things?

Again he remembered Ehsan's prayers of protection, the comfort he felt in evoking God's name before stepping out, the hope that he would not have to face this world alone. He did not want to give this up. He did not want Hosaam to rob him of that, as well, of the hope that his grandmother had instilled in him since he was a little child. He would not let his brother gain even more control over him.

He reached into his pocket, grabbed Ehsan's money. "Let's go," he said, getting up.

"Where to?"

He did not know. "Let's walk around for a while."

They strolled down the street, he all the time scanning the still-open stores. He was looking for something, but did not know what. Then he remembered a store they had passed on their way there, and, leading her by the hand, he made his way through the streets and found it, still open, displays of silver jewelry hanging off decorative brass branches in its window.

"Wait here," he said. Inside, he scanned the shelves and display cases, frantically looking for something, a sign, something to prove to him, and to her, that miracles still happened. On one of the hangers, he saw it waiting for him, and he reached out and grabbed it: a large, tear-shaped pendant, a turquoise stone mounted in antique silver. On the back of the mounting was etched a butterfly, its wings spread out.

He paid for it with Ehsan's money. Outside, he put it on Brittany's neck.

"What's that?" she asked, laughing.

"Proof that miracles do happen."

She held the stone in her hand. "It's beautiful."

"Look at the back," he said.

She flipped it over and chuckled. He watched her, thinking that this moment was a miracle in itself, that, if nothing else ever worked his way, at least he could always remember her laugh, soft and tender, erasing the pain of the past hour, the past year.

"Thank you," he said.

"For what?"

"Everything."

She smiled and, leaning forward, planted a kiss on his cheek. "You're a good guy, Khaled," she said, and, because she said so, he felt it could very well be true.

16

ENGLISH: We are sorry for your loss.

ARABIC: Only God can remain.

I am here to tell you how truly sorry my family and I are.

No. That won't do.

I am here, today, to share in your grief.

Neither will that, of course. *Share in your grief* will not do. It's not their grief alone, after all. It's his, as well, isn't it?

I am here today to offer my respects and to assure you that your grief and mine are one and the same.

That won't work, either. It would sound as if he were claiming to be on the same footing with them, as if he was as much of a victim as they were. Which he was, of course, but they wouldn't like that.

I am here today to offer my respects and to assure you that my heart has been heavy with grief, a grief that only the prospect of your forgiveness could alleviate.

Samir looked at this last line and smiled. That was starting to sound better. He had been in his office ever since he left home in the morning, only stepping out for a quick lunch at Shark's diner before locking himself in again. Though he had not planned to leave home before his scuffle with Nagla, he felt the privacy had been beneficial, helping him concentrate. He wondered how he could have written this speech at home, Nagla and her mother a constant distraction. Thinking of his wife made him wince; he had been too sharp with her, had undoubtedly hurt her. He would have to apologize. Perhaps. But this was not the time to think of that.

He sat back in his chair, reviewed what he had written so far. He would have to assure the Bradstreets that he would be willing to trade his own life for that of their daughter and his son. That he wished there was anything he could do to change this, anything he could have done. And he would have to let them in on how much he blamed himself for all of that, but this, he thought as he pulled the pen away from the paper, would have to be done tactfully. He felt they needed to know, yes, but he could not say it in a way that would be an invitation to lay further blame on him. Also, he didn't want to humiliate himself unnecessarily. God knows, he sighed as he put the pen back to paper, the entire affair was humiliating enough, without him adding to the embarrassment.

> *In this day of grief, in this day of remembrance, I would like to*
> *remind you of my family's history in Summerset. We have been*
> *a part of this community for almost two decades. I have taken*
> *upon myself the responsibility of treating many of you, and I*
> *believe I have done so to the utmost of my ability. My wife has*
> *served on school committees, and has volunteered, countless*
> *times, in community projects. My children . . .*

He paused, lifting his pen again, and leaned back in his seat. He had to bring the children in, of course. Up till now he had been gaining in confidence. He thought he expressed himself rather nicely. Doctors, he now remembered, were often literarily inclined. Many of the most famous authors in Egypt were doctors. Also, he felt the words he put on the page reflected how clear a vision he had for this speech, how confident he was in the message he wanted to convey. But including the children was tricky. Maybe if he mentioned them by name. He crossed out the two last words and went on:

> *My daughter, Fatima, has represented her school in many competitions, and has recently won first place on Math Marathon and has placed highly on the Spelling Bee finals, as well. You all know her; you all know how disciplined, kind, and dedicated she is. He paused. Between disciplined and kind, he drew an arrow and wrote well-bred. He smiled. Fatima was the one who would always make him proud. It is her dream to become a doctor, too, to live and practice in this community she calls home, in the only community she has ever known. Khaled, my son, is also . . .*

He paused again, leaning away from the paper and looking at it, narrowing his eyes. What could he say about Khaled? He'd have to be careful, here. Of course Khaled was the one they'd all compare with Hosaam. No one would fear Fatima, he was certain. But Khaled was a different story. Samir sighed. If only Khaled had taken up sports. Wouldn't it have been wonderful if he could write something about that? This they would have appreciated: some athletic achievement, being a star pitcher for the high school, for instance, or a reliable quarterback. The Americans and their sports, he sighed. But Khaled, he was not interested in any of that stuff. Which really irritated Samir, because Khaled was the most American of all his kids, but why did he have to be so selective in his Americanism? Why couldn't he be good in sports?

Khaled, my son, has never known a home other than Summerset, either, and the events of this past year have been very hard on him, as well as on his sister and mother. My children have both been harassed at school. They do not tell me, but I know. They have been called names. They have been chased down streets. I saw it once with my own eyes, though I never told anyone about it before.

Samir's hand started shaking. He held the pen a bit harder, tried to maintain a legible handwriting. He could always copy it out clearer, later on.

I saw my son running down Maple Street, being chased by four boys. He is a fast runner, Khaled, and the boys did not catch up with him. But one of them stopped and pulled out a baseball, flung it at him. It hit my son in the lower back, and I saw him arch his back and fall down to his knees. I saw him pull himself up again and run, holding his side. I saw the tears streaming down his face. It is a sight I wish on no parent. Nor do I ever wish any of you to witness a day when your own child, your own flesh and blood, takes an innocent life as well as his own.

My neighbors, my friends: I come here today to implore you for your forgiveness. My son has committed a sin that God will certainly punish him for. And if my family or I have had any share of the blame, this past year has been punishment enough for all of us. I therefore implore you to forgive us the sins my son has committed. I implore you to remember that Fatima and Khaled are not to blame for what their brother has done. I implore you to remember that we, too, have been grieving, and that our grief is doubled by our shame and regret. And, more than anything, I implore you to accept my personal, heartfelt, sincere apologies. May God bless us all, and help us through this diffi-cult time.

Samir, putting his pen down, looked at the notepad. He had been thinking this over the entire morning, and was pleasantly surprised at how easy it was to put his ideas on paper. Maybe he should write more, he told himself as he looked at his work, smiling. There were many venues for writing he could pursue. He might even write an editorial to the local newspaper, in observation of the anniversary of his son's death. He wondered if he could use some of this material in it.

Getting up from his desk, Samir held the notepad in his hand and, pacing, started reading out loud. He read the whole thing once, then again, and then a third time. With each reading he grew more pleased with his work. He felt it was sincere and genuine, and that his audience would certainly feel his pain, as well as that of his family. He could imagine Jim and Cynthia looking up at him, sad, of course, but not angry anymore. Certainly some of those in attendance would be touched by his words. Some might even be moved to tears. He looked over the part about Khaled's assault, wondered if he should elaborate, then changed his mind. This memory, just like many others, he did not want to dwell on.

Going back to his desk, Samir picked up the pen one more time. With a trembling hand he read over the first line, then crossed out the word *I*, replacing it with a *We.* He then edited the rest of the sentence, and read it over again. *We are here today to offer our respects and to assure you that our hearts have been heavy with grief, a grief that only the prospect of your forgiveness could alleviate.* This sounded much, much better. Of course. He had no doubt that Nagla would accompany him; he knew her too well. But, looking at this, he now saw the necessity of including the kids, as well. They would all go together, one family, united.

SUNDAY

17

ENGLISH: Rest in peace.

ARABIC: Death is rest.

The alarm clock's buzz interrupted Nagla's dream, and she flung her arm out from under the covers, slapping the snooze button and killing the noise. Of all mornings, today was one when a dream could be of major significance, a message with the potential to foretell the future or, at the very least, shed light on the present. She closed her eyes again, tried to recall her vision: did it involve a green field? Was Hosaam truly there? She tried to focus, hoping she might recall the elusive prophecy she was certain had been bestowed on her during the night.

Beside her, Samir turned, and she knew he, too, was awake. She remained motionless, even after she felt him sit up in bed.

"Why'd you set the alarm clock so early? It's not even six in the morning," he asked.

"I'm going to the cemetery. I didn't want to oversleep."

She had hardly had any sleep all night, only fits of slumber interrupted by sudden jerks, as if someone were standing by her bedside specifically to yank her out of her dreams whenever she started to doze off. She must finally have fallen asleep out of sheer exhaustion, which might have explained that dream. Her mother always claimed that exhaustion brought people as close to the transcendent as possible.

"How long will you stay?" Samir asked. She knew what he really wanted to say: that she needed to be back in time for them to go to the memorial service together; that she needed to confirm to him that she was, indeed, going to the service; that she had not meant it when she claimed she would not accompany him there.

She slid out of bed and walked into the bathroom, running the water in the sink and starting to brush her teeth. He had left home after their scuffle over the *shoreik* the previous morning and had not come back till late in the evening. "I will send you packing," he had told her. She knew he remembered his words as well as she did. They had not spoken since then.

She brushed vigorously, scrubbed her teeth and gums, spat out blood.

"Would you do it, Samir?" she asked. She could sense him standing behind her.

"Do what?"

"Send me packing?" She placed the toothbrush in its holder, splashed her face with water, and saw him, in the mirror, stepping out of the bathroom and leaving her alone.

She ran the water in the shower, waited for it to warm up before stepping in. Letting the hot water knead her back, she tried, again, to remember that dream. Dream interpretation was, according to Ehsan, a science that few could boast of understanding but that existed, as evidenced by the Qur'an. The prophet Yousef, peace be upon his soul, had been its most famous master, predicting both a crucifixion and a royal pardon out of the bird- and wine-dotted dreams of two prison inmates. Nagla was certain that the prophet had taken the secrets of dream interpretation with him to the grave, yet she could not help but wonder whether dreams still revealed prophecies, even if the knowledge to interpret them was no longer granted to humans.

Whatever Nagla knew of dream interpretation came to her secondhand from her mother: dreaming of grilled fish was bad, but dreaming of live fish predicted good fortune, especially if the fish sparkled in silvery hues. Having a child was good if the child was a girl, bad if it was a boy, since girls were known to bestow fortune on their parents, a compensation for the financial burden daughters inevitably became. Dreaming of the dead had layers of interpretation: seeing a dead person walk off with a live one foretold sickness or death for the latter; receiving something from a dead person was good, but having him or her take something away from a live one was a prelude to impending grief. Seeing the prophet Muhammad, peace be upon his soul, in a dream equaled seeing him in real life and was a privilege reserved for the righteous (Nagla had, of course, never dreamed of the Prophet). A vision of the dead could tell of their status in the afterlife: seeing the deceased in his or her youth, full of health or in seeming happiness, indicated that the person's sins had been forgiven, that he or she had safely made it through life and was now in peace and under the good grace of the All-Merciful. Nagla, failing to remember the exact dream she had, started making up her own: one of Hosaam, in white robes (a sign of purity and virtue), giving her a hug and a pat on the back, whispering something comforting in her ear—though she could not imagine what that whisper might entail.

Stepping out of the bathroom after her shower, she saw Samir sitting on the bed, arms crossed. She felt him watch her as she put on her jeans and shirt and started brushing her hair.

"You cannot blame me for words spoken in anger."

She did not reply.

"It's quite insulting, you know. Acting like you don't know me after all these years. Like you truly believe I could do anything to hurt you."

She combed her hair, paying no attention to the slight drizzle she caused as droplets of water fell to the carpet. Once she had untangled her hair, she wrapped it up in a towel and threw it over her shoulder. She tried not to think of her hair color, its blackness glistening with moisture.

"I need coffee," she said, walking out of the bedroom.

In the kitchen, she waited for the coffee to brew. Outside, daylight had not yet broken, and she could see a light burning in Cynthia's kitchen. She kept her eyes on the coffee machine, tried to avoid looking at the house next door.

If she were to follow the path of honesty that had, only yesterday, seemed like the only possible one, if she were to cling to an iota of self-respect, then she should stand her ground, insist on not going to the memorial service, and point out to her husband the cruelty of his language, even if it was, as he was claiming, the result of anger. She tried to imagine how such a conversation could progress and grimaced. The coffee machine released the last few droplets of hot liquid and steam, and Nagla grabbed her mug and walked up to the window. Cynthia was in her kitchen. Nagla could see her shadow moving around, probably making her own coffee. Cream, no sugar, accompanied by one slice of toast and a dab of strawberry jam.

Upstairs the water ran again, and she knew Samir had stepped into the shower. She should, of course, tell him what she truly thought—but what kind of Pandora's box would such a confrontation open? What else would need to be discussed? Could a two-decades-old marriage be zipped open, its contents spilled to be inspected and probed without, in the process, killing those involved in it? Where would she even start? She shuddered to think of what would be said.

Her mother would advise her not to bring ruin on herself—*ma tekhrebish ala nafsek,* she could almost hear her say. Nagla knew that such a confrontation with her husband had a very high risk of escalating to something beyond her control. For a split second another one of the questions that had haunted her for the previous days tried to squeeze itself into her brain: So what? But she dismissed it. She was sick of questions. Instead, she imagined what her mother would say to calm her down, if she were to speak to her: Samir had said worse before. He didn't truly mean it anyway. He was under so much pressure. He was only trying to do what he thought was best for his wife and kids. *You are his wife; you are obliged to stand by him. To support him. This is your duty.*

We lie to protect our families, Ehsan had told her.

We lie to protect ourselves, Nagla revised her mother's statement.

We lie because the truth is too much trouble.

Nagla contemplated this last thought. Perhaps. But wanting to avoid trouble was not as cowardly as it seemed. In fact, she sensed wisdom in it, a rising above the trivial. An embrace of peace. A surrender to tranquillity.

Her mother would agree. Cynthia wouldn't. Nagla wasn't sure what Ameena would think, but, whatever her opinion on that matter was, she would probably back it up with a quote from the Qur'an.

Softly, Nagla stepped out onto the deck, her coffee mug in hand. She sat in her usual chair, her back to the Bradstreets' house, and lit a cigarette. She still loved the early morning hours, still enjoyed sitting on her deck, even though the idea of finding joy in such close proximity to the site of unthinkable tragedy seemed blasphemous.

But she didn't want to think anymore.

She sipped her coffee, took one deep draw from her cigarette, and watched the trees that had started to redraw their shapes amid the dissipating darkness. She wanted this weekend to pass. She didn't want to hang on to people's words and search for meanings behind them, not Ameena's, not her mother's (the truthful ones or the false), and certainly not Samir's. The assumption that every word had layers of meaning was, she decided, exhausting beyond human capacity. Dream interpretation made sense because it validated the very existence of dreams, marking them as the coded messages they had to be, whether they came from the subconscious (according to Freud—Nagla still remembered *something* from her college years) or from God (according to Ehsan). Dreams were simply more manageable than words.

Behind her, she imagined that Cynthia was holding her own coffee cup with both hands, letting its hot surface warm her fingers as she waited for daylight to come.

Back in her room, Nagla found Samir already fully dressed, pacing the floor. She walked into the bathroom and started drying her hair.

"How long do you plan to stay at the cemetery?" Samir asked again. "We don't want to be late to the service."

She wrapped one long strand of hair around the hot-air brush, held it in place until she could feel her scalp sting under the heat. Behind her, her husband stood by the door to the bedroom. She watched his reflection in the mirror.

"I don't want to have to go there without you, Nagla."

She turned the hair dryer off, listened. "What?"

"I said I don't want to have to go without you." She listened again, closing her eyes, trying to detect a tone she could have sworn had seeped into his voice, a layer of quasi-warmth, a pleading, perhaps, or a resignation barely detectable. Then again, she might have imagined things.

"Don't worry," she finally said, turning the hair dryer back on. "I'll be back in time."

Ehsan carried the *shoreik;* Nagla carried the cleaning supplies. They walked, Nagla leading, along the winding path bordering the cemetery until they reached Hosaam's grave. Ehsan threw herself on the wooden bench at the edge of the path, wiped her sweat as Nagla knelt by the grave, putting on latex gloves, pulling spray cans and sponges out of the shopping bag.

Nagla had expected to find the graffiti. It had first appeared a few months earlier, after they finally had the gravestone installed, and ever since, she kept the cleaning supplies in the trunk of her car. She would clean, and the graffiti would eventually reappear, redrawn with renewed creativity. This time they had done an impressive job. *Have fun in Hell* was sprayed in red and neon yellow, the two *l*'s shaped like spikes spitting flames.

"Here, let me help you." Ehsan started to get down on her knees next to her daughter.

"No, Mama, please, don't." Nagla pushed her mother back up. "I can handle this. Besides, I don't have gloves for you. This stuff is harsh," she said, nodding toward the cleaning supplies.

"But I have to do something!"

"Just read him some Qur'an, will you? Aloud?"

She sprayed and scrubbed meticulously while her mother's voice resonated behind her, starting with a couple of prayers for the dead and the living, then settling into a low, melodic recitation, her voice now smooth and silky, now cracking with emotion that Nagla tried to tune out. Again she tried to remember her dream. What had she seen? A meadow? Not similar to the park, but sunny and vast with patches of daffodils. She was probably making this up. She sighed, scrubbed the stone harder, dabbed at the rainbow-colored solution dripping around her son's name.

Behind her a car door slammed shut. A young woman in jeans and a T-shirt walked over to a grave a few spots away. There, she lay down, outstretched, her face buried in her arms. The grave was fresh—no headstone yet, the patch of ground barely sprouting grass.

Nagla, preoccupied in watching the visitor—no one ever came here this early in the morning—did not notice her mother's hurried voice as she wrapped up her Qur'an recitation, the sudden silence. By the time Nagla jumped up, tearing the gloves off her hands, her mother had already reached the woman.

"Mama!" Nagla hissed, hurrying after her mother. Ehsan ignored her, leaning down closer to the woman and pointing into the opened container filled with *shoreik* as she pushed it toward the young woman, who, still lying on her stomach, had lifted herself half up and was looking at Ehsan with moist eyes.

"I'm so sorry," Nagla said to the young woman, pulling her mother by the arm.

"*Feih eih?*" Ehsan said. "I'm just offering her some *shoreik*!"

"You can't do that here, Mama!"

"That's okay," the woman said, getting up.

"*Da fetir el-rahmah!*" Ehsan said.

"What is she saying?" the woman asked Nagla.

"She is saying this is the bread of . . . no . . ." Nagla looked for the words. More than two decades in the United States and the words still stumbled on her tongue. And her mother called her American. "Pastries, yes. She says these are the Pastries of Mercy. We bake them in Egypt for the dead. To pray for mercy for the dead."

"And the alive," Ehsan added in English, her accent heavy, "the" sounding like "zee."

The woman looked down at the pastries, sniffed. "That sounds good. May I have one?" Ehsan, beaming and giving Nagla an I-told-you-so look, pushed the container closer to the woman, who pulled a pastry out, bit into it. Instantly her eyes watered, and Nagla wondered whether there was an ingredient in the *shoreik* that made people react that way, a serum of nostalgia.

"They're good," the woman said. "Sweet."

"Ask her who is buried there," Ehsan said in Arabic.

"I can't, Mama!"

"What did she say?" the woman asked. Nagla looked at her, sighed. She was taller than Nagla but younger and athletic. Her eyes were similar to Fatima's, her hair just as thick and curly, only a reddish blond, not black like Fatima's.

"She wants to know who's buried here."

The woman chewed at a piece of *shoreik,* swallowed. "My husband," she said, tears instantly pouring.

"Name?" Ehsan asked.

"Mark."

"Mother name?" The *th* sound was an emphasized *z*: *mozer.*

"Excuse me?" the woman asked. Nagla glared at her mother.

"Alashaan aldoaa!" Ehsan told Nagla.

"She says she needs to know his mother's name so she can pray for him," Nagla said. "We pray with the mother's name. Like Mark the son of . . ." Nagla searched for a name. "Mary, for example. Mark the son of Mary. That's how we pray for someone. We have to mention the mother's name."

The young woman nodded. "Judith."

"Mark, son of Judith," Ehsan repeated. She pointed at herself, and then pointed at the sky. "I pray for Mark, son of Judith, okay?"

"Okay. Thank you," the young woman said.

Nagla pulled at her mother's arm, murmured apologies again before leading her mother back to the seat by Hosaam's grave. Once seated, Ehsan pulled out small prayer booklets and started reading out loud, praying once for Hosaam, the son of Nagla, and then again for Mark, the son of Judith. Again one of Nagla's convictions was confirmed: a lifetime of watching American movies had not taught her mother anything about American social norms. Yet every single breach of American notions of etiquette that Nagla witnessed her mother commit resulted in a connection with someone, a momentary intersection between her mother's life and a stranger's that, paradoxically, Nagla could not find fault with, perhaps even envied.

"I thought we could only pray for the Muslim dead," Nagla said, putting the gloves back on. She watched her mother wrap up a prayer and could not help but smile.

"Says who?" Ehsan asked.

"Says everyone, as far as I know."

"Then they're all wrong," Ehsan blurted before looking down at her prayer book again. "People will deny mercy long before Allah does."

Nagla looked at the gravestone. She had managed to scrub off most of the word *hell*, but she could still see it, faintly imprinted on the marble. She fished a small brush out of her bag, sprayed more graffiti remover, and started scrubbing.

"Mama?"

Her mother finished the verse she was reading before replying, "Yes, *habibti*?"

"Do you think..." She paused, searching for words. "Do you think God takes insanity pleas?"

Ehsan sighed. Nagla heard her close the book in her lap. "I don't know, *habibti*. He is the Most Merciful, though. He wouldn't have called himself that if he didn't want us to hope. And they do say only the sane can be held accountable." She paused, and then added in a whisper, "Of course, we cannot know who will be considered sane and who won't."

Nagla nodded. "It's just that sometimes I think he might forgive him the suicide, but not—" She sniffed, wiped her eyes on her sleeve. She pulled a tissue out of her pocket, blew her nose.

Ehsan sighed and said nothing. Nagla scrubbed on, until she heard her mother fumble with the shopping bags. She turned around, expecting to see Ehsan rush toward more cemetery visitors—but there was no one new. Behind her, her mother stood, a cup of hot tea in hand. A thermos was on the bench. Nagla could smell the aroma of mint.

"Here, take a break," Ehsan said, handing her daughter the cup. Nagla sipped the tea, watched her mother sit back and fish another cup out of the bag for herself. She wondered what else could be hidden in there: a picnic basket with lunch for six, maybe, or a portable propane tank like the one her mother used on outings in Egypt, just in case they ran out of hot tea. Nagla smiled.

"Mama, I've been meaning to tell you—" She paused. Ehsan looked at her, waited. "Thank you," Nagla said. "For everything."

"For what, *ya benti*? *Alshokr lellah wahdoh*."

Ameena had said the same: thanks should be given to God alone. Nagla dismissed the questions before they assaulted her. No more.

"For everything you've done for me, this past year." Nagla could not remember the last time she had cooked a meal for her children, the last time she had cared about cleaning house or shopping for groceries. Had her mother not been living with her for the past year, her house would have been dripping cobwebs, her children emaciated.

Ehsan nodded and sipped her tea. "When your father passed away, *Allah yerhamoh we yebashbesh eltoobah elly taht rasoh*, your aunts practically moved in with me. Not my sisters—his. Three of them, all older than I was, all married with kids. For two weeks I could hardly turn in my own home without bumping into one of them."

"Did you like having them around?"

"I hated it. Each day I would wake up determined to tell them all off. But then one day we sat in the evening, sipping tea, just like we're doing now." She smiled at her daughter. Nagla, lighting a cigarette, listened.

"You and your brothers were playing in a bedroom with your cousins, and one of your aunts mentioned how your father used to love *fesikh*. And then the other mentioned that, since Easter had just passed, the salted fish was, for sure, for sale everywhere, and before I knew it they sent two of your cousins out for *fesikh* in the middle of the night." Ehsan laughed, shaking her head. "It was ten in the evening before they came back, the stench of the fish rising up the stairway before they made it to our apartment. We smelled them before we saw them. As did the neighbors." Smiling, she took a sip of her tea before continuing. "We spent over an hour, your aunts and I, picking out the bones and marinating the fish in oil and lemon, all the while talking about your father. *Remember that time he took us all to the park, a basket of* fesikh, *scallions, lemon, and fresh-baked bread in hand? Remember how his mother insisted he go and buy more lemons, chiding him for bringing so few? How he ended up sending one of the girls over to beg the family sitting by us for a lemon and then pretending to scold her for it? Remember when he was a teenager and he stole his uncle's car, drove all the way to Cairo and came back three days later? Remember the thrashing his father gave him?*" Ehsan laughed. "The later it got, the more scandalous the stories became. And your oldest aunt, Jameela, kept murmuring: 'Astaghfiru Allah; mention the good of your dead; don't expose that which Allah has kept hidden; don't bring disgrace to those whom Allah has shielded from scandal.'"

Nagla raised her eyebrows. "And you let them speak ill of *Baba*?"

"They weren't really speaking ill," Ehsan quickly retorted. "It was all in good fun. Nothing he wouldn't have minded people sharing, if he were still alive."

"And what did you contribute? Stories about how good and kind he was to you?" Nagla smiled, trying to mask the sarcastic tone that had crept into her voice. "Let me guess: you told them how he used to stay up all night by your side when you were sick. How he used to bake *basbousa* for you just because you loved it."

Ehsan sucked at her lips. "Go ahead, make fun of me. My fault for trying to make your father look good."

Nagla smiled, shook her head, and inhaled the aroma of mint rising from the tea. "This talk of food is making me hungry."

Ehsan reached into the bag and fished out a pastry, handing it to Nagla. She chewed, aware of her mother watching her. She looked away. The young woman was still lying by the grave, motionless.

"I wanted to tell you," Ehsan started. "I don't know what your brothers told you, but your father was a good man."

"Sure. He was a good man. Samir is a good man. They're all good men."

"Don't be so bitter, Nagla. Be content with what Allah has given you."

"Don't get me started," Nagla murmured, chewing on a piece of pastry.

"Bent!"

"Sorry, Mama."

Nagla waited, watching the young woman. "I think your pastry might have knocked her out," she smiled. "Americans can't take our food. Too rich for them."

"Nothing wrong with my food," Ehsan assured her. "She's resting, poor soul. Probably feels better after having eaten something."

In silence, Nagla finished her pastry, stubbed her cigarette. She had to admit the pastry did make her feel better. Perhaps there was some truth to the claim that those pastries brought about mercy.

"It's just that he had no luck, your father." Ehsan watched the young woman. "You know how it is. No one can get more than what God has written for him."

"So you invent stories about him to make up for his lack of luck in life?"

"I don't invent stories!" Ehsan arched her eyebrows. Nagla did not comment. "Besides, what difference does it make? I wanted to make sure you and your brothers remember him well. I only hope you would do the same for me after I die. That's all that stays, after all. Stories."

Nagla placed her cup on the bench next to her mother and went back to scrubbing the gravestone. She was almost done, could hardly see the outline of the spray-painted words. If she had her mother's knack for stories, she would tell some about Hosaam that might make people think better of him. Not made up ones like her mother's, merely selective ones. To emphasize the good. She sighed, scrubbing on. In a way, that was what Samir was trying to do, she realized. Tell his story. She wished she shared his conviction that people would listen, if they spoke.

"What happened?"

Nagla looked up. The young woman was standing behind her, looking at the gravestone. For a moment Nagla wished she could shield her son's name, just in case the woman knew what he had done, but it was too late. She searched the woman's face. What did she mean? What happened to her son? To her life? No, the woman pointed at the gravestone, the outline of the graffiti still faintly visible.

"Graffiti." Nagla took her gloves off, stood up. Stared at the gravestone the woman was still examining.

"People can be so cruel," the woman finally said. Nagla nodded. The woman looked over her shoulder at the grave she had been sitting by.

"We were married for seven months," she said.

They stood, facing each other, the woman looking at Nagla as Nagla avoided her eyes. Again Nagla felt, as she often did, that something needed to be said, but she did not know what to say, so she remained silent.

"Well, thanks for the bread," the woman said, both to Nagla and Ehsan. Ehsan smiled broadly, looked at Nagla. Doubtless happy the bread had not, in fact, been too rich for the American.

Nagla sat next to her mother, watched the woman walk back to her car. Ehsan watched her, too, and when the car pulled off, she murmured, "May Allah grant us all peace and patience."

"Amen."

She sat Indian-style by her son's grave while her mother finished *ed-deyyet Yasin,* reading the same sura over seven times in a row, back to back, then capping it off with a long prayer. Over the past year, the days that Nagla spent by her son's grave infused the place with a strangely comforting familiarity. The visits had become a necessity, so much so that she had joined her husband in resisting a move away from Summerset, even though Khaled had wanted it; poor Khaled, who longed for nothing more than to live in a place where no one would recognize him. If he deserved such luxury, she did not. She deserved the incriminating stares, the malicious words that people occasionally shouted at her after her son became the town's black sheep, her guilt duly recognized as equal to his, if not surpassing it. She deserved to be hated. She bit at her lower lip, took a deep breath. Besides, Khaled would soon leave for college. She saw his application packets arrive in the mail, watched, with relief, as he sat in his room filling them out months before they were due. At least he would not follow in Hosaam's footsteps and announce he was not going to apply to college anytime soon. She rested her head on her open palm, stared at the grass ahead of her. The racket Hosaam's announcement had caused. Samir had been livid. He had stood in the middle of the living room, stomping his feet, his voice probably heard blocks away. But Hosaam had only stared. And she, as always, had made excuses for him. *The boy is burned out after years of study. Let him take a break. Let him rest.*

Yes. She deserved to be hated. Besides, if she were to move away, who would look after her son's grave? Who would keep the gravestone clean of obscenities? Was she to abandon Hosaam after his death just as she had failed him in his life?

Nagla traced her son's gravestone with her eyes, outlined the patch of grass on his grave. Slowly, she ran her fingers over the grass, which now stood green and dry in the late morning heat. Coarse and prickly, it reminded her of Hosaam's hair when it was cut short, the way it brushed against her palm whenever she patted his head in passing, as she always did, even after he had grown taller than she was, even after the gesture had irritated rather than pleased him.

Everything reminded her of him. The rattle of car keys. A laptop left

19

ENGLISH: For we must all appear before the judgment seat of Christ; that every one may receive the things done in his body, according to that he hath done, whether it be good or bad.

Bible

ARABIC: Then to Him shall you return, and He will then declare to you all that you have done.

Qur'an

Khaled made his way across the thick woods, zigzagging through the forest he had known since he was a child. He inhaled the smell of the pines and the dry soil and listened to the sound of twigs and leaves being crushed under his boots. The familiar mixture of smells and sounds soothed him. His stride fell from the frantic trot that had whisked him through his parents' backyard and into the park to a steady walking speed, and he could almost pretend he was on one of his many hikes, exploring the vast park in search of butterflies.

He knew the way because he had taken it before. Steadily he walked, cutting through the trees, through the meadow where he and his brother had once tried to access Ali Baba's cave, and through a second set of thicker trees, their branches intertwined, snagging his clothes. He was grateful he had put on the hoodie. With every step he felt his mind become clearer, falling into a serenity that led him by the hand, showing him the way. He did not stop to question his destination, accepting it the moment he became aware of it.

He reached the spot he had been looking for, the way there as familiar to him as if he had been treading it every day, even though it had been a full year since he was here last. He slowed down when he could hear the sounds of people talking, the hum of engines slowing to park, the clicking as car doors slammed shut. He found the same location he had stood in a year before, when he, one day after his brother had died, had walked that same route to stand transfixed, staring at a square patch of grass enclosed in yellow tape, the square's center stained a dark brown from which he could not avert his gaze, a black hole that he knew would pull his entire life in, crushing him. Today, the meadow by the park's Visitors' Center was lined with white folding chairs probably used most often for weddings. Scattered throughout the chairs, people sat in groups, huddled together and talking, while others exited cars parked nearby. In front of the chairs stood a podium, and, a few yards to the side, a young tree lay on the ground, its roots wrapped in a dark mesh. Beside it, a hole had been freshly dug in the soil, ready to receive it.

They were going to plant the tree in the wrong spot. The hole was a good ten feet from where Khaled had seen the patch of blood-soaked grass. Perhaps this was done on purpose—to get the tree closer to the center of the clearing, or to avoid the exact location. Ehsan would probably think the area contaminated now, suffused with a sort of evil that would allow nothing to grow in it. He looked at the spot again, expecting to find dry grass. The grass was fine, green and lush. He looked away.

Quietly, he lowered himself, sat on the ground, his legs bent in front of him. He knew no one could see him; the location he had chosen stood behind the clearing and high above it, the top of a hill that fell sharply ahead of where he sat until it joined the main road that ran through the park. To his right and a good twenty feet below him, he could see the parking lot overflowing with cars, the most recent arrivals parked in one long row on the grass.

He found his father's car before he could find his family. He looked through every row, recognizing people whose backs were turned to him: neighbors; high school teachers; Imam Fadel, the preacher at the mosque; kids from school. Garrett and his mother sat on the edge of one row of seats. Police officers stood at the corners, their cars parked by the road beside the news vans. A cameraman fiddled with his camera, already perched on its tripod. In the very last row, settled together and to one side, Bud Murphy sat with his entourage. Samir's car was there, but Khaled's family was nowhere to be seen. He began to think that he might have mistaken the car for a similar one when the entire crowd fell to a hush. All he had to do was follow the collective gaze.

His father had gotten out of the car and was standing by it, waiting for Nagla and Fatima to get out and close their doors. Khaled watched them, wondering why they had waited in the car for such a long time, feeling a pang of guilt that he immediately dismissed. They walked toward the heads now turned their way, against the outburst of whispers that exploded from the silence. Samir plowed through, his step slightly faster than usual, the increased speed recognizable only to those who knew him. Behind him, Nagla walked, clutching her purse, with Fatima trailing her. They crossed the line of trees that separated the parking lot from the clearing and then walked across the grass to the seats. There, Samir stood still, scanning the area. Nagla, catching up, stood by his side. The place was packed. Already people were getting up in the back, shifting in place. Samir leaned toward Nagla, whispered something, and then they walked to the back, Fatima following. Halfway there, Samir stopped, spotting a few empty seats in the middle of one of the rows. They made their way to them under everyone's scrutiny, his father bumping against people's knees.

Cynthia, Jim, Pat, and Reverend Fielding were standing by the podium that had been set in the middle of the clearing. They, too, watched the family as they arrived. As soon as Samir, Nagla, and Fatima were seated, Pat turned halfway to whisper something to the other three before heading away from them in brisk steps. Immediately Cynthia sprinted and held her back, shaking her head, her whispers urgent, emotional. The reverend, too, walked up to Pat and spoke to her, Jim following suit. She listened, openly staring at Samir and Nagla.

Khaled watched it all but remained in place. Already his serenity was gone, the anxiety of the previous week, of the previous year, returning in a gush. Now that he was sitting here, he started wondering why he had come. Why did he need to see this? Had he not managed to break free of his father's grasp and his brother's control? Why was he here, and not miles away, on a train headed to New York? He could still cut his way through the park and make it to the train station. No one would see him.

He got to his feet, still staring at the crowd, but did not walk away. People had fallen quiet, and Reverend Fielding was now alone at the podium, Jim, Cynthia, and Pat having taken their seats in the front row. The reverend cleared his throat, and people looked at him, waiting. In the back, the cameraman stepped up to his tripod, ready to film the speech. The reverend started talking.

"We are gathered here today not to mourn, but to remember, in love, a precious life tragically cut short."

Khaled looked around. The microphones carried the reverend's words his way, but he had to strain to hear them. He decided not to. He knew, now, why he had not wanted to be here, and why he felt no need to join his family in their self-imposed suffering and humiliation. He took a few steps back. Whatever was to happen had already been set in motion, and his presence here would change nothing. Already he felt a pang at the sight of people glancing toward his family, leaning closer to their neighbors and whispering, the neighbors nodding in approval. He knew what people were thinking, their judgmental stares needing no verbal expression. Khaled had hoped that, given time, Hosaam's crime would have been accepted as the isolated act of violence that it was, a reflection of nothing other than his own madness. Now his entire family would be labeled deranged.

Still he could not tear himself away. He stared at his father's bald spot, shining in the midday sun, at his mother, sitting with her head bent, at Fatima's own head resting on her mother's shoulder. In the front row, Jim and Cynthia sat motionless. Khaled imagined Cynthia holding Jim's hand, or maybe his and her sister's. Pat sat on her other side. His parents sat with a gap between them, a space whose vastness Khaled now saw clearer than ever. He stared at Samir, trying to evoke Ehsan's words of understanding and to find excuses for his father, but he could not. Question after question forced itself into his head, and with each one his anger with his father grew sharper: Why was he always so stubborn? Why did he think he had the right to tell everyone what to do? Why did he think coming to the memorial was the best way to handle this situation? Why couldn't he listen to Nagla when she told him, repeatedly, that he would only pile more humiliation on his family? Khaled had heard them arguing, but of course his father never listened to anyone. Why was he so disrespectful of his wife and his children?

What was he doing?

Khaled took a few steps forward, held on to one of the trees. His father had just pulled something out of his pocket and was looking down, staring at it. Samir's neighbor, an elderly woman who had remained very still, was also looking down at the object in his hands. Khaled took a few steps to the left, trying to get a better view. A piece of paper. Samir was looking at a piece of paper, yellow notepad paper, just like the ones his father kept in his office.

Khaled sank to his knees. Of course: his father intended to give a speech. How had he forgotten? Wasn't this part of the reason Samir had wanted to attend the memorial in the first place? Perhaps it was the main reason; perhaps dragging his family along was not a show of support for the Bradstreets but for him as he walked up and preached to the crowd. Khaled tried to calm down and clear his head, think. He looked at the people around his family, at the townspeople among whom he had grown up. How many were there—a hundred? Two? Three? He could not tell. How would they react to his father's speech? Would they even let him speak?

At the podium, Cynthia had taken the reverend's spot. Her voice was so low it hardly reached the audience, in spite of the microphones. Khaled strained to listen. She was describing Natalie, remembering her, telling stories. Her words reminded him of Ehsan's stories of his brother, of her husband. He mistrusted stories of the dead, disliked their tendency for revisionism. "Natalie's capacity for love and compassion was limitless. When I think of her now, I feel God created her solely as a vehicle to transmit his compassion to all she touched." His father, his speech in his lap, was doubtless getting ready to tell stories of how Hosaam was, before, or of how he hoped he was going to turn out, stories of sports achievements, of medical school aspirations.

Khaled looked around, tried to imagine how this crowd would react to his father's attempt at describing Hosaam, to any mention of Hosaam, and felt his head grow dizzy, his stomach turn. Now he could see people he had not noticed before: the high school football coach who had cornered him one day in an empty hallway, lifting him by his collar and hissing that he would kill him with his bare hands if he ever came near any of the town's girls; the elderly police officer whom he had seen crying in the patrol car after he had walked out of the Bradstreets' house that day; two of the men who had helped Jim carry Natalie's casket—he had seen pictures—and who now sat with their own daughters, Natalie's friends and playmates since childhood. As Cynthia spoke, people were dabbing at their eyes, the sight of the bereaved mother opening wounds that the passing of one year had not healed. These were his townspeople, his teachers, his neighbors—but his brother had caused them so much pain. His father was determined to show this town that his family still belonged—what he failed to see was that, as far as the townspeople were concerned, they were a cancer that brought nothing but suffering. All his father's words would do was remind people of how cancers should be dealt with.

Khaled looked around. His position, high above, was isolated, with no way down to reach his family. On his right-hand side the hill grew higher and then fell sharply. On the left the decline was more gradual, the hill sloping until it finally joined the road a couple of hundred feet ahead. Khaled looked back down and saw that Cynthia was done speaking; she and Jim were now heading toward the tree, where the town's mayor was waiting to help them lift it. Khaled watched his father, saw him straighten up and tuck the paper in his breast pocket. Already Jim was lifting the tree by its trunk. The cameraman had moved closer, camera poised on his shoulder, set to film the tree planting.

"Excuse me," Samir yelled, lifting one hand in the air. Around him, people shushed, but he, persistent, stood up, his hand still lifted. Nagla tugged at his jacket. He ignored her. "Excuse me," he yelled again, louder this time.

"Sit down!" someone yelled. Samir did not. The cameraman turned around, pointed his camera at Samir, who was making his way out of the row of seats. Around him, people hushed, hissed, tugged at him, tried to hold him back—but he continued. Behind him, Nagla followed, trying to grab hold of him. He ignored her still.

Khaled took one more frantic look around him. He would have to take the long route. Planted in place, he struggled to tear himself away—he did not dare miss what was going to happen next. But he would have to follow the long slope down. He would have to tear himself away from his family if he wanted to join them.

He started running. He strained to listen to the escalating commotion, but could hear nothing above his own breathing and the sound of twigs breaking under his feet and brushing against his face and arms. He ran faster. He thought he heard his father's voice. The hill sloped down and down. Still the end of his road was too far away, and, once he made it there, he would have to run all the way back. He ran, scanning the side of the hill. Midway to the end, the side slope seemed gentler. He could probably walk down there. He veered to the right too quickly, stumbled over his own feet, and fell.

He tumbled down. Frantically, he tried to grab at something. His hand found a tree root, clutched it. The root skinned his palm, and he let go in pain. He rolled down the rest of the hill, came to a stop at its foot. He jumped up, ran limping to the clearing, brushing thorns and dirt from his face, his hands. He could hardly breathe and became suddenly aware of the heat now that he was out of the shade. He pulled his hoodie over his head as he ran, the twigs that stuck to it scratching his skin.

By the time he reached the clearing no one was seated anymore. People were stretching their necks, looking at the commotion in the front. In the back row, Bud was standing on top of one of the chairs, laughing, and, his phone in hand, capturing the commotion on film. He would post it online so that everyone could bask in Samir's humiliation, in Khaled's. Khaled ran alongside the edge of the crowd. He found Garrett, grabbed him by the shoulder. Garrett turned around.

"Hey, where have you—Jesus Christ, what happened to your face?" Garrett asked.

"Get Bud's phone," Khaled said, pointing to the back. Garrett turned, saw Bud, and nodded, heading his way.

Khaled ran to the front. The closer he got, the tighter the throng of people seemed to be around a center that he knew held his family. Getting nearer, Khaled could hear his father's voice.

"I just want to say a few words!" Samir pleaded.

"*Baba*, wait," Khaled yelled, pulling at people's arms, trying to reach his father. Craning his neck, Khaled glimpsed Imam Fadel, who seemed to be struggling to lead Samir away from the crowd. Khaled searched for his family and saw Fatima's braid ahead, heard his mother's words, in Arabic, louder and clearer the closer he got to her.

"*Kefaya ya Samir!*" Nagla yelled. "You're making a fool of yourself."

"Let me be, Nagla! I just want to talk."

"No one wants to listen to you!" she yelled again.

"*Baba*, please," Fatima's voice came. Khaled, hearing his sister, plunged into the middle of the crowd.

"Get your stupid father out of here," someone shouted at him on his way.

"I'm trying. I'm trying," he said.

He had almost made it to his father when Samir, breaking free of the imam's grasp, made a dash toward the podium. "*Baba!*" Khaled hollered, but he could no longer reach his father. He couldn't even see him, nor could he see his mother or Fatima. Quickly, Khaled jumped on one of the seats and then, hopping from one seat to the next, made it to the center of a row only a few feet from the podium. His father had reached it, was holding his speech in his hand, tapping on the microphone, bending down to look for its power button. "I just have a few words to say! Is this so wrong? Can't you listen to me say only a few words?" A couple of feet away, Reverend Fielding was holding Jim back, words sputtering from his mouth. Around Samir, everyone gathered: Nagla still yelling at him in Arabic, "You're making a scene!" Fatima still pleading. Imam Fadel had made it there, as well, and was trying to pull Samir away while everyone else around him talked, some trying to restore order, some shouting at Samir, others gathering around Jim. In the back, still holding the young tree, Cynthia was talking to Pat, sobbing as she spoke. The calm that had presided a few minutes ago had imploded, releasing a constant hum of noise interrupted by occasional shrieks from Samir and Cynthia, who stood on opposite sides of the crowd, each surrounded by a group of people, the space between them empty, a no-man's-land promising imminent conflict.

Khaled looked around. The cameraman, probably taking his cue from Khaled, was up on a chair as well, filming the whole thing. Khaled, desperate, looked at his father: his face sweaty, his shirt out of his pants, his tie crooked. The speech he held in his hand was crumpled now, but he still held on to it, still tried to yell louder than anyone else, still tried to reach for the microphone. "If you would just let me speak! Only a few words!"

"*Baba,* enough!" Fatima shrieked, her voice much louder than usual yet hardly loud enough to break through the noise erupting around her.

Khaled stared at his sister. He had to do something. *"Baba!"* he shouted, trying to get his father's attention. *"Baba!"* Nothing.

Khaled jumped two rows to the front, made it as close as he could to the podium. He tried to think, looked down, and saw he still had his hoodie in one hand. Holding it by the sleeve, he lifted his arm and started swinging the hoodie in circles. A few people noticed him and watched, waiting. His father, struggling with those closest to him, was not looking. The cameraman still did not see him.

"Hey!" Khaled yelled. "Hey!"

The cameraman turned around. Now his lens was pointed at Khaled. Khaled kept turning the hoodie in the air, the circular, rhythmic motion reminding him of the whirling dervishes he had once seen in a street festival in Egypt. In the blazing heat, the hoodie provided a gentle breeze that might have cooled him down, had the motion not made him sweat even more. He looked around, saw he had gotten everyone's attention, even Cynthia and Jim's, even Fatima and his mother's, and, yes, even Samir's. Slowly, Khaled let his arm come to a stop, brought the hoodie down.

He wanted to say something, felt everyone was expecting him to, but did not know what to say. Even if he had known, he was too out of breath to speak.

So he waited, like everyone else.

They all waited for something major to happen. Khaled remembered Ehsan's assertion that God would take care of things, so he waited for some sign from God saying that all would change, that all would be better, perhaps. He looked to the sky, up between the trees whose branches intertwined on top of the podium, expecting to see something. Maybe rays shining through the branches and onto the podium. Maybe thousands and thousands of monarch butterflies, suddenly lifting off from their habitats in the middle of the trees, jubilant in their successful migration back from the south. For a moment, looking up, he thought he saw something moving, and he believed that this might happen still, that God might make it happen, that He might intervene to stop this humiliation, to send him a message, a sign, a flock of butterflies summoned just for him, like the single cloud that gave Muhammad shade or the crow that gave Solomon news of the Queen of Sheba. The sea splitting to let Moses and his people pass. The ground spouting water under Ismail's heel. Nature, controlled by God, just to serve him.

Ehsan would deem this possible. Ehsan would see it happening. Ehsan might even have the power to make this happen.

Then again, she might not.

Looking up, Khaled saw nothing but the blinding sun shining through the moving branches. Looking around, he saw faces watching his. He had caught their attention, yes, but he could do nothing else, because he controlled nothing. He did not control the butterflies, nor did he control the movement of the wind to make it shake the branches violently enough to send every nesting bird flying. He could not even make his own father stop humiliating himself, just as his father had been incapable of making Hosaam turn into the son he had imagined him to be. He knew perfectly well that there was absolutely nothing he could do, but somehow all those around him still looked at him, still expected him to have the answer to it all, just because he had stood on a chair and waved a hoodie around. Even Cynthia had stopped crying and was looking at him. Even his own parents stared, as well as the imam and the reverend. He looked behind him. Garrett was standing next to Bud, who still held his phone up. They were both watching him. Khaled, looking first at Bud's phone, then at the newsman's camera, realized he was finally in control—everyone was waiting for him to act.

But he did not know what to do.

And it struck him, standing there on the chair, cameras and eyes turned toward him, that this was not the defining moment of his life, that, for better or worse, that moment had happened exactly a year ago, that Hosaam had controlled it, and that all he could do from then on was react. Which, in a way, made him just like his grandmother, whose prayers were calculated to regain control by beseeching the All-Powerful to act on her behalf and shield her from whatever life threw her way.

But life was trying to snuff him out of existence. A year ago, his brother had pulled a trigger and unleashed a hurricane that had been pummeling Khaled ever since, snatching him off his feet and tossing him in the air, twirling and twisting him about, watching him grope for an elusive ground.

He would probably remain suspended in midair for the rest of his life.

There was nothing he could do. A sudden exhaustion overcame him, an urge to surrender to the winds.

Standing there, a couple of hundred pairs of eyes fixated on him, Khaled understood why Ehsan prayed. Why she hoped for control yet accepted having none. Why she embraced the private peace that surrender evoked.

Surrender, he told himself.

Surrender.

Or—he paused, looking around him, forcing himself to meet people's eyes—learn to ride the winds. Learn to fly.

He looked for Fatima and his eyes found hers. She nodded once, then pushed her way to her father and spoke to him, in Arabic, so quickly and with such a heavy accent that even Khaled could not understand her. But Samir did. Khaled could see it from the way his father's face blanched, the way his mouth gaped. Khaled jumped off the seat, made his way through the crowd, which had fallen silent and, seeing him approach, had cleared a path for him. He reached his father at the same moment Jim did.

The two men stood staring at each other, their pleading looks eerily similar.

"I just—" Samir started. "I just—"

"I know, Samir. I know what you're trying to do. But now is not the time." Jim's voice was shaking, not with anger so much as with an emotion that Khaled could only recognize as exhaustion.

"I wanted—"

"Not now, Samir. Please." Jim looked at Khaled, who walked up and held his father by the arm.

"Let's go, *Baba*."

"But—"

"*Men fadlak, Baba*," Fatima pleaded, pulling at her father's other arm. "Please."

Khaled and Fatima, each on one side of Samir, pulled him away. He resisted at first, but then Khaled's eyes met his, and Samir's look turned into one of wonder that made Khaled feel as if his father had not recognized him until just now. Khaled wished he could tell his father what he had only now realized: that they were all trying to undo something that Hosaam did, hoping that, by their hands or by God's, fate would change course and all would be well again. But they were damned no matter what they did, not by God, but by a nineteen-year-old boy who had lost the will to live, and, perhaps, by their own failure to see it coming, to prevent disaster rather than scramble in a futile attempt to change the past.

First surrender. And then learn to fly.

Slowly, Khaled, Fatima, and Samir made their way out of the crowd, passing by the tree that still lay on its side, Cynthia standing by it, her face buried in one hand. Nagla, following her family, paused, and, for a moment, Khaled thought she was going to walk up to Cynthia—but she did not. Instead, Nagla overtook her family, headed toward the car.

Khaled did not turn around to see if people were watching them, nor did he remember to check if the cameraman was still shooting footage of his family. He aimed for the car, kept his eyes on it, and ignored the aches he started to feel shooting up in various parts of his body, from his calf to his shoulder, from his right palm to his temples. Behind him, he heard Bud yell something about his phone, heard Garrett's "It was an accident, I'm sorry!" and grinned, for the first time today.

A few feet from his father's car, he stopped, allowing Imam Fadel to take his place. Slowly, the imam and Fatima led Samir to the car, and Khaled watched as they sat him down in the passenger seat. There Samir stayed, both legs out of the car, shoulders and head down. The imam knelt by his side, talking to Samir, leaning close to his ear as he spoke, reminding Khaled of how Ehsan used to recite the Qur'an in his ear whenever he woke up crying in the middle of the night, softly humming the verses to drive away nightmares, her breath brushing against his temples.

Khaled saw his father's face through the glass of the opened passenger door. Samir had stopped talking, had stopped wiping his sweat, letting it now run down his cheeks and forehead. His face seemed older, ashen, and Khaled noted for the first time how his father, when looking up, seemed to have a sagging double chin, and how the corners of his mouth twisted down, as if he were about to cry. As the imam spoke, Fatima, who had been standing behind him, turned toward Khaled. He nodded. She, walking around the car, whispered something to her mother, who looked at Khaled and, grabbing her purse, walked up to him, followed by Fatima.

"What did you do to your face?" Nagla said, reaching out to touch Khaled's cheek. Her hand was shaking.

"Nothing, Mama." Khaled pulled away from her. Nagla opened her purse, rummaged through it, and pulled out a disinfectant wipe.

"Here," she said. "Let me clean this up."

"I'll do it, Mama," Fatima said, grabbing the wipe from her mother's hand. "You go back and take care of *Baba*, will you?"

Nagla glanced at her husband, then, sighing, back at Khaled.

"I'm fine, Mama. Just go."

Khaled and Fatima watched her walk away before Fatima took the wipe to her brother's face.

"Ouch! Just give this to me," Khaled said.

"What did you do, walk into a tree?" Fatima asked as she watched him try to clean his face. She had been crying, and her lower lip was still trembling. She bit it.

"It seemed like the better option," Khaled said, nodding toward the crowd behind them. Fatima chuckled. Her eyes and nose were red.

They made their way to the car together, Fatima walking up to her mother, who sat in the driver's seat. Imam Fadel was still talking to Samir, who took occasional quick glances toward his son and daughter.

Khaled paused a few yards from the car, looked up at the trees. One tree close by had a trunk that must have been a good five feet wide. Khaled traced the branches with his eyes, from top to bottom, all the way to the roots and then up again. The tree was magnificent, a fortress immune to wind, the ideal harbor of a small miracle.

It would have been perfect if those flocks of butterflies had appeared, if God had intervened to straighten up a mess that He had not started. Ehsan would never give up on this kind of miracle. She would feel entitled to it, would insist that wanting God's help should guarantee its arrival. But, Khaled thought, maybe Brittany was right; maybe miracles did not happen, at least not anymore. Ehsan would be infuriated by such an assumption; she would consider it blasphemous.

Then again, perhaps they were both wrong.

Perhaps the miracle lay in Khaled's gaze up, in the anticipation of butterflies, in the faith that he was not alone. In his willingness to surrender to crushing winds, and in the hope that such surrender would teach him how to fly.

"Islam," Ehsan had repeatedly assured him, "shares the root of the word *surrender*." He would have to write this down. And then, perhaps, he would talk to Ehsan about miracles that did not involve divine intervention.

In the car, he leaned his head back, shut out the engine's hum as his mother maneuvered her way out of the parking lot. Khaled avoided looking at his father, who sat with his head against the door, motionless. Eyes closed, Khaled put his hand out and found Fatima's, squeezed it, and listened only long enough to make sure she had stopped crying.

EPILOGUE

The house had been empty for six months. Khaled pulled onto the driveway and, stepping out of his car, looked around. The street seemed deserted, engulfed in a mid-morning calm that only the absence of humans can invoke. Still, someone might have been peering from behind a curtain. He hurried to the front door, only once glancing toward the Bradstreets' house. He saw no one.

He turned the key and walked in, surprised at himself for having expected the door to squeak, for having half anticipated layer upon layer of dust and flocks of bugs buzzing around the rooms. But the house was spotless, a sweet and slightly musty smell lingering in the air. Someone had been here, of course. Fatima, perhaps. Or Aunt Ameena. He pinched the edge of one of the sheets his mother had draped over the furniture, bent down, and sniffed, recognizing, with an ache, his mother's favorite laundry softener. On the dining room table stood a wicker basket filled with mail. Aunt Ameena.

He would not stay long. On the phone, his mother had dictated a short list of things he needed to get her *men elbeit*: a box of jewelry in her nightstand drawer; a thick envelope tucked on a shelf in her closet. Sprinting up two steps at a time, Khaled remembered another word that Ehsan had read to him from one of his Sunday school books: *al-manzel*. Was there a distinction between *elbeit* and *al-manzel*? Did one mean "home" and the other "house"? To him, the words were interchangeable, the second more formal than the first but neither intimate.

For the previous six months, his parents' home had been the small apartment in Al-Ibrahimiyya, where his mother had grown up and where Ehsan had lived. This had been their longest "vacation" to date— his parents still called their trips to Egypt vacations, even after Samir had retired and their stays in Egypt grew so long that Khaled and Fatima started wondering why their parents bothered to keep the house in Summerset, why they bothered to come back from each trip to Egypt and pretend they intended to stay. Yet neither Khaled nor his sister dared suggest that their parents move back to Egypt for good. The implications were thorny: that their kids no longer needed them; that they had never truly belonged here anyway.

On his way out of his parents' room he stopped in his own, looking around. Nothing had changed in the years since he had left. Seven years? Six? He had to pause and calculate. Had he stopped by on any other day, he might have found something here he still wanted: the old book on lepidoptera on the shelf, maybe, or the stack of CDs he had left behind when he went to college. Today, though, he had only Ehsan on his mind. Walking up to his desk, he opened the bottom drawer and pulled out an old composition notebook. The black-and-white marbled cover had faded to a sepia tone, and the pages had curled up in one corner. He laid his mother's jewelry box and the envelope down on the desk and leafed through the notebook. Ehsan had picked it up for him during one of her grocery-store trips. He must have been eleven or twelve; he had just started middle school, and she, arriving from Egypt after a two-year absence, had declared his Arabic deplorable. "You cannot learn Arabic unless you write it down," she had said, walking into his bedroom and placing the notebook on his desk. Each day, she would teach him something new, a word, a proverb, or an expression, and ask him to write it down in the notebook followed by its English translation. *Ahlak,* one entry said. *Your people,* his father had translated for him. *Your family.*

He headed toward the city in the relative calm of midday traffic. He had not planned on driving to New Jersey on the same day he was to fly out of JFK, but his mother had told him of the things she needed only the night before, her request preceded by apologies and affirmations that the things were "not that important, really." He suspected she had waited so long because she had not believed he would really do it.

"Why do you want to come?" his father had asked him for the tenth time only two days earlier. "It's useless, really. Just a waste of your time and money."

"Nice to know you miss me, too," Khaled said.

"You know that's not what I mean. Your mother and I can come over and visit once you settle down. We could be there next month, if you want us to."

"I still want to come, *Baba*."

"For what? A month ago, two months ago, I might have understood. But now—it's seriously of no use. Besides, it's not really safe here, right now."

"It's safe enough for you and Mama to be there."

"That's different. We can blend in much better than you can."

Khaled listened as he looked out the tenth-story window of the apartment he was about to vacate. Arguing with his father over the necessity of a trip to Egypt at this time was useless, as all arguments with Samir always were. He understood what his father was referring to, of course: that he had missed everything already—Ehsan's illness, her stroke, the months she spent in bed. For the entire spring term he had been convinced that she would wait for him. Working on his thesis, preparing for his exams, waiting to hear from the various PhD programs he had applied to, he had been certain that Ehsan would manage to hang on just long enough for him to finish his last term of his master's program. He had even booked the ticket months in advance, a direct flight from JFK leaving only five days after the term ended.

Heading into the Holland Tunnel, Khaled glanced at the notebook his grandmother had given him all those years ago. From the moment he knew he would be stopping by the house, he had intended to retrieve it. He imagined Ehsan would have wanted him to, though he was less certain she would approve of his plans for the notebook. He had lain in bed the night before thinking this through, contemplating especially why he would not give it to Fatima, who, he had to admit, would have probably liked to have it. But Ehsan had never given her a similar notebook, and passing it on to her might have ended up being a tactless reminder of Ehsan's favoritism. Besides, he did not want to stop by Fatima's place again, not after he had spent the entire preceding afternoon reassuring her that she did not need to fly to Egypt, even as he tried to explain why he did. He had finally managed to convince her that the trip came at an appropriate time for him but not for her; leaving now would mean she would have to abandon the summer internship she had finally secured. She needed the research experience. With any luck, she might even cowrite a paper or two, which would help her tremendously once she finished medical school and started looking for residencies. He had managed to spend two hours with her and not once say what was truly on his mind: that this trip was something between him and Ehsan, a final chapter in a story they both started a long time ago and that he now needed to see to its conclusion. He could not risk seeing Fatima again, because he was certain that, this time, his discretion would fail him, and he did not want to hurt her feelings.

Driving out of the tunnel, he glanced at the dashboard and saw that it was barely past midday, which meant he had a good six hours until his plane left. Even in New York City's traffic this should give him enough time for a detour. He picked up his cell phone and dialed Brittany.

"Hey, Dr. Al-Menshawy," Brittany said.

He laughed. "Not until five more years. If I stopped by, would you be able to dash out for a moment? I have something to give you."

In the city, he pulled up at a fire hydrant and texted her. He watched her walk out of the office building and down the block to where he was parked, and he smiled. He missed the purple streak in her hair, still could not get used to the sight of Brittany in a pencil skirt and a silk top. At least she had kept the multiple earrings on one ear, and her nails were painted a matte black.

"Haven't left yet?" she asked, leaning in through the passenger window.

"I'm on my way to the airport." He reached out and handed her the notebook.

"What's this?" She held it in her hand, her eyes glistening. He smiled.

"Something I want you to keep for me till I come back." Then, after a pause, "If you have the time, you can glance through it. If you want to, that is."

She smiled, tucking the notebook under her arm. "Will you stop by again before you head to California?"

He nodded. "I still have a couple of boxes lying around in my apartment, and I have till the end of the month."

She leaned through the window and all the way across the passenger seat, somehow managing to hug him across the distance. "I'll miss you."

He hugged her back, careful not to wrinkle her shirt, inhaling the scent of jasmine and dew-covered leaves that hung on her hair.

Even before liftoff, he could feel the nostalgia engulf him. Across the aisle sat a young woman, a boy next to her, a baby in her lap. She was cooing to the baby, who was already getting restless, and he could see her lift the baby and, putting her lips to his ear, murmur words that he did not need to hear to know were verses from the Qur'an. He imagined that was exactly what his mother had done to him on all those trips they took to Egypt when he was young. A few rows ahead, he could see a heavyset woman, dressed in black, her white head cover draping across her shoulder, her slow movements betraying her age.

Ehsan had not managed to pull off the miracle after all. She almost did; she had lingered until two weeks earlier, and had finally died only a few days before the spring term ended. He was shocked when his father told him; so deeply had he believed she would wait for him that her death, expected by everyone, totally blindsided him. Sitting in the airplane, the hum of the engines growing to a deafening pitch, he contemplated again how foolish it was to think she would be able to control the time of her own death. For the previous days he had been furious at himself for entertaining such a thought—had he learned nothing? For years now he had known better than to expect miracles; yet, when it came to his grandmother, his scientific mind-set seemed to be clouded by memories of incense and protective incantations. He had always thought of her on her own terms, as if she existed in a parallel universe where the rules she believed in worked for her, even if not for those around her. In such a world, the little details as well as the feelings people harbored for one another *could* change destinies: his status as her favorite; his promise to her that he would be back to see her as soon as he could; the ticket that he had purchased using her money, the two thousand dollars she had sent him (God knows where she got that much money from) when he got his BA two years earlier, crisp hundred-dollar bills tied up in a sealed envelope. The money he had lied to her about, assuring her he had spent it toward his graduate school tuition. If Ehsan had played by her own rules, she would have waited to see him. She would have died as he held her hand.

For the hundredth time in a week he reminded himself that no one could play by such rules, that Ehsan might have believed whatever she wanted to believe, but that some things were simply out of humans' control. But then, as the plane climbed higher, it occurred to him that perhaps she had, in fact, managed to do things her way after all. She had died on the dawn of a Friday, at the time when angels come down to earth and bless those who are awake early in devotion to God. She had been buried that same day, in accordance with Islamic tradition; a swift interring that was the best preservation of the dignity of the dead. And, as his mother had described, her voice cracking over the phone, Ehsan had been ready for burial precisely in time for the Friday prayer, and her funeral service was performed not only by her family and friends, but by thousands and thousands of people who had flocked to the mosque for the weekly midday prayer and, finding a funeral service in progress, had rushed to perform the prayer that begged for mercy for those who have died and those who will eventually join them. Khaled, listening to his mother describe the scene, saw the prayer rugs spread in rows out on the streets and heard the whispers of attendees wondering who was this woman, lucky enough to die on the holy day and have that many people pray for her, a sure sign of her virtue. This, he was certain, would have pleased Ehsan immensely.

But perhaps he was wrong again. Perhaps the success of Ehsan's rules of life lay not in the time and manner of her death, but in the fact that he, sitting in an airplane high above the Atlantic, understood perfectly well what those rules entailed and *still* felt an insurmountable urge to go back to a country he could hardly remember, a country he felt he had never truly known. Samir was partially right, of course: flying back to Egypt two weeks after the funeral was futile, and traveling there during the Arab Spring was probably foolish, especially for a quasi-Egyptian who spoke Arabic with an American accent.

Yet to Ehsan, who believed that the dead boasted of their visitors, such a journey would have made perfect sense. And he *would* go visit her grave. He would sit by it and talk to her, just as he used to see her do by the grave of his grandfather. He imagined himself sitting in the cemetery and talking to a tombstone in broken Arabic, and he chuckled. But he *would* do it. And he could almost hear her, boasting, trying not to sound too prideful, exclaiming, "See? My grandson flew all the way here from America to visit me. He can barely speak two Arabic words, the poor boy (though Allah be my witness, I did try to teach him), but he still knows enough to come here and sit by my grave, to try and recite the Qur'an with his heavy American accent. I taught him well, didn't I?" And Khaled would tell Ehsan, and whoever else listened, that he still kept some of her incense tucked in one of his drawers, that he still gravitated toward the trays of stuffed grape leaves in Mediterranean restaurants, that he still thought of her often, and that, when he did, he saw her cooking. He saw himself walking into his parents' house to the smell of eggplant *musakkah* and cold beef with gravy, of white buttered rice and *molokheyya* spiced with garlic and coriander, of hot, minted tea and *mehallabeyya* for dessert. And he still imagined she walked around at night, after everyone was asleep, twirling her incense holder, letting the fragrant smoke fill the air, reminding him that he was not alone.

ACKNOWLEDGMENTS

I owe my entire professional existence to Jane Hill, my mentor and friend, who gave me the confidence to call myself a writer and the means to make it all happen. She believed in me long before I believed in myself, and for that she has my eternal gratitude and love.

Sincere thanks and an abundance of hugs go to the incredibly generous Marie Manilla, who led me by the hand through the first drafts of this novel and who continues to guide me in everything that has to do with the writing life.

I still smile with joy whenever I remember that Lynn Nesbit is my agent, a fact that proves I am one of the luckiest people alive and that certainly tips the scale toward the probability of miracles actually happening.

Ann Beattie, the instigator of miracles, has my sincere thanks for her unmatched kindness.

I am forever indebted to Allison Lorentzen, my editor, for believing in this novel and for her guidance and ardent support.

Many thanks go to John Van Kirk both for his writing advice and for pointing out the fascinating ending of *The Arabian Nights.*

Thank you, Zohreh T. Sullivan, for encouragement when I needed it most.

My friends and former professors: Michael Householder, Whitney Douglas, and Kelli Prejean, and, of course, my amazing fellow teaching assistants for those two crazy years: Anna Rollins, Cat Staley, David

Robinson, John Chirico, and Sarah Krause—thank you all for making me feel like I belong.

I am humbled by the support of the following incredibly gifted poets and writers: Bob Hill, Mary Moore, Carrie Oeding, Rachael Peckham, Eric Smith, and Art Stringer.

Thank you, Crystal Canterbury, for always being there for me and my kids and for having a pure, pure heart.

My Egyptian friends, too many to list: German school alumni, architects, musicians—thank you all for the cheering that spans the globe and for the gift of lasting friendship.

Two of my childhood English teachers hold a special place in my heart: Hoda Hamdy for visiting me when I was sick and explaining the week's lessons to me while I lay on the sofa in my parents' living room, and Amal El-Nayal for years of guidance and inspiration.

Finally, my love and gratitude go to:

My family in the United States: my husband for decades of love, for his unflinching support, and for the gift of freedom; my kids for being who they are.

And my family in Egypt: my father for his unconditional love and constant encouragement, my sister for her prayers, and my mother—for placing that first book in my hands, for being the first to take my writing seriously, and for a lifetime of giving. *Habibti* Mama: I miss you with every single breath.

A PENGUIN READERS GUIDE TO

IN THE LANGUAGE
OF MIRACLES

Rajia Hassib

An Introduction to
In the Language of Miracles

Samir and Nagla Al-Menshawy have settled in the sleepy suburb
of Summerset, New Jersey, to raise a family, leaving behind their
native Egypt for their own version of the American dream. At
first, it all seems to be going smoothly. The couple bonds with the
Bradstreets next door, and Samir's medical practice is bustling. The
Al-Menshawys' three children make friends in the community,
assimilating into American life. In high school, their oldest son,
Hosaam, even starts dating his lifelong friend Natalie Bradstreet.

Then the unthinkable happens—Hosaam and Natalie are killed—
and everything shatters. Patients abandon Samir's practice, kids
bully his children Fatima and Khaled, and their house is vandalized

repeatedly. Where they once saw the promise of their affluent life, they now see closed doors and shaming stares. Worst of all, no one in the family can come to terms with their inexplicable loss.

A year has passed. Samir refuses to consider moving, and only wants to clear his family's name to make a safer life for his surviving children. Nagla blames herself for not recognizing the signs of Hosaam's descent into depression, and not doing more to save him or Natalie. Khaled, who always resented his domineering brother, is still angry for the shadow Hosaam has cast over his life and seeks refuge in New York City with a like-minded friend. Fatima grows increasingly devout, also spending more time outside the home. If the family once fit in to suburban New Jersey life, they are now more alienated than ever. Nagla's mother, Ehsan, comes from Egypt to help, but her traditional ways only seem to spark more tension and highlight just how divided the household has become.

Everything comes to a head when the Bradstreets announce that they're holding a memorial service for their daughter. The Al-Menshawys must decide whether it's a chance for public redemption or a brutal reminder of what cannot be undone.

Rajia Hassib's stunning debut novel follows the Al-Manshawys in the five days leading up to the service. A classic immigrant story with a decidedly contemporary plot, *In the Language of Miracles* explores the Arab-American experience and what it means to belong in a distrusting world. In crystalline prose, Hassib captures the intricate family dynamics at play—secrets, lies, unfulfilled hopes, and crushing regrets—as her eminently likable characters struggle to move beyond tragedy.

ABOUT THE AUTHOR

Rajia Hassib was born in Egypt and moved to the United States when she was twenty-three. She holds an MA in creative writing from Marshall University, and her writing has appeared in *The New Yorker* online, *Upstreet*, *Steam Ticket*, and *Border Crossing* magazines. She lives in West Virginia.

A CONVERSATION WITH RAJIA HASSIB

What brought you to this story of a family torn apart by a violent act?

My mind often seeks symbols in order to deal with that which troubles it most, and the family torn apart by violence seemed like a perfect microcosm for the experience of Muslim Arab Americans post-9/11. Because I came to the United States shortly before 9/11, I witnessed the painful backlash that many Muslims suffered from after this heinous terrorist attack, and I became deeply interested in how this backlash has often caused Arab Americans and Muslims to contemplate their own role in this event. I know that while most felt victimized by the hostility aimed at them in retaliation for something they neither caused nor approved of, many others started questioning if there was anything we, the peaceful Muslims, could have done to prevent such an outcome or should now do to help stop the spread of extremism. That kind of self-examination sparked my interest in this story depicting a family that is forced to deal with tragedy in a similarly public way.

The experience of coming to America from Egypt echoes through the ways the different family members cope with loss. As the author, what did you hope to capture in these varying perspectives? What did you most want to get right?

I'm always most concerned with authenticity: I wanted to make sure I presented the influence of immigration on the different family members in an honest way, even if this did not reflect the ideal that first-generation immigrants like me often hope for. This particularly applied to the younger generation's relationship both to its old culture and to the parents and grandparents who still live by the rules of that culture. While most parents will attest to the wonder of seeing their children grow into their own distinctive selves, the experience of immigrants magnifies this situation. In addition to developing their own personalities, the children of immigrants also diverge from their parents in cultural and linguistic aspects that often widen the gap between the generations. At a time of tragedy or distress such as the time the novel presents, these differences will ultimately influence how the younger and older generations cope, and those varying coping mechanisms will, in turn, put further strain on their relationships. I wanted to make sure I got that right, because any attempt at softening such differences would have made the characters seem contrived and unrealistic and would have simplified their struggles.

This book is very much situated in a post-9/11 world. How might the story have been different if it was set before 2001?

Unfortunately, the post-9/11 world is one where Islam is often associated with violence. Pre-9/11, a story such as this one would have been tragic, of course, but I doubt people would have jumped to the conclusion that Hosaam's actions were a predictable result of his ethnicity or religion. Today, any such violence committed by a Muslim is almost always blamed on the perpetrator's religion. While extremists certainly try to present their violence as religiously justified, I have always believed that people who deliberately kill other people do not become violent because of their religion; they are inherently violent and just use their religion (or politics, or ideology) to justify their crimes. It therefore pains me to see how often people fall back on stereotyping when discussing violent acts. How many times have we witnessed news anchors, analysts, or even people we know and love claim that a certain act of violence was predictable because of the perpetrator's race, ethnicity, skin color, or religion? On some level, I understand the drive to do so—it makes people feel better because it separates them from the violent person by underscoring his position as an "other" who belongs to a "different" group of people. In the post-9/11 world, Muslims are the ones seen as most "different" and, in particular, violent. We are now similar to the post-WWII Germans or the Cold War–era Russians—the villains in every action movie, the ones everyone is afraid of. This position, and the assumption of guilt that comes with it, makes the trials of the Al-Menshawys harder than they would have been had they belonged to a different race and religion—or had the novel been set before 9/11.

Not much attention is overtly paid to Hosaam's mental health—instead, his family seems to blame other factors for what's happened. Can you talk about your decision to leave it out of the discussion?

I made a conscious, deliberate decision to spend as little time as possible focusing on Hosaam's mental health, motivations, or on the troubles that led to his act of violence. I had two reasons for doing so. The first had to do with my sense of who the protagonists of this story truly were. Just as Khaled always resented Hosaam's control over his life, I, too, didn't want Hosaam to appropriate a story that belonged to his family. I felt—a bit harshly, perhaps—that he had escaped the consequences of killing Natalie and had left his family to suffer the backlash of his crime, and I thought that, in doing so, he had relinquished his right to be the center of this story. I was more concerned with how his actions affected his family than with why he had committed them in the first place, and I wanted to maintain this focus. The second and more important reason had to do with my gripping sense of the finality of the violent death Hosaam chose for himself as well as for Natalie. This kind of violence never truly affords closure for those left behind. I do not believe the families of those who either kill themselves or, like Hosaam, decide to take other innocent lives with them ever come to a full understanding of what truly motivated their loved ones to commit something so horrendous. I believe that living with those unanswered questions is, perhaps, one of the heaviest burdens those families bear, and I wanted the reader to share in this experience by leaving some of the questions unanswered for him or her, too.

Both of the family's surviving children react quite differently to Hosaam's death, but Khaled seems to take it much harder. Can you talk about your decision to focus on Khaled's journey instead of Fatima's?

Khaled is the one people will more readily identify with Hosaam. He is the brother of a young man who committed an atrocious act and would therefore face different kinds of challenges than his sister would. Externally, those challenges will stem from how people would fear him—they would suspect him of having the same violent tendencies his brother did. This is the kind of treatment male Arabs got after 9/11. My husband, a doctor who at the time was in his early thirties, experienced the shift in scrutiny in airports, for example, much more visibly than I ever did—it's a simple matter of gender preconceptions, of assuming that males are more likely to be violent than females. Khaled would also suffer an ironically similar internal struggle: the fear that whatever unhinged his brother was lurking in his own DNA. This, again, is a fear that Fatima would most likely not experience. Fatima would have little reason to fear that she would, one day, pose a threat to her future spouse (a gender issue, again), whereas Khaled already fears for Brittany, sometimes wondering if whatever demons caused his brother's love for Natalie to take such a violent turn may one day haunt him, as well. So I chose Khaled because I felt he would embody the survivor's struggles more acutely.

How did your characters evolve over the course of writing this novel? How did they surprise you?

My characters evolved considerably over the multiple drafts of this novel. I think characters have this in common with plot: they reveal more about themselves with every new revision. Understandably, this is a process of discovery, which means that the characters I know the least about when I start out end up evolving the most, whereas the characters I know quite well at the beginning remain relatively static. In this novel, Ehsan, for example, did not evolve much because I knew exactly who she was and what her role would be. On the opposite side of that spectrum stand both Khaled and his mother. When I started, I thought Khaled would be more fed up than anything else—I imagined him angry with his father and with society for comparing him to his brother and determined to distance himself from both. I was pleasantly surprised to see his character develop into one that actually sought connections rather than severed them: he repeatedly reached out to Brittany, and he truly cared about his entire family and, in particular, about his grandmother. So he didn't end up being the typical rebellious teenager I first thought he would be. His mother, Nagla, had an equally interesting trajectory: she started out passively wallowing in grief, and then, slowly but surely, developed a kind of inquisitive and introspective quality. That, too, was a development I had not foreseen.

Inevitably, in an immigrant story, generations will clash over ideals and social norms. How do you make this struggle feel new to readers?

I think the key here is to balance the unexpected with the familiar. On one hand, the reader may come to the novel with preconceived ideas about what Muslim kids would clash with their parents over, and I think it's refreshing to avoid conforming to the stereotype when presenting this clash. For example, I don't think many readers will expect to see young Muslim girls embracing the idea of the head cover in defiance of their parents, as Fatima does, though I know that this is often the case in real life. I'm particularly disinclined to try to win over the readers by presenting the parents as "others" who embrace crazy ideas while presenting the kids as victims who want nothing other than to be good, normal Americans. Any presentation that easily separates characters into "us" versus "them" is, in my opinion, too simplistic. So one way to make this struggle new is to stay true to the Arab and Muslim culture while veering away from the stereotype. But at the same time I think it's important to balance that with the familiar. Khaled and Fatima's struggles, though cast in the light of a different culture, stem from the same identity issues teenagers of all cultures, religions, and ethnicities grapple with. I hope that highlighting this familiarity while avoiding the expected stereotypes would make my presentation of the generational struggles feel interesting to the readers.

The specifics of Hosaam's death are not revealed until midway through the book, making it something of a mystery. Why did you choose to shape the narrative in this way?

I wanted to delay the revelations of the specifics of Hosaam's death as much as possible because I wanted to see whether the reader would assume that Hosaam's violent crime was either culturally or religiously motivated. I will confess to hoping that the reader would actually think so and would, as a result, question his or her own inclination to make such an assumption based solely on Hosaam's religion and ethnicity.

Also, in terms of structure, I thought it would be more fun to keep the reader guessing for some time, just to add a level of suspense. Since this is a character-driven narrative, there are no great mysteries or huge reveals to build up to, but I thought that leaving a few details untold and revealing them in time would, hopefully, make the reading experience more enjoyable.

The guilt and hurt the family feels—not to mention the public shaming they must endure—seem almost insurmountable. How can survivor families find their way back after this sort of tragedy?

The only way I can offer some advice on this is by returning to my belief that the particular experience of the Al-Menshawys mirrors the state of most Muslim Arab Americans after 9/11. As a part of this community that has been grappling with similar questions for over a decade now, my sense is that some tragedies do, indeed, leave insurmountable pain in their wake, and that one way to deal with that is not to strive to heal fully from that pain, but rather to learn to live with it, to accept it, and to focus on those aspects of one's identity that this tragedy has not fully contaminated. I don't think anyone who suffers such a horrific loss as the one the Al-Menshawys faced can ever be fully healed. But I do believe, truly and honestly, that life can go on even for those who have been so painfully scarred. And I think realizing that—embracing that final stage of grief generally referred to as acceptance—is the key to finding the way back.

This book is your very auspicious debut. What can we expect from you in the future?

I'm currently working on a novel set in the years following the 2011 Egyptian revolution. In the novel, an Egyptian woman married to an American journalist comes to terms with her husband's inadvertent implication in a terrorist attack that caused her sister's death. It is an intimate story that allows me to grapple with issues of cultural and religious identity, of the intersection of the personal and the political, and of the complexity of unconditional love. I'm enjoying every moment of writing it, and I hope the readers will enjoy it, too.

Questions for Discussion

1. The novel opens with a memory of when Khaled was sick and his grandmother tended to him at his bedside. What significance does this memory have for Khaled and the story to follow?

2. The memorial service and the question of whether to attend it hang over the Al-Menshawy family for days. What would you do if you were in their position?

3. Throughout the book the author has included proverbs from Egypt and the United States. What do these bits of wisdom reveal about the two cultures? How are they similar and how are they different?

4. How does the author evoke the family's isolation and loneliness? What details best capture that experience?

5. Each family member blames the others for failing to support one another or make decisions that reflect their best interests. Who is right, in your opinion?

6. What role does Ehsan play in this story? How does her presence in the household change the way Khaled and his mother deal with their personal tragedy?

7. As a teenager, Khaled seems most vulnerable to both bullying and other people's suspicions. What gives him strength and hope?

8. In many scenes there are debates over religious rites versus superstitions, and whether either can truly heal people. What do you think the author is trying to say about the value of these practices in our lives?

9. Why does Samir feel so strongly about staying in Summerset? What changes his mind?

10. The story ends with Khaled several years later. What has he learned and how has he changed over the course of the book?

To access Penguin Readers Guides online,
visit the Penguin Group (USA) Web site at www.penguin.com.

P.O. 0003621334